LOVE AND DEATH IN
SILICON VALLEY

LOVE AND DEATH IN SILICON VALLEY

To Judith

Best Wishes

Joseph D. McNamara

JOSEPH D. MCNAMARA

Library of Congress Control Number: 2012903819
ISBN: Hardcover   978-1-4691-7654-3
               Softcover   978-1-4691-7653-6
               Ebook   978-1-4691-7655-0

To order additional copies of this book, contact:
Xlibris Corporation
1-888-795-4274
www.Xlibris.com
Orders@Xlibris.com
110450

CHAPTER ONE

A COLD BEER or a Naproxen? Rusty Carter's right shoulder bursitis hurt like hell. But at 11 a.m. he savored the thought of a chilled Amstel. It had been three unusually grueling sets of tennis on a hot July morning.

Doc Hoffman had said no booze combined with Naproxen. Since his coronary angioplasty, Rusty listened. He stood indecisive in his tennis outfit, soaking with sweat, absently gazing out the kitchen window into his small backyard.

Dark shadows appeared around the fully blooming Bougainvillea vine climbing the rear corner of the house. His eyes widened. Two men in ski masks moved from the shade. Both had AK-47's.

The older one placed his assault rifle on the brick patio. He leaned over the back door lock. The other, a kid, glancing nervously around, held his weapon at ready.

What the hell? Carter had retired as county sheriff four years earlier. Burglars didn't wear ski masks and carry assault rifles even in zany California. And they were wearing gang colors.

It was time was time to get out. Fast!

He hurriedly grabbed a knife from the kitchen rack and dashed toward the front door. Elderly Mrs. Hernandez across the street was always home. He'd use her phone to call 911. His cell phone was in the back room.

His hand on the front door handle, he hesitated. The gunmen might have company. He peeked through the front curtain.

Damn! A well-dented Chevy Impala, four-door sedan, badly needing a paint job, sat in his driveway. A young Latino's eyes in the passenger seat were riveted on Rusty's front door. He and the driver probably had at least Mac 10's. Maybe even another assault rifle. Plenty of firepower.

Rusty sighed. He was pinned in. And his two old service .357 Magnums were locked in the back desk in plain sight of the two thugs breaking in. Not that they'd be much good against AK-47's.

Rusty returned to the kitchen window. The larger masked man bending over the back door's flimsy catch lock wouldn't take long. But the double bolt above it would hold until the intruder realized that all he needed to do was break the windowpane.

He could simply reach inside and slide the door open. Since Lucy had died of cancer two years ago, Rusty hadn't bothered to set the house alarm system which he had only installed to pacify her longing for security.

Belatedly, when he had raced to the front door and the illusion of escape, he realized he hadn't taken a sturdy carving knife but the thin, razor sharp serrated bread knife from the rack. Still, no knife was a match for assault rifles, and there was no time for 911.

Carter took a deep breath. Two heavily armed thugs were in front and two in the rear.

And here he was, a day after his forty-second birthday and almost twenty-five years in law enforcement, once again about to face the dark angel that hung over cops' shoulders.

He felt a flash of adrenaline and rage at these two punks in the rear and their pals in the front invading his space. He had no chance, but he wasn't going easy.

He heard the glass breaking in the back door as the goon finally understood that all he had to do was put his hand through the hole and slide open the double lock bolt. Rusty moved quickly into the modest sized bedroom that he and Lucy had shared during their twenty years of marriage.

The two intruders would have to come through the short narrow hall from the rear entrance in single file to get to the bedroom. Rusty positioned himself just inside the closed door that the first gunman would have to push open.

They were mumbling to each other in Spanish. They'd already made enough noise to alert anyone inside the house.

They must have looked at the deserted driveway and into the empty detached one-car garage and figured that no one was home. Rusty had taken his aged pick-up truck, habitually parked in front of the garage, for servicing.

Henry Wilson, his lawyer and today's tennis partner, had picked him up at the car place and driven the half-mile to the courts. The truck wouldn't be ready until later in the afternoon, so Henry had dropped him at home, ribbing him that he didn't deserve the ride because they had lost the match in the third set tie-breaker.

Rusty felt a chill run through him. He stood, back against the bedroom wall, on the balls of his feet. The gunman pushed the door open with the barrel of his rifle.

Rusty was on him instantly. With his left hand, he grabbed the barrel of the assault weapon and swung it upward.

A volley of shots tore holes in the ceiling. Rusty brought the blade of the bread knife viciously across the underside of shooter's exposed gun hand, slicing deeply into his arteries. Blood shot into the air.

The gunman screamed, "My wrist! My wrist!"

He dropped the gun. Rusty hit him with a shoulder block, driving the thug into his young accomplice a step behind him.

What saved Rusty was the first man's panic. His severed arteries sprayed blood all over the hall. Frantically, he jumped away from Rusty, bumping backward into his partner.

The second guy, sighting on Rusty, managed to raise the weapon above his accomplice's shoulder. It threw his aim upward. He pulled the trigger.

Before he could again bring the weapon to bear, Rusty was just able to grab the barrel and twist the gun toward the ceiling. There was no time to go for the kid's gun hand. Rusty tried to ignore the searing pain in his left hand from the heat of the gun barrels.

The former sheriff swung the bread knife as he would have his tennis racket, hitting a nasty backhand slice into his opponent's back corner. This time it wasn't a tennis ball. Rusty had aimed with lethal accuracy at the man's throat.

Using the full strength of his six-foot one frame, he cut through the carotid artery. Torrents of pumping blood splattered throughout the narrow hallway.

The first gunman was still on his feet, futilely grasping his wrist, trying to stop the hemorrhaging.

"Help me! Help me!" he cried.

Rusty kicked him in the stomach, sending him reeling backward to the floor of the small anteroom they had broken into. The second man was unable to talk, but he, too, had dropped his weapon and clasped his hand to his throat in a hopeless effort to stop the bleeding.

Rusty grabbed the portable phone from its cradle, sticking it in his pocket. He picked up the AK-47's. Now, with equal firepower, he rushed to the front door ready to take on the two hoods in the driveway, should they charge forward.

But they sat in their car, anxiously staring at the house after hearing the shots. No heroes out there, he thought.

The retired lawman started to dial 911, but hesitated. He could still hear the two men in the rear, moaning. He tried to remember his first aid training. Did you live two minutes after a severed artery, or three? By applying direct hand pressure until they weakened, they probably had an extra minute or two.

Rusty lived within a mile of a hospital with one of the best trauma centers in California. Ambulances were constantly coming and going. No hurry on calling an ambulance for these two bastards.

He checked the rifles in case the two in the front had the balls to see what was up with their buddies. Minutes crawled by.

Finally, Rusty slipped open the front door, hoping to get a sight picture with the AK-47 on the guy in the front passenger seat. But the young Latino riding shotgun had seen the door open.

He splintered the entrance with a burst of gunfire. Rusty dove rightward to the floor. The son-of-a bitch did have an assault rifle.

Flat on his stomach, Rusty winced in agony. He'd had a just two years five years earlier. Now, for the first time since the surgery, he experienced severe angina. He tossed the AK-47 to the side.

Fumbling in his pocket, he reached for the tiny container of nitro pills that he always carried. He shoved one under his tongue.

His heart felt like it was going to burst. Even worse than when they had inflated the balloon in the unsuccessful angioplasty tried before the bypass.

He placed another pill under his tongue. What had they told him? Wait five minutes after the first pill. If you don't feel relief, try a second.

Take a third if the pain doesn't subside. Call 911 and hope that you make the ER.

But all the emergency treatment in the world wouldn't work if he was helpless like this and the gangbangers in front walked up to the open door an emptied their guns into him.

Rusty wasn't waiting five minutes between pills. He took the third pill before the second was even fully dissolved.

The Chevy in front screeched away. The angina was easing a bit. Rusty dialed 911. He lay in the open doorway, his heart still thumping way too fast.

When the emergency operator answered, he identified himself as the retired sheriff. Ignoring the pain in his chest, he told her men with assault rifles had fired through his front door. He gave a description of the car, the license plate, the direction of flight, and a warning that the escapees probably had assault weapons.

"Tell the officers to be careful! Did you copy, Central?"

"Copied, Sheriff. I'm transmitting for immediate dispatch right now. We have anti-gang units in the area. Stay on the line."

Rusty rested his head on the front door mat, trying not to pay attention to his struggling heart. Idly, he wondered why sheriff anti-gang units would be in an area that never had gang activity. After a while, the dispatcher came back.

"Sheriff, are you there?"

"Right. I had bypass a few years ago. I think I'm having a heart attack."

"Hold on if you can. I'll send a trauma unit."

Shortly, she was back. "Hang in there, Sheriff," she said with that eerie calm dispatchers have. "We're on the way."

He closed his eyes, hoping the pain would lessen and that he'd catch his breath. He stayed still.

The dispatcher was still talking, trying to soothe him. The angina should have been easing more, but it wasn't.

"One other thing," he finally said.

"What else, Sheriff?" For the first time, he heard a trace of anxiety.

"Two bad guys broke into my house. Shot it up. I fought them with a knife. They're bleeding a lot, need help."

"Got it, Sheriff." She was calm again when she realized he wasn't talking about himself. "You just stay with us. The coronary paramedics and patrol units are only three blocks away. I'll dispatch another ambulance for the suspects."

Maybe the paramedics would be in time to save Rusty from cardiac arrest. Maybe not. Still, he had done the best he could.

CHAPTER TWO

THREE HOURS AFTER the shooting, Sheriff Sally Henson sat in the opposite corner of the hospital room, distancing herself from the rest of them. Rusty was propped up in bed, hooked to an EKG monitor being closely studied by Doc Hoffman, another tennis buddy, and his heart surgeon. Rusty's burned left hand was thickly bandaged.

An IV dripped yellow stuff into the vein in his right arm. Tall, slim and appropriately somber, former Chief Assistant District Attorney Henry Wilson stood next to Doc Wilson. Henry, another tennis buddy occasionally did legal work for Rusty.

A youngish Latino woman, whom Rusty assumed was Sally's driver, sat motionless against the pastel blue hospital wall directly across from Rusty. She was dressed in an azure business suit that almost seemed to have been chosen to make her blend seamlessly into the background of the hospital wall.

Her smooth dark hair was close cropped, barely covering her ears, but very fem. Completely still, her unblinking brown eyes focused steadily, but without expression, on Rusty.

The door burst open and Pablo Garcia rushed in. The muscular former Army Special Forces captain's angry eyes focused on Sally.

"What the hell, Sally?" he exclaimed.

"Ah. The fourth musketeer has arrived. Your defense platoon is present and accounted for, Rusty." Sally's attractive face was flushed underneath her long blondish hairdo.

Rusty had never seen her this agitated during the five years she had been his undersheriff while he groomed her to run as his replacement.

"I just heard that dope-pushing pimp of a D.A., Herrera saying on the radio that he was demanding a full investigation of how the sheriff's department killed two young Latinos in a matter of minutes, like those gangbanging bastards didn't deserve it!" Pablo roared.

"Exactly! You see what I mean, Rusty," Sally said. "I need your help on this. I've got three hundred people demonstrating in front of headquarters right now against 'deputy murderers.' Every TV crew in the Bay Area and a couple of the national vultures are giving full coverage.

She took a deep breath, "Without your cooperation, I can't even say that it was your 911 call that enabled our anti-gang unit to take out the two fleeing gangbangers in the Impala after the idiots made the mistake of firing on the officers."

"Who's she?" Pablo rudely interrupted, pointing at the young woman seated in the wall chair. The woman ignored Pablo. Her eyes never shifted from Rusty.

"Well, now that Rusty's palace guard is all here, let me introduce Lieutenant Maria Lopez-Hogan, commanding officer of the Homicide Investigation Unit," Sally said.

Rusty blinked. The young woman sitting so still was C.O. of the most prestigious detective unit? She didn't even look thirty. Her name was vaguely familiar. But a lieutenant, already? She must be very good for Sally to have jumped her that far in the brief four years since he had retired.

"Sheriff Sally," Doc Hoffman said firmly, "my patient is suffered trauma and is under medication. He's in no condition to make legal statements."

"As his attorney, I have to agree, Sally," Henry added in his quiet way.

"Yeah, Sheriff Sally," Pablo said, "why don't you just say that that dirtbag Herrera ought to keep his trap shut, and that punks with masks and assault rifles who think they can invade peoples' homes are going to get their asses fried one way or another?"

"Rusty, tell your buddies to get real. This isn't a movie. Giving the rabble rousers a couple of days of full stage will build a momentum that we won't be able to overcome. And remember, any D.A. can get a grand jury to indict a loaf of bread. And since you rather publicly declined his request to endorse him when he ran for office, he's not exactly fond of you," Sally said.

Rusty felt curiously mellow. Doc must have been dripping morphine into his veins.

"She's got a point, guys," he said. "I can describe what happened in a couple of sentences."

"That's with the understanding that he is medicated and it's a general, not a formal statement," Henry Wilson added.

"O.K.," Sally agreed.

Briefly, Rusty summarized the attack.

"Good," Sally stood. "That gives us enough to issue a press release. We'll e-mail a copy to you, Henry."

"Er, Sheriff," Lieutenant Maria Lopez-Hogan, still sitting, said softly to Rusty, "they didn't ring your bell or knock on the door?"

"No."

"Your Ford pick-up truck wasn't in the driveway?"

"Right. I dropped it at the shop for maintenance this morning. Henry drove me."

The lieutenant turned to the physician. "Doctor, is it your opinion that Sheriff Carter had a heart attack?"

"He had a cardiovascular event, Lieutenant. That's all that I can tell you until we do further testing."

"One other little thing, Sheriff Sally," Pablo folded his bulging arms, "there's a half asleep deputy sitting on his fat ass outside the door. Is that your idea of security? I remind you that the four of us macho pigs were your biggest supporters when you ran for sheriff. And Rusty really pissed Herrera off when he ran around campaigning for you and refused any comment on Herrera."

Sally strode right up to him, stopping with her face inches from his. "In case you haven't noticed, Pablo, Lieutenant Hogan and I are two armed and trained police officers. We're leaving, but I assure you that I have already added additional adequate security for Rusty. Now, if you think you know better, I suggest that you file to run for sheriff next year!"

She stalked out of the room with Lieutenant Hogan in tow.

Pablo grinned widely, "God, she is one tough broad, Rusty. You were right to pick her!"

Rusty leaned back on his pillow. "A suggestion, Pablo. Don't ever let Sally hear you refer to her as a broad."

"And a suggestion for you, Amigo. Don't trust that female lieutenant one inch. She's a silent bear trap just waiting for you to make a misstep. The jaws will snap shut right around your neck. You'll find yourself in San Quentin waiting for the big sleep needle instead of getting a medal for terminating two punk killers."

CHAPTER THREE

A T NOON THE day following the Friday shootings, Rusty, dressed in a short-sleeved shirt and summer slacks, sat in the mandatory wheelchair which the hospital required for discharging patients who no matter how healthy, had to be wheeled to the front door before being spewed back out into the masses.

The previous evening, Doc Bill Hoffman had pulled rank and jumped Rusty ahead of other patients awaiting echocardiogram ultra-sound exams. After the test, Rusty had enjoyed a fairly restful sleep while the Doc studied the results and consulted with other heart specialists.

At seven a.m., the Doc visited, scanned the EKG readings from the bedside machine, gave Rusty's heart a listen with his stethoscope, took his pulse, and flipped through the chart attached to the foot of the bed, listing all the information that nurses had obtained while interrupting Rusty's slumber.

"Rusty, I'd like you to stay another night for observation. The MRI didn't show any indication of new heart damage. However, the trauma and prolonged angina during your combat, warrant caution. But Pablo is driving me crazy. He's bad enough on the tennis court. He didn't even want you to stay last night, had men with guns here. I not only had to listen to crap from the hospital security and Sally, but Pablo called hourly. He was in the hospital twice during the night, paging me."

Rusty smiled. "Pablo can get carried away."

"Indeed. Against my better judgment I agreed to release you to his compound, but you'll be hooked to an EKG monitor and have twenty-four hour nursing for another day. And maybe our madman tennis friend will let me get some sleep tonight."

Rusty wondered what Pablo, the master builder, would have thought of the luxury, multi-million dollar homes in the gated community that he had built being referred to as a compound.

Waiting for Pablo to pick him up, Rusty read the Saturday morning newspaper. Sally had been right. The media picked up D.A. Herrera's hyperbole and ran with it. Because of the delay in getting Rusty's statement, the sheriff's department's press conference didn't take place until well after 5 p.m. Few reporters were still working and the news was too late for the morning papers.

The whole front page was a headline: **D.A. DEMANDS INDEPENDENT INVESTIGATION OF SHERIFF'S DEPARTMENT'S KILLING OF FOUR LATINO YOUTHS WITHIN FOURTEEN MINUTES.**

The text of the stories wasn't much better. "The Silicon Valley Sheriff's Department refused to release the names of the deceased, and said it would have no official statement until the preliminary investigation was complete this evening.

"Sources close to the investigation said retired Sheriff Rusty Carter killed two of the youths with a knife. The other two were shot multiple times by plainclothes detectives in a nearby crowded shopping mall. Witnesses at the mall described chaos, flying bullets, store windows being shattered, screaming shoppers, and crashing cars.

"Former Sheriff Carter, who has been retired two years, was unreachable for comment, and indeed, no one in law enforcement would confirm his whereabouts. His house on quiet Rosebud Lane is cordoned off as a crime scene and jammed with law enforcement vehicles. Sheriff Sally Henson, who served as undersheriff for Carter and was endorsed by him when she ran for election, said through a spokesperson that she would make a full statement as soon as possible."

Rusty knew that radio and television would have paralleled the newspaper coverage. He looked up at a knock on the door. Before he could respond, Lieutenant Maria Lopez-Hogan came in.

"Good afternoon, Sheriff," she nodded, and settled into a chair.

She noticed his newspaper but made no comment as he put it aside.

Rusty asked, "Busy night, Lieutenant?"

"Quite. Sheriff Sally asked me to stop by and brief you on what we have so far. Your attorney, Henry Wilson, let her know that you've been discharged and are moving to Mr. Garcia's residence. I wanted to catch you before you left."

Rusty observed that she wore a tan, short-sleeved blouse tucked into tight blue jeans. Saturday morning uniform, he mused. She carried a large leather purse which undoubtedly housed her Department-issued Glock and extra ammo, since nothing else could have fit into jeans that tight.

She looked even younger than she had wearing a business suit. Today, she wore makeup. He realized that the somber young woman was not only shapely, but also damned pretty. As Homicide boss, she must have been up all night. Probably only had time to go home and shower and change. Yet she showed no sign of fatigue. Her eyes were as watchful as they had been yesterday.

"It's been just twenty-four hours since the incident, so we don't have all that much in here." She held up the manila case file.

"I understand."

"We have tentatively ID'd all four of the deceased suspects as members of the Sureños. Gilbert Sanchez, age 38, Jose Fernando, age 17, were the two at your house. Sanchez is an old customer of ours, spent about half of his life in the joint, fairly high in the organization, capitán level. Fernando, two years in California Youth Authority, armed robbery with a firearm, fired an "accidental" shot at the owner."

"Seventeen?"

She waved her right hand, "Yeah. His AK-47 was even younger. So?"

He shrugged. She continued, "Vincente Santoro, age 30, Sal Velasco, age 16 were the two taken out near the mall by the anti-gang deputies. Santoro's previous convictions: assault with firearm, meth sales, possession of firearm by convicted felon, rep as a shooter for the gang. Did time in various joints for around eight years. Velasco, in the country only a year, no record. Three undocumented, Fernando born here in San Mateo."

"I don't remember any particular beef with the Sureños. What in the world were they doing at my house?"

"I'll tell you what we know in a minute, Sheriff, but first Sally wanted you to be aware that D.A. Herrera routinely assigns his own investigators to roll-outs on deputy involved shootings."

"That was policy even before Herrera. It actually added to our credibility to have experienced outside investigators. Of course, they were straight."

"Right. It's a little different with Herrera. Sheriff Sally says that Herrera is treating the break-in at your house as a deputy involved shooting. He's assigned D.A. Chief Investigator Paul Henrich, retired after twenty with the Alto Department, which has a total of fifteen officers, to monitor the investigation of the break-in deaths. Heinrich was president of Alto P.D.'s union which endorsed Herrera for election. Heinrich spent his career in uniform, patrol and traffic enforcement, no investigative assignment."

"Great."

"Assistant Chief D.A. Investigator Rick Jones, head of the union for Bay City P.D., twenty-two officers, no investigative experience, is monitoring the anti-gang unit shootout."

"Don't tell me. Jones also headed the union which endorsed Herrera and retired, like Heinrich, to take the job after Herrera won."

"You got it. Herrera will be privy to all of our investigation reports."

"Anyway, what the hell interest could the Sureños have in me five years after my retirement?"

"That's what we haven't released to the press. They wanted to be inside to surprise you when you came home. The trunk of the getaway car contained restraints for your arms and legs and duct tape to cover your mouth."

"What?"

"The Sureños gang was out to take you prisoner, Sheriff!"

CHAPTER FOUR

PABLO STEERED RUSTY'S wheelchair out the door of the hospital room. "You hate hospitals as much as I do, Rusty?"

"Yeah."

"Then why don't you get out of this stupid wheelchair and walk out of here as a man? I feel like some asshole orderly."

"It's probably just malpractice cover-your-rear-end stuff by the hospital, Pablo."

"Screw the hospital. While you lay on your butt slumbering in a morphine haze, the rest of us have been working all night."

Rusty neither wanted to know what "work" Pablo had been up to, nor to argue with him about hospital red tape. He rose from the wheelchair and, under the disapproving eyes of the nurses, walked down the exit stairs with Pablo.

"No doubt the sheriff's department kept your two antique Magnums for evidence, Rusty?"

"It's procedure, Pablo. The guns have to be tested by ballistics."

"Right. And it's procedure to scrape you off the fucking sidewalk full of lead if the gangbangers show up and blow you away." Pablo's face reflected his disgust.

Pablo drove his non-descript six year-old Toyota SUV in loops through the hospital parking lot. The guy who could afford any car in the world was paranoid about security for his wife, Teresa, and their two children, ten year-old Enrique, and Sonia, who was six.

Pablo adored Teresa, who laughed at his fearfulness. She humored him, because you didn't really have much choice when Pablo made up his mind about something.

"The only ones following us are the two undercover cops who might as well be in uniform in a marked cruiser. Sally called me. I told her forget about it. My own people would take our back. She threatened that if any of us even went through a stop sign the cops would take us all down. Keep my guys out of it. What the hell is wrong with her, Rusty?"

"You've got to chill on her. Herrera's putting her under terrific pressure."

"Yeah. Well, we're turning the table around. Henry and me and the Doc had a strategy session last night. My people have been working the phones all morning. We've got the money and support to recall Herrera and run Henry for D.A. in a special election."

Rusty sighed. This was Pablo. Search out and destroy the enemy. But this wasn't military combat. The strategy could just as well come back and bite you in the ass, confuse and politicize the gang attack on Rusty and get Herrera publicity and support he never would get on his own.

"I saw that female hawk lieutenant leaving when I came in. What was she grilling you on this time?"

Rusty hesitated. But Pablo had a right to know. He was endangering his family by providing a sanctuary for Rusty.

"She said the gang getaway car had restraints and a gag in the trunk."

"Those little cowardly mother-fuckers! So they think this is Baghdad. Well, I'm ready to give them a taste of reality."

"They may be crazy, Pablo, but you know they're not cowards. Unfortunately, too many of them are bravely suicidal."

"I'm perfectly willing to accommodate those wishing to be martyrs. The only good terrorist is a dead one."

"Yeah. Well, let's the four of us talk this over before we end up behind bars, joining the white supremacists for protection against the Sureños."

When they came to the uniformed armed guards manning the gate to Paraíso, the luxury oasis created by Pablo, the crew knew better than to skip asking for Pablo's I.D. or not to check the computer readout on his windshield sticker even though the greenest rookie employee recognized Pablo on sight.

Pablo deftly drove through the deliberately confusing, winding dead-end cul-de-sacs until he came to his home. He had intentionally made it more modest, at least on the outside, than the others in the complex. Again, his intense security concern was not to draw attention.

In Special Forces, he had operated behind enemy lines. Some old habits never die.

Inside the home, Rusty patiently let the nurse make a fuss over getting him into bed and hooked up to the monitoring machine arranged for by Doc Hoffman. In truth, he admitted to himself, he was exhausted, his legs a little wobbly. He hoped it was from the medication and not new coronary problems.

Pablo sat on the edge of the bed. "You're a better man than I am, Gunga Din. Beating two AK-47's with a bread knife. Man! You could have been my point man anytime."

Rusty braced himself for what was coming next. Pablo had won all kinds of medals for his Special Forces work. It was classified, but Pablo didn't toss around compliments. He wanted something.

He reached inside his jacket, pulled out a handgun and offered it to Rusty. "Glock, ten-millimeter, sixteen rounds. About time you retired those Magnums and got yourself some additional rounds."

Rusty made no move to take the weapon. "Look, Pablo, I wouldn't feel right being responsible for this, with Teresa, your two kids, and workers around the house."

"Forget that horseshit. You're not a politician anymore. I take Teresa and Enrique to the range. They're probably better shots than you are. Sonia and the staff know better than to touch a gun, except Jorge and Antonio, whom I trained. Stick the Glock under your pillow. Help you and me sleep better."

Rusty sighed. He didn't have the strength to argue with Pablo. He'd overdosed on Pablo just being around his intensity for the last couple of hours. But it wasn't fair to put Teresa and the family in danger. Rusty stuck the weapon under the pillow. He would have to disappear for awhile as soon as he was able.

The door opened. Little Sonia screamed, "Uncle Rusty!" Pigtails flying, she would have sailed onto Rusty's chest if Pablo hadn't deftly caught her in mid-air. Enrique followed, his normally fun loving face solemn. He had seen TV news accounts.

Teresa gave Rusty a peck on the cheek. "It's been almost a month since you've been over for dinner, Rusty," she gently scolded. Then, ignoring him, she glanced through the nurse's notes on a clipboard hanging from the foot of the bed. A practicing physician before surrendering to Pablo's full-scale courtship assault, she then turned to the EKG printouts.

Pablo had stepped respectfully back a step, waiting for her opinion. He held little Sonia, still struggling to get to Rusty's bedside.

Itsy Bitsy, the family's nervous pint-sized terrier pooch, had no such trouble. He leaped onto the bed, sniffed suspiciously at the IV and moved up to Rusty's chest, the ideal position to lick his face while wagging his tail furiously. Rusty scratched behind the mutt's ear. As always, he wondered how the little dog, a mere bite for the family mastiff Bruno, managed to bully the huge animal.

"Is Uncle Rusty sick, Mom?" Sonia asked.

"No," Teresa said, "he just needs to take it easy for a couple of days."

Pablo cast an inquiring glance at her. She wasn't about to comment about Doc Hoffman's patient, but she directed a nod and a slight smile at her husband.

She turned to Rusty. "We'll get these two wild ones out of here, so you can get some rest. The wildest one," she pointed at Pablo, "you chase away, Rusty. I mean it."

She nodded at the nurse sitting in the corner and hustled the kids out of the room. Itsy Bitsy settled down, rested his head on Rusty and gazed into his eyes. He knew Rusty was good for continuous affection, whereas others in the busy household couldn't be depended upon for the level of attention Itsy craved.

Pablo turned to the nurse. "Doc Hoffman talked to you, right? Rusty needs to walk a little." He gestured to the heart monitor. "Can you unhook him? I'll have him back in a few minutes."

Rusty groaned. He knew neither the nurse nor Pablo would have pushed him to walk if Doc hadn't advised it. Pablo guided him slowly past the swimming pool to what looked like a dark green pool house sitting a considerable distance from the pool area. Up close, Rusty saw that it was actually a thick concrete structure.

Pablo pressed his palm against a small, rectangular, opaque square of green glass that was screened from view by a large hedge of rosemary. A heavy metal door slowly ground open and lights turned on in the windowless structure.

Inside, Pablo pushed a button on the wall and the door slid shut behind them. Only when it was completely closed did he pull aside the solid, dark green curtain that hid the small room from view.

Rusty was startled. It was an arsenal. Perhaps twelve feet by twelve feet, the room contained open wooden crates of weapons and ammunition. Wooden dollies raised them above the damp floor. A dehumidifier hummed in the background.

One box contained three military M 4's. He wondered if they were legal. The laws against assault weapons had been allowed to expire recently. Rusty hadn't paid attention to just what could be sold and what couldn't. He picked up one of two expensively made scoped sniper rifles with night vision fittings.

"Deadly accurate at a thousand yards and maybe double that if in the hands of an expert," Pablo said.

Another container held a dozen Glock 10's. At the far end of the aisle, as they were about to retrace their steps, Rusty paused and looked into an open crate of various ammunition for the weapons. Two hand grenades sat on top.

"So when and where does the invasion start, Pablo?"

"It started yesterday at Rosebud Lane, Amigo," Pablo answered.

CHAPTER FIVE

RUSTY RELUCTANTLY ENDURED Pablo's insistence on programming his palm onto the arsenal's admittance list. Only he, Pablo and his two closest helpers, Jorge and Antonio, could gain access.

Pablo's paranoia strengthened Rusty's resolve to relocate as soon as possible. He required space to think clearly, to end this madness before it got completely out of hand.

He needed no encouragement the next day to follow Doc Hoffman's advice to escape Pablo's stronghold for a couple of hours by accompanying the tennis group as a spectator at their doubles match. Barry Fitzsimmons, retired after thirty-five years in the Sheriff's department, filled in occasionally when one of them couldn't make it. He was taking Rusty's place.

During the last three months, the group had been playing at a public park. The private club they belonged to was undergoing construction. Before they left home, Pablo provided Rusty with a holster for the Mac 10.

Rusty almost refused to carry the weapon. But his friend, Pablo, had been there for him from the first hours of the attack. Then too, Rusty had to concede that even he felt a growing apprehension. Something ominous was unfolding. Pablo neatly fit an M 4 carbine into his tennis bag before zipping it shut.

At ten a.m. on a weekday, the courts were pretty much deserted. The warm sun and fresh air felt good, but Doc Hoffman firmly directed Rusty to take the elevated referee's chair protected from ultraviolet rays by a large umbrella.

Rusty watched the four men playing good amateur tennis. Doc Hoffman, the most slender of them, must have been in his early seventies. A former college player, he possessed classic strokes and court savvy. Like Henry, Doc's quick reflexes more than made up for muscles of the younger players.

Barry Fitzsimmons and Henry Wilson most likely weren't going to see sixty again, and Pablo was three or four years younger than Rusty. All had stayed in top shape.

Rusty soon lost interest in the game, ignoring joking appeals from Pablo to call the lines in his favor. Rusty wondered about the Sheriff's Department. Through the enigmatic Lieutenant Maria Lopez-Hogan, he was getting bits of information. Clearly, however, there were puzzling gaps.

He hadn't expected Sally to bring him fully into the investigation. Yet there were too many things unexplained. Anti-gang units in the area of his house where no gang activity had ever taken place. Not a word on what the gang units' intelligence had come up with, nor any information from the Department's sizeable Central Intelligence unit, or whether the feds had picked up anything useful.

The foursome was playing next to an unoccupied court. It flanked the square box of the gym centered in the middle of the county park and recreation center. Absentmindedly, Rusty glanced at three men who huddled on the unoccupied court.

Standing a few feet from the side exit of the gym building, they stared at the tennis foursome. He guessed the three must have just emerged from the gym. He hadn't seen them come through the street entrance fence his group had used.

The three didn't have tennis rackets or any gear. In fact, they weren't wearing sports clothes at all. They split and slowly began walking toward the foursome's court.

One of the newcomers stayed close to the other court's net as he approached the tennis players. Another wandered over to the street fence and moved toward the game court. The remaining guy walked straight-ahead.

He was heading right at Pablo, crouched at the net, ready to leap and smash a weak return of his partner's serve.

"Pablo!" Rusty yelled, drawing the Glock from his holster.

Pablo glanced to his left, spotting the approaching group. "Hit the deck!" he shouted to the other three tennis players, and raced toward his tennis bag.

There was no time to climb down from the ref's chair. Rusty carefully aimed the Glock at the individual approaching from the street. If there was gunplay, he didn't want Pablo spraying fire from the carbine into the busy street. The three approaching men were squinting into the sun and didn't immediately react when Pablo dashed to his bag, and the other players flattened out on the ground.

A moment later, however, the intruders were firing wildly at the suddenly scattered targets. Rusty had braced his Glock on the armrest and calmly, steadily opened fire, being very careful not to let the weapon kick up and send rounds out into the street where people were coming and going.

All three of the interlopers were firing rapidly, but erratically. By comparison, Rusty and Pablo seemed to be shooting in slow motion.

Rusty wasn't sure how many shots he got off before his target fell. Probably around five. The Glock held sixteen, counting the one in the chamber. When his guy crumpled, Rusty immediately swung around ready to shoot at the other two.

He should have known better. Pablo lay in a prone firing position with his legs spread, just as if he were taking practice on an Army firing range. He had already taken the two down.

Doc Hoffman rose to his feet and headed toward his ever—present small black physician's bag. He was going to administer to their assailants.

"Just a moment, Doc.," Pablo said. "Let me make sure they're not going to do any more shooting."

The doc ignored him and headed for the guy Rusty had shot. Henry and Barry stood dazed.

Pablo started to stop Doc, then suddenly turned to Rusty. "You O.K.?"

"Yeah."

"Then get down from there. What the hell do you think you are, a professional target?"

Rusty carefully climbed down. He kept the Glock in his right hand, checking the horizon. Doc Hoffman was kneeling over the fallen shooter.

Suddenly, the air was again filled with the chatter of assault rifles. Rusty crashed to the ground. Pablo was on top of him, covering him.

"Damn you. You almost broke my legs."

Pablo didn't respond to Rusty's complaint. He stayed on top of Rusty. His carbine pointed at the street searching for the shooters.

An unmarked police car with a flashing red light stuck on its roof and its siren blaring, raced down the street chasing a dark sedan that was still spraying lead onto the tennis court.

The sedan hit something in the street, it stopped and the doors flew open. More shots were fired. Instantly, booming shotgun fire from the police car replied. Abruptly, a stillness filled the air.

Looking backwards across the net, Rusty saw Barry fall into a sitting position, holding his right thigh. Blood was spreading onto the ground beneath him.

"Doc," Rusty yelled, "Barry's been hit!" He rushed to Barry's side, glancing back to see if Doc had heard. Rusty was surprised to see Pablo running full speed toward the Doc. Pablo had left his weapon behind.

"I think it went clean through," Barry said.

Rusty looked at the wound and whipped off his belt. "Tourniquet," he told Henry, handing him the belt. Rusty turned and took off after Pablo.

Rusty was suddenly aware that the courts were filled with uniformed deputies with drawn weapons. Two sergeants and six or seven deputies. And there had been two cars full of plainclothes cops. How the hell did they all get here so fast?

He reached Pablo, kneeling over Doc and the shooter. The Doc had been trying to save a man who tried to kill him. Now, Doc Hoffman, ever so still, looked up at them.

A slug from the drive-by gangbangers' car had pierced his skull just above his right eye. Instant death, Rusty knew, gazing into the staring blue eyes that had so often scrutinized him and restored his health.

Pablo reached over and gently closed Hoffman's eyes. Then, still on his knees, he made the sign of the cross and began praying softly in Spanish. Rusty sat silently next to him, holding his head between his hands.

A uniformed sergeant approached. Softly, he said, "I'm sorry, Gentlemen."

Pablo didn't even look at him. Just kept praying in a low voice.

"I know how you feel, Gentlemen, but the whole area is a crime scene. It has to be done. Could you please move over to the fence where the deputies are?"

"Go get fucked," Pablo said, and kept quietly praying.

"Sheriff?" the sergeant pleaded.

Rusty nodded, and handed him his Glock. He pointed to where Pablo had left his weapon. "He," nodding toward Pablo, "returned fire with that.

"The Doc was trying to help this shooter when the drive-by took him down. And you've got a retired deputy wounded over there. He's bleeding out. You got ambulances responding?"

"We got everything responding, Sir. I'll make sure the deputy's first." He spoke into his shoulder mike and slowly walked toward Barry and Henry.

This had all happened because the gang was after him. Rusty sat in despair. They had lost Doc. An irreplaceable part of their lives was gone.

Rusty's rage at the gangbangers was mixed with determination that none of his other friends would be hurt, and an equally powerful emotion. Whoever was responsible for the attacks would pay.

CHAPTER SIX

D OC HOFFMAN HADN'T been religious. Following his wish, a funeral service was held in a non-denominational chapel after his cremation. The hall held six hundred people, but the aisles were crowded with standees.

Rusty sat between Teresa and Pablo. Ten year-old Enrique was next to his father and Henry. Rusty had been invited to be one of a long line of speakers, but he was too numb with grief to take the podium. Physician colleagues, prominent officials, and a number of heads of non-profit organizations spoke of Hoffman's skills, dedication and charitable medical work.

Rusty couldn't concentrate as the well-deserved compliments droned on. He found the ubiquitous security surrounding the ceremony an oppressive reminder of the violence suddenly engulfing them.

The atmosphere wasn't improved any by the relentless and obscene media description of a "machine-gun civil war between gangs and the Silicon Valley Sheriff's Department." His own name was in every story with mysterious insinuations as to his role in the combat.

Finally, it was over. They rode in the funeral limousine back to Pablo's home. Teresa sat between him and Pablo in the rear seat. She had worked with Doc and held him in both professional esteem and deep affection. Tears in her eyes, she rested her head on Pablo's shoulder, holding both his hand and Rusty's. Rusty was unable to take comfort from her gesture. He was running on empty.

Henry rode in the front, next to the driver. Reaching the Garcia residence, Teresa embraced both Rusty and Pablo. She pecked Henry's cheek, and led Enrique into the west wing of the house.

The three men settled into Pablo's den. He salted three glasses and poured Tequila. The first drink was a solemn toast to the Doc. Slowly, Pablo refilled the glasses. Unhurriedly, they began a silent ritual of getting drunk in honor of their departed friend.

Pablo's eyes settled on Rusty, who could almost sense Pablo feeling the presence of the Doc. Pablo suddenly corked the bottle as if Hoffman had reprimanded him for feeding Rusty too much booze.

Pablo shelved the bottle and turned back to them.

"You haven't said a fucking word since the shoot-out at O.K. Corral, Rusty."

"He's dead because of me. As you said, I was the target."

"Bullshit!" Pablo exploded. "I don't want to hear that liberal guilt crap. Blame the victim. You're a victim, Dummy. Every one of those bastards deserved to die and they did. It was their fault."

"He's right, Rusty," Henry added, now fully composed. "Doc died doing his duty. It was what he loved, being a doctor. The killers were responsible, not you, or us."

"And we're the ones that got hauled down to the Homicide Unit to be grilled once again by that scorpion disguised as a lady lieutenant," Pablo added.

"Now, Pablo," Henry interjected. "I was there as your attorney. I assure you that your statements were an accurate description of legal self-defense."

"Well, her questions sure didn't sound friendly to me."

"She was doing her job. Actually, those concise, pertinent questions nailed down our case for self-defense much more definitively than if she had tossed softballs that D.A. Herrera could have twisted."

Pablo grunted. Rusty thought back to the state of shock he had been in after seeing the Doc dead. He hardly remembered the headquarters session. Lieutenant Maria Lopez-Hogan had been thorough, but it seemed to him that a couple of times when her eyes were on him there had been genuine flashes of sympathy and, and . . . Could it have been anguish? He hoped Henry was right.

He bummed a sleeping pill from Pablo and went to bed shortly after 9 p.m.

Rusty's deep, restful sleep brought on by the sleeping pill was interrupted when he felt a strong arm lock onto his hand wrapped around the Glock under his pillow.

"Easy, Rusty. It's me, Pablo."

Rusty let go of the Glock and sat up. The bedside clock showed 4 a.m. "What's wrong, Pablo?"

"The witch lieutenant is here without her broomstick. Says she has to talk to you." Pablo stood back as he watched Rusty come awake and ease, fully dressed, from the bed.

JOSEPH D. MCNAMARA

Rusty followed Pablo into the foyer. Lieutenant Maria Lopez-Hogan stood next to the front door. A light grey, three quarter length jacket covered her cream-colored blouse and slacks against the pre-dawn chill. For the first time, Rusty saw deep fatigue lining her face.

"Sheriff," she said grimly to Rusty, "you need to come with me. We have a report that your house is on fire."

"I'll come too," Pablo added.

"Mr. Garcia, may I respectfully suggest that you stay with your family," the lieutenant said. "We don't know much about the fire yet, but the Sureños lost four of their members in their raid on Sheriff Carter's house and had seven more killed today. We've been trying to keep an eye on them, but they've scattered. You have to consider that you and your family are targets, too."

"Listen, little lady, I was taking out bad guys before you got to high school. I have good security for the complex. My two men on guard here right now are better than anyone you've got on your SWAT team. And, I'm going to let Bruno into the outside house perimeter to greet any gangbangers that are stupid enough to come here. In fact, let me introduce you to Bruno."

"No, Pablo!" Rusty protested.

But it was too late. Pablo had opened the door to a small room bordering the foyer. A huge, snarling black mongrel dog leapt toward Lieutenant Hogan with its formidable teeth bared. Pablo quickly grabbed the chain around the dog's neck and had to use his full strength to restrain the vicious animal before it reached her.

She didn't wince, simply reaching into the side pocket of her jacket. For a horrible moment, Rusty was afraid she would try to shoot the dog. It was too close. The animal's jaws would have closed on her lovely throat before she could have brought her weapon to bear. Rusty hated the beast, even though Pablo had somehow managed to have it sniff Rusty enough to realize that he was not to be attacked.

But the lieutenant squatted down to the dog's level. "Hello, Bruno," Rusty heard a melodic note previously absent from her terse speech. Slowly, she removed her right hand from her jacket. Palm down, she stuck it right into proximity of the growling beast's bared fangs.

Pablo's face showed amazement when the animal abruptly quieted and sniffed curiously at the young woman's hand. She turned it over. The dog eagerly licked a brownish substance from her palm.

"Sit, Bruno," she commanded when the dog had finished eating. It sat, docile, its formerly wild eyes that had focused on her jugular now eagerly looked at her hand for another tasty treat.

Still squatting next to the dog, the lieutenant gazed up and met Pablo's eyes. "What is it they say about generals always fighting with strategies from the last war, Captain?"

For once, Pablo was speechless. Rusty followed Maria Lopez-Hogan out to her unmarked police vehicle stopped in the circular driveway. Two other unmarked police cars surrounded it. Each contained two plainclothes deputies. They were to have a motorcade to Rosebud Lane.

CHAPTER SEVEN

"WHAT DID YOU feed the dog?" Rusty asked, as they pulled out of the driveway.

"You'll find out when you return."

He turned sharply to her. "You didn't cause harm to Bruno?"

"Just the carpets. Your friend, Pablo, is a little too sure of himself, even for an Alpha male."

"Well, at the risk of sounding Alpha, Lieutenant, you're weaving on the road. I can drive if you like."

Her jaw tightened. "We're almost there. Try to keep your nerves under control until we arrive. I've been driving a long time without an accident. You have three on your record."

Rusty grunted. He had been constantly defending her against Pablo's barbs, but she didn't make it any easier.

He was stunned when they pulled into the normally dark, quiet, Rosebud Lane that had never boasted a sidewalk. The street was clogged with fire, police, and ambulance vehicles.

A small crowd of pajama and bathrobe clad residents stood quietly watching the inferno that had been his house. Any number of people were on their lawns, aiming water from their garden hoses at large, fiery embers landing on their roofs, trees, and shrubs.

Lieutenant Hogan badged a uniformed deputy controlling the traffic. He waved them on. She drove gingerly through the fire lines, avoiding hoses. She stopped opposite the blaze. The house was gone.

Instead, the conflagration, in a deep pit that had been the foundation, sent flames reaching high into the night black sky. Only the chimney and a couple of stubborn burning wood support beams, about to topple, remained upright.

County fire trucks poured huge jets of water into the blazing foundation and adjacent garage without any sign that the flames were diminishing. Two other fire vehicles aimed their hoses at nearby trees and houses.

Standing next to the police car, Rusty could feel the intense heat. The lieutenant, who had alighted from the driver's side, closer to the fire, could feel it, too. She walked around the car and stood next to Rusty.

Rusty knew he should feel deep emotion looking at the ruins of the home where he and Lucy had spent such happy years. She had turned it into a sanctuary from his stressful world.

The sheriff of a huge, rapidly growing county, managing a large police agency, lived under pressure twenty-four hours a day, every day of the year. So many times, Lucy had been at his side at the endless community dinners, meetings, and Department ceremonies that were required of him.

He wondered at his lack of feeling.

The Lieutenant lightly touched his arm. "I'm sorry, Sheriff. All those mementos of your life, gone. But the house itself. You couldn't have gone back there. All the cleaning in the world couldn't have removed the thought of the blood of those two who desecrated your home."

Mrs. Hernandez appeared at their side. "Sheriff! Thank god you're safe." She hugged him. He put his arms around the trembling old lady. She had raised her children here, lived her whole adult life here. Lucy had gone out of her way to help her as age diminished the woman's abilities. As sick as she was herself, Lucy took Mrs. Hernandez shopping, to doctor visits and even helped her cook.

He noticed that Lieutenant Hogan was watching. He released Mrs. Hernandez.

"I was so afraid that you might be in there, Sheriff. It's terrible. Did the evil ones do this?"

Rusty looked at the still spectacular blaze. There was no way this had been an accident, but he remained silent.

"Did you happen to see or hear anything before the fire, Mrs. Hernandez?" Lieutenant Hogan asked.

"Nada. The engines woke me up. It was already too late. It was blazing."

She turned back to Rusty. "I always felt so safe with you across the street, Sheriff. I'm old. I don't want to move, but I'm afraid. Should I sell my house? Go to one of those group homes?"

Lieutenant Hogan spoke rapidly in Spanish to the old lady. Mrs. Hernandez listened intently, nodding her head a number of times.

"Mucho gracias, Tienta," she said, after a few minutes. Then she briefly hugged the Lieutenant and shuffled in her bathrobe and slippers back to her house, all the while dabbing at tears with her handkerchief.

"What did you tell her?" Rusty said.

"That it was O.K. She doesn't have to sell her house."

"Lieutenant," he said, tired, and still fighting off the sleeping pill, and unable to keep the irritation out of his voice, "you talked to her for a few minutes. You obviously said more than it was O.K."

He regretted his words when she looked at him. He read the total exhaustion in her eyes. She leaned with one hand against the police car.

"I told Mrs. Hernandez that she was safe. The evil ones were only after you. Now that you're gone, she doesn't have to sell her house."

She had made no attempt to keep the anger from her voice. Rusty looked back toward the blaze which was finally beginning to diminish. There was nothing left to burn.

He sighed. "It's gone. Can we leave?"

"I have to wait for the deputy fire chief to officially confirm that it was arson. I can have the deputies take you back to Mr. Garcia's."

"I'll wait. If you have time, I'd like to buy you a cup of coffee in the all night diner a couple of blocks away on the Avenue."

She nodded. The Deputy Chief had taken off his helmet and was approaching.

"Definitely a pro job. They must have planted multiple incendiaries in key locations. A couple of minutes after ignition it was already uncontrollable. Accelerants were placed in strategic spots. We were lucky to keep it from spreading and taking out the entire block."

They sat opposite each other in a booth over black coffee. For a moment after giving the order to the waitress, Lieutenant Maria Lopez-Hogan leaned her head back and closed her eyes.

Rusty thought, if Lucy had been able to have children, our daughter would have been almost her age. He placed his large hand over hers resting on the table.

"I'm sorry I spoke that way, asking what you said to Mrs. Hernandez, Maria. It's just that losing the Doc like that . . ."

She didn't move her hand, but opened her eyes and looked into his. Rusty squeezed her hand. "Don't take offense, Lieutenant, I really appreciate you coming personally to pick me up, but would you do me a big favor? Let two deputies in the front car take me back to Pablo's, and let one of the two in the other car drive you home. You're out on your feet."

She yanked her hand from under his. Her eyes were no longer sleepy. "Speaking of Mrs. Hernandez," she pulled a small notebook from her side pocket and pointed a pen at a notation, "she called 911 at 1103 hours on the day of the attack on you."

He felt like she had slapped his face. Sighing, he leaned back in the booth. "Look, I know that you and Sally can't let me be part of the investigation, but you're telling me less than what you'd tell an ordinary victim."

She continued, "Mrs. Hernandez was confused. Didn't I.D. herself. Told the communications operator, 'There's noise, but I don't think he's home. Hold on.' The call taker was sharp. She came up with the address on the call-locator, realized that it was across from your address. All of the operators have a list in front of them of key possible targets."

Rusty simply looked at her.

"Then, Mrs. H. is back on the phone at 1105 hours. She's excited. Says it had sounded like shots, and there's a strange car with two men in your driveway. But she's apologizing, telling the operator it could just have been kids down the street. They shoot firecrackers all the time. Mrs. H. is babbling on, saying she saw you drive your truck away and it's not there now. So you must be out. She keeps interrupting the operator."

"So?"

"So, finally she screams, 'More noises! I'm going to look.' By now, it's 1110 hours. The operator signals the supervisor who comes to her console. By the time she gets filled in by the call taker, it's 1111 hours. Mrs. H. never gets back on the phone."

Rusty frowned at her.

"At 1114 hours, you call and report the gangbangers' shooting and driving away. Communications dispatches. The operator gets back to you. At 1116 hours you report that you're having a heart attack. Two minutes later, at 1118 hours, you finally mention two guys bleeding out in the rear of your house. Putting it all together, that makes it fifteen plus minutes after Mrs. H heard the first shots, indicating that's when you sliced and diced them with the bread knife. Fifteen minutes after you opened their arteries, that you decided to call an ambulance for them."

Rusty stood. "I want to go back to Pablo's now."

She followed him out of the diner and spoke briefly to the deputies in the lead car. Rusty started to get into the rear, but she beckoned him aside.

"You didn't hear this from me, Sheriff, but Herrera's convening a grand jury next week. Not even Sally knows yet."

Rusty resisted asking her, if that's so, how come she knew? In the rear seat of the police car, he looked back and saw Maria Lopez-Hogan giving her car keys to a deputy. She then got into the other car to be driven home.

He realized he had been wrong to think of Maria Lopez-Hogan as an innocent young woman in a harsh world. She was smart, experienced and tough. He had been foolish to brush aside Pablo's warnings that Lieutenant Lopez-Hogan was not a straightforward cop without a hidden agenda.

CHAPTER EIGHT

I T WAS EIGHT a.m. when the cops dropped Rusty off. He badly wanted a shower to get the smell of the fire off him. He spotted a note on his freshly made bed.

It was from Pablo, informing Rusty that he had taken Teresa and the kids down to Malibu for their annual two—week vacation visit to her mother's ranch. Sure, except Rusty knew they always went there in August, not early July.

Pablo would be back in a few days. Rusty was to make himself at home, AND TO STAY HOME.

After showering, and changing to clean clothes, he decided it was time to visit the Padre. Rusty hesitated, then left the Glock under his pillow.

He sought out Antonio, asking for a ride to the car maintenance shop to pick up his truck. Antonio, no doubt having been instructed by Pablo to keep Rusty safe, was reluctant, but did as he was asked.

Rusty paid the bill for the truck, acknowledging the sympathetic remarks about his troubles from the owner, whom he had known for years. Behind the wheel, he drove carefully through the run-down city streets where the equally run-down St. Sebastian Church stood in what had once been a thriving middle class neighborhood before the gangs Sureños and Norteños had arrived.

That was the odd thing about the local gangs. Neither had any contact with the statewide Sureños and Norteños, who for unknown reasons stayed out of Silicon Valley County.

Another puzzling oddity was, despite their names, the Silicon County gangs hadn't split on a north south axis. The Sureños claimed the turf on the east side of the county, the Norteños, the west side.

His old truck was well known both to deputies and gangbangers, neither of whom he wished to encounter at the moment. As he had often done during his years as sheriff, he ignored the parking lot and pulled to the rear of the church.

He drove around fifteen feet down a dirt path into the tiny ancient abandoned cemetery, leaving the truck where it couldn't be easily seen. Gangbangers were apparently superstitious about ghosts, and there was no particular reason for a police cruiser to venture among the graves.

During his many confidential dealings with the Padre, they had both agreed that it was best that their meetings went unobserved both by law enforcement and the gangs the Padre regarded as the major part of his ministry.

The rear door of the church was locked. Rusty didn't want to try the front entrance, which was visible from the street. In the past, he had entered the rear and used the narrow hall leading from the sacristy directly into the rectory.

Now, he found the front of the church locked, as well. He was forced to walk along the sidewalk to the next-door rectory and stand in the open, waiting for the doorbell to be answered.

Finally, the door opened. At first, he almost didn't recognize the stooped-over old man. The Padre had stood erect, over six-feet with the broad shoulders of the college fullback he had been before entering the seminary. In just the last couple of years, age had caught up with him.

"Sheriff," the old priest greeted him, "you haven't been here since Lucy's funeral. Come in. Come in. You always came through the sacristy," the aged man said, limping into the living room with the aid of a cane.

"The doors were locked, Padre."

The priest, obviously hurting, sank into a worn chair.

"A sign of the times we live in. We lock the people away from God and then wonder why society is the way it is."

He pointed to an old TV set. "I've been hearing about your problems." "People criticized our peace efforts. Still, I'd like to believe you and I did some good. Saved some lives. But times have changed since you retired, Sheriff. I doubt if we could do much now."

The Padre had frequently carried messages and truce negotiations from Rusty to the leaders of the Norteños and Sureños during especially tense times when both gangs and the sheriff's deputies had been in a three-way war.

"It's why I came, Padre. I have no idea why the Sureños have suddenly made me a target four years after I left policing. I thought you might have heard something when meeting with them."

"Meet with them! Not for a couple of years. Even a man of God is no longer welcome among these boys."

Boys! The Padre's use of that word to describe the young killers had always grated on Rusty, but he had never told the Padre.

He wondered why the priest was now shunned. Most of the new "boys" arriving had been from Mexico, Central America, or South America. Many gang members had been born here, offspring of immigrants from the same countries. Catholic countries.

Notwithstanding the criminality of the gangbangers, they had always had what Rusty believed to be a childlike reverence for priests. The county hadn't had much of a black population, so there had never been black gangs to worry about. The few attempts to form them had been brutally crushed by both Latino gangs.

"Next month I'm leaving. Ordered into a retirement home in San Diego. The higher-ups are closing the church. The church where you and Lucy were married, Rusty. The church where we laid her to rest, God bless her soul, just a couple of years ago. She took communion every Sunday and a couple of times a week. We both prayed that you would come with her but . . ."

"She really appreciated your visits when she got sick, Father. I never did thank you for that."

Rusty heard the hoarseness in his voice. He had never shown, but often felt anger at this old man's excuses for vicious thugs, his silly belief that there was no such thing as a bad boy. Yet, devout Lucy had held him in great respect.

Rusty guessed when it was all said and done, that the priest was a good man, although the Sheriff had never completely trusted him when it came to warning gangs of pending police actions. They used each other, he supposed.

Rusty brought himself back to listening. The old Padre was obviously sick, and his voice was weak. Rusty leaned forward to hear.

"Sheriff Sally is a good officer, I think. But outside of a courtesy visit when she was first appointed, she's never come here."

Her mistake, Rusty thought. Leaving intelligence gathering to the Intel cops, instead of hearing the nuances from community leaders with your own ears.

"I visited Jacko to say goodbye a month ago. The change was startling. The boys outside his center were actually threatening, even though I was dressed as a priest. If the Indian and Jacko's son hadn't come to escort me, I believe they would have attacked me."

Jacko was head of the Norteños, a shrewd man, capable of great violence, but one who Rusty had always found it possible to deal with. The Indian, six-four, lean and muscular, with a shaved head, and huge arms visible under the gray muscle vest he always wore, was the enforcer.

The Indian was lightning fast, with gun, knife, or his powerful body. Of course, he wasn't a Native-American Indian, but his hawk-like face and copper coloring undoubtedly were due to an Indian-Mexican background.

Jacko's son, Ralph, was the Indian's apprentice in violence, his shadow, and thought to be Jacko's heir as gang leader.

"What did Jacko say?" Rusty asked.

"It was shocking. He told me I must never come back. He couldn't prevent me from being killed. He said they have been overwhelmed with these newcomers. It was our immigration policies, drug armies in their home countries, whatever," he hesitated.

"And?"

"Jacko said by the time these boys arrive at fourteen, or fifteen, they have already killed with assault rifles, machetes, been kidnapped and made child soldiers, indoctrinated into killing, and the ones born here were now no better."

"But Jacko is still boss?"

"I think Jacko has become a frightened figurehead. Only his aura, and that of the Indian and Jacko's son keep the barbarians—his word—at bay. I really came away feeling that he is almost a prisoner. That the three of them can't leave. He hinted that Ricardo Campas, a powerful rival with the Sureños, was planning a coup against him."

Rusty thought about it. Padre was an old man. Rusty had never completely trusted his judgment, even less so now, in his condition. This was a strange situation he was describing.

"Did you know Campas, Padre?"

"A little. He was close to Ralph, though. Jacko must have thought well of him, at first. He chose him to attend the education center. Although, something happened there. Soon Ricardo went back to the other gang."

Rusty tried without success to picture Ricardo. But there had been so many throughout the years.

"Lucy donated generously, Rusty. I say a mass for you every week at her request. I know you're not religious. I think you'll admit though, I never preached at you."

Rusty nodded, intensely disturbed at the old man's sudden intrusion into his deep private sorrow about Lucy.

The priest continued, "Since this is the only chance I've had, or daresay will have, I'll follow her wishes to tell you what we prayed for. I know you well enough to understand that you'll resent what I say, but I did promise Lucy."

Rusty's stiff body and stern face gave him no encouragement, but the Padre was not to be deterred.

"It was Lucy's prayer that you would remarry, Sheriff. She knew how much you would miss her, but it was her fondest hope that you would find another wife. She wanted you to be happy. She said you needed a good wife and had a lot of life to live."

Rusty was so furious that he averted his gaze and fought from telling the priest "How dare you!" He took a deep breath and regained control. The old man probably didn't have that long to live. Why let his anger cause more pain?

He stood, "Adios, Padre."

"Let me follow you to the door, Sheriff. They tell me I must lock up all the time until I leave."

Slowly, they walked to the door.

"One last thing, Sheriff. Jacko told me that you probably would be coming to see me. He said I should tell you, whatever you do, not to try to visit him. It will mean death for you as well as him, the Indian and his son. He said you should look to your own Department for the answers."

Rusty left the rectory and headed for his truck. Despite the Padre's warning, he was going to visit Jacko and hear exactly what he had to say.

CHAPTER NINE

RUSTY PULLED HIS truck right up in front of Jacko's main headquarters, The Boy's Job Training Center. A group of watchful Norteños stood near the entrance. He got out and walked toward the front door. Any subtlety would have been fatal with this group.

A pint-sized teen-ager blocked his path. Other youths closed in. Rusty stood very still.

There weren't any chicas around. A good sign. They carried guns for the male gangbangers who were constantly being stopped and frisked by cops. Still, every one of the young males, and some who hadn't been young for years, carried a legal knife.

After a full minute of stalemate, the group dourly parted when the Indian moved through them. He hadn't aged at all. The man who never spoke a word still inspired fear.

But Rusty saw the difference that the Padre had described. There was fear, yes. But none of the respect and awe that had formerly surrounded the Indian. Years ago, the group would never have dared show their displeasure.

The Indian patted Rusty down. It was more for the group's benefit than the thorough pat-down the Indian would have given if he were serious. He gestured Rusty through the front door, protecting his back.

Inside, Jacko's son, Ralph, stood, no longer the skinny fifteen-year old Rusty remembered, but a full-grown man. He held an AR-15 rifle with an extended banana magazine. Thirty-six rounds. It wasn't for protection from cops. Maybe from the group outside, or the Sureños.

He handed the weapon to the Indian, who moved to the window where the curtains had been slightly parted to provide a view of the front. Ralph led Rusty to a comfortable leather chair facing Jacko, lounging on a worn couch with his booted feet resting on the small, scratched, glass coffee table separating him from Rusty.

Jacko waved Ralph away, but his son paid no heed. Another dramatic change from past meetings. Instead, he took the chair next to Rusty.

Rusty hid his surprise. In the five or six years since he had been here, Jacko had withered. Not as bad as the Padre, but the intensity of his body language was no longer there. His wrinkled face sagged.

The Padre was probably early eighties, but Jacko was only in his sixties. The shrewd brown eyes were still there, though.

"Have you not spoken to the Padre, Sheriff?" Jacko asked.

"I just left him, Jacko."

"Did the old man forget my warning, or have you gone loco, Sheriff?"

"I heard him."

Suddenly, Ralph leaned forward, his eyes blazing. "You have been most stupid. Even if the SWAT team is mobilized two blocks away, these animals will kill all of us before cops get in here."

"My associates outside," Jacko said, "seem to regard being killed as a memorial to their bravery, which will never be forgotten even though they have already forgotten their friends, shot down a year or two ago. You have doomed us, Sheriff."

"Let's worry about that later, Jacko. I didn't come without a plan. I came for some information. Why are the Sureños suddenly trying to kill me?"

"The answer lies somewhere within your old Department, Sheriff. But Ralph has a proposal. He says the only way for us to survive is to kill you and allow the group out front to take your body to the Sureños as a peace offering."

"You were always able to handle the Sureños, with a little help from us, Jacko."

"Thanks to the federal, state, and local task force, which, last year, busted forty of our members for Meth trafficking, we are totally outnumbered by the Sureños. Never mind that they deal more meth than any Norteños ever dreamed of." The old fire was in Jacko's eyes now.

"Surely, the Sureños can't blame me for whatever the task force is doing. I retired years before the task force was formed," Rusty said.

"I know that, Sheriff, but since you left, there is no communication with the police, only more harassment, arrests, and news stories. The result is what you saw outside, increased recruitment for both gangs. A surplus of jungle animals with cunning and unlimited guns and dope to sell, but no brains."

Jacko got up and moved slowly and painfully to his old battered desk. He opened the middle drawer and came back, handing Rusty a single sheet of paper.

It was a three-week-old newspaper clipping that Rusty had seen. A large group picture sat above the brief story. The governor of California was in the center, with Rusty in a suit and tie on his left. A cluster of uniformed police chiefs and a couple of Feds in suits were in the background.

The caption read: "Politically Influential Former Sheriff Endorses Governor's Federal and Local Police Anti-Gang and Drug Task Force." The story continued, saying that former Silicon County Sheriff Rusty Carter had helped plan the crackdown on the county Norteños that resulted in at least forty of them facing life in prison for drug dealing and various other crimes.

The article concluded: "The sheriff, who kept gang violence to a minimum during his tenure, reportedly will help plan a similar movement against the Sureños, the other large gang whose violence has alarmed this county."

Rusty grunted. "Look, Jacko, I owed the governor a political favor from the old days when he endorsed me after the Deputy's Union gave me a vote of No Confidence and campaigned against me in the election."

"Politics. I remember it well."

"Right. For some reason, the governor thought it would help if I posed with the group in his Sacramento office. The newspaper doesn't know its ass from a hole in the wall. I haven't had anything to do with law enforcement since I retired."

"Turn the paper over, Sheriff."

Rusty did. He stared at an old picture of himself in uniform. Printed under the picture in huge block lettering was "$50,000 For This Man Dead." At the bottom of the page was graffiti signing. Rusty frowned at it.

"It's the Sureños' sign, Sheriff."

"It's crazy, Jacko."

"Yes, but they are crazy. They believe that you personally are aiming the task force to do to them what it did to us."

"Christ! Fifty thousand. No wonder they've been going wild. Why did they want to kidnap me?"

"To torture the Task Force plans against them from you before they killed you."

"So, as Ralph figured, I'm worth $50,000 and a way out for all of you."

"I haven't forgotten the vote of No Confidence, Sheriff. Your narc Captain, Jeremiah Christian, and his men planted enough Crack Cocaine on me for a mandatory life sentence. You saved me."

"They were wrong all the way. They didn't belong on the Department for what they did."

"Yes. But it was a slam-dunk case against me, until you investigated my lawyer's complaints. You had the charges dismissed and tried to fire the guilty cops. It would have cost you the election if the governor hadn't backed you so strongly. So tell me your plan so that I can compare it to Ralph's."

Rusty jabbed the newspaper story with his finger. "This actually helps our chances of getting out of here alive, Jacko."

CHAPTER TEN

T HEY LEFT THE building. Ralph's face was full of resentment as he led the way. He kept his right hand in his pocket. Next came Rusty, hand cuffed from behind. He noticed that the size of the crowd had more than doubled. Word of his arrival had spread.

There were angry shouts. They subsided when the gang saw that Jacko, a step behind Rusty, held a shotgun to the former sheriff's head. The Indian brought up the rear, the AR-15 casually sweeping from side to side along with his dead eyes.

The same kid, joined by an older, much larger gang member blocked Ralph's progress.

"Easy, Ralph," Jacko whispered.

Ralph slowed his pace. Rusty felt sweat dripping down his neck into the middle of his back. It was his plan, but he knew it was risky as hell. Jacko had been right. A lot of these gangbangers had a death wish.

Right now, it could go either way. If the group of thirty or so gang members surged, the shotgun, and whatever Ralph had in his pocket and even the AR-15 couldn't save them from this mob.

Jacko held the flyer offering $50,000 for Rusty's death up in his left hand.

"Look," he commanded, swinging the paper around so that the entire circle saw it. "We are going to deliver this Pig and come back with $50,000 dollars. We will have enough rifles to win. Viva Norteños!"

There were a few shouts of "Viva Norteños." Then it swelled into a roaring chant.

The two members blocking the path heard. They stepped aside. Ralph unhurriedly got behind the wheel of Rusty's truck. Jacko opened the passenger door. He pushed Rusty roughly inside and got in after him, letting the crowd see that he still held the shotgun to Rusty's head.

The Indian vaulted over the pick-up's rear folding door. He rested the assault rifle on the side panel, rather pointedly aimed at the crowd.

The truck pulled slowly away. It turned a corner, taking them out of sight of the crowd. Jacko lowered the shotgun and uncuffed Rusty.

"Nice and easy, Ralph," Rusty said, more calmly than he felt. "No traffic violations. We don't want any attention from cops right now."

Ralph still wore a sullen look, but followed the advice. Rusty was sweating. Part one of the plan had worked. They had escaped the mob. But now he wondered. The three men could easily revert to Ralph's original plan, or simply kill him and dump his body into one of the empty lots they were passing.

"Jacko," he asked, "what ever happened to the other program that you had on the east side?"

"Two years after you left, the county criminal justice committee that you chaired dropped our funding. It was too bad. The Youth Reclamation Project had twenty kids complete the program over four years. Sixteen graduated high school and college. One's a doctor, another a dentist, five teachers, two cops in the CHP. Nineteen out of twenty made it out of the life."

Jacko had handpicked five or six a year from the new kids trying to join the gang. He sent them, instead, into the live-in program. The deputy's union and some prominent ambitious politicians thundered against funding that "rewarded" gang members.

Rusty had been able to squeeze a grant award of seed money from the county committee allocating federal criminal justice grants on the basis that private sector funding would match the public dough. With Pablo's help, they managed to double the seed money.

Over the next two years the justice committee secured a small campus and doubled the funding when they saw top business leaders serving as mentors, in addition to providing internships and funding.

Rusty privately made it clear to Jacko that if he didn't run the program on the level, the sheriff's department would make it impossible for him to head the Norteños. The cops may not have been able to eliminate the gang, but they could make life so miserable that a new leader was bound to emerge.

Behind the scenes, Jacko became the program's strongest supporter. Some of the methods he used to "motivate" the staff, and dissuade various unions from kneecapping a non-union operation, drew vague complaints.

But, since no one ever dared to lodge a formal charge, the sheriff's department never investigated. Given the achievement of the kids, California declared it a model program three years after it started.

JOSEPH D. MCNAMARA

Unlike the mob they had just escaped, Jacko's program enrollees had seen success models. They took advantage of the opportunities offered.

"What about the twentieth guy?"

"Oh, you've heard of him, Sheriff, Spanish Ramundo."

"Boss of the Sureños?"

"Yes. The man who offers $50,000 to see you dead. He also wants me killed, but I don't command nearly the price. Of course," Jacko smiled slightly, "I don't get my picture taken with the governor."

"Why did you say the answer lies in the sheriffs' department?"

"It was an unmarked sheriff's car that threw the leaflets into the streets both near our and the Sureños' headquarters. Also, we spent some money.

"Just like detectives, we got the flyers analyzed. A retired deputy in the private detective business liked our money. The flyers came from the copying room on the second floor of the Sheriff Department's headquarters."

Shocked, Rusty didn't know whether to believe him or not. He changed the subject. "The Sureños still hang out in the little empty store on East Fourth Street?"

"No. They're too big now, thanks to the Task Force cutting us in half. How could all those cops be so dumb to not know that we held each other in check?"

"The feds live in a different world, Jacko."

"They should stay in it. Like General Motors and Ford, we never sue, we use a different business model. Giving the Sureños superiority could only make everything worse. And now you're seeing it."

"Sureños give up the store on Fourth?"

"Spanish Ramundo's not so bright. It's probably why he didn't make it in my education program. He still meets with some of his top captains there. Three o'clock sharp, every two days."

"Not too cool."

"No. They sweep it for bugs. Have good lookouts, but it's foolish to be so predictable. If we had known what they had planned before my authority was weakened by the task force . . ."

"Would have used your different business model?"

Jacko smiled. "Better than making the lawyers rich, no?"

Rusty's uneasiness grew. They had been driving for twenty minutes. He didn't care for the angry look still pasted on Ralph's face. Didn't care for it at all.

Why hadn't they released him? Finally, Ralph pulled into a shopping mall. He got out and left the motor running. The Indian jumped from the back of the truck. The AR-15 was now hidden under his long jacket. Jacko did the same with the shotgun.

He stood by the open window. Rusty braced himself for a sudden blast of gunfire from any or all of them. But Jacko stood there, hesitating. He still had something to say.

"One other thing, Sheriff. You've heard of the Phantom brothers?"

"Two brothers from Juarez who are super hit men?"

"Juarez, Guadalajara, Acapulco? Who knows? No one can identify them. But word on the street is that Ramundo sent for them after he kept missing you. They're here. $50,000 is enough to lure them. Adios, Sheriff. Please drive away. Don't try to see where we're going."

Rusty got behind the wheel and drove out of the mall. He had a pretty good idea where Jacko was going. There was a large bank in the mall. Jacko probably had one or two oversized safe deposit boxes filled for a rainy day. It was a good guess that they also had a car stashed somewhere in the mall parking maze.

Rusty drove away. These three were out of his life. He no longer had to look over his shoulder for them. But Jacko's information left little doubt that Rusty was a prime target of the Sureños.

Then too, he had to be concerned with D.A. Herrera, traitors in his former Sheriff's department, and the ever-present, enigmatic Lieutenant Maria Lopez-Hogan.

CHAPTER ELEVEN

DRIVING SLOWLY AWAY from the three deposed gang leaders, fatigue hit Rusty like a tsunami. He had been hyper since being awakened by Pablo and being driven to the fire by Lieutenant Hogan.

Doc Hoffman's funeral, his home going up in flames. Dueling with the unfathomable Maria Lopez-Hogan, the poignant revelations from the Padre about Lucy's last wishes, the dicey escape from the mob of gang-bangers, and sleep deprivation, super hit men after him. It overwhelmed him.

He pulled to the curb. He had to close his eyes. In a moment, he jerked awake. Behind the wheel, he drove toward Pablo's. The last mile was tricky in the growing dusk as drowsiness again came over him. Somehow, he made it into the circular driveway.

An anxious Antonio, assault weapon slung over his shoulder, regarded him with concern. He tossed Antonio the keys, knowing that the conspicuous pick-up had to be parked in a less visible place.

Rusty found the luxurious house empty and silent, except for Itsy Bitsy, who gave him a lavish greeting. One of the staff had left a turkey sandwich for him on the kitchen table. He drank fresh milk from the refrigerator and ate while dusk faded into darkness. He showered and went to bed, falling instantly into a dream-filled slumber with his hand around the butt of the Glock under his pillow.

It was late morning by the time he opened his eyes. He smelled coffee from the kitchen. Making his way there, he found a smiling middle-aged woman who introduced herself as Mrs. Gladys Monahan.

She had been with the Garcia's for five years. She insisted on feeding him waffles covered with maple syrup to complement the coffee. Surprisingly, he found that he was hungry. Under her approving gaze he finished all of the waffles.

He went to Pablo's closet and borrowed a short sleeved sports shirt, tossing his own into the hamper. He wore the shirt over his slacks, covering the Glock holstered to his belt. It was almost one p.m. Time to visit the children.

After leaving the Army, Pablo had turned developer at precisely the right time for California's housing boom. His father had taught him the business before Pablo went into the service. Smart, tough, supercharged with energy and talent, and honed by his combat experience on the fine distinction between success and failure in big risk taking, Pablo had become mega-rich within a few years.

He didn't forget the community he came from. Soon he was an important civic leader. Known for his generosity, he was never an easy touch. He demanded results from charities he supported. Rusty, equally devoted to community involvement, although without funds, became close friends with Pablo.

The two men were part of a support group for a new children's' hospital. That's how Pablo met and immediately fell in love with Teresa, a respected pediatrician. Rusty and Lucy were part of their wedding party.

The two women were as close to each other as the two men. Childless herself, Lucy was drawn into volunteer work with terminally ill children in the children's hospital that Pablo built.

During Rusty's last five years as sheriff, Lucy retired from public school teaching. She devoted two days a week to reading to the terminally ill children.

Rusty joined her for an hour or two a week. He became a favorite, and was known as Sheriff Thursday by the children in the special ward for those under ten. Even after Lucy was gone, Rusty hardly ever missed a Thursday afternoon session with the severely ill youngsters.

Now it was Thursday. He was damned if he was going to miss being with the kids because of threats from a bunch of gangstas. He locked the Glock in the glove compartment. Stopping at the nurse's station outside the ward to pick up the day's storybooks, he saw that the two nurses were red eyed. He stopped.

"Who was it?" he asked.

"Little Robby Rivera," the nurse told him. "This morning."

He paused. You never got used to it. There were no miracle cures. Sure, sometimes the treatment succeeded giving the youngster a few more years, and they "graduated" to another ward for those over ten years of age.

Inevitably, the kids would ask Rusty what happened to their absent friend, Robby.

"What should I say when they ask?"

"Just say that he moved on to another ward, Sheriff," the nurse said, dabbing at her eyes with a tissue.

Inside with the kids, Rusty did what he was told when asked. Some of them bought it and some didn't. He quickly moved on to reading. In a way, it was strangely calming to be with these bright eyed, eagerly listening, courageous children, knowing that they were enjoying the session.

But there was always a downer after leaving them. What had these poor innocent kids done to deserve such an abbreviated future? He said goodbye, promising to come back next week.

Rusty paused for a moment outside the door to compose himself before returning the books to the nurses. He looked sideways. A woman had been standing outside the transparent glass window that allowed nurses to look and listen in.

It was Lieutenant Maria Lopez-Hogan. He wondered how long she had been watching. She was paying close attention to the children. He saw her make the sign of the cross.

After a moment, she turned to him.

"I'm sorry, Sheriff. I have a subpoena obtained by D.A. Herrera and signed by Judge Tang ordering us to immediately report to the courthouse, to the Grand Jury hearing on the third floor."

Rusty turned away from her. He walked slowly to the nurse's station and returned the books. He and the Lieutenant moved to the elevator.

In the lobby, he asked curtly, "How did you know where I was?"

She spoke in her flat, expressionless, cop voice. "You turned a half-ass, incompetent, racist, and corrupt department into a national model. You don't know anything about me. Where I live, what kind of wheels I have, nothing. But you're a legend! I know more about you than you'd ever guess."

He was brusque. "These visits here were never publicized."

"No. But some of us were quite curious about the Super Sheriff."

In the rear parking lot he said, "I assume I'm not under arrest, but still have a right to call my lawyer."

"Of course."

He took out his cell phone and called Henry's private number.

"Wilson."

"Henry, Rusty. Lieutenant Hogan just flashed a subpoena signed by Judge Tang ordering me to report immediately to a Grand Jury hearing."

"You saw that it was signed by a judge?"

"Yeah."

"Well, then I guess you have to appear. Whatever you do, don't waive or sign anything until I get there. We can discuss your options."

Lieutenant Hogan waved to get Rusty's attention. He looked at her.

"Would you excuse me for a couple of minutes? I need to use the restroom." She walked back toward the hospital.

"What was that she said?" Henry asked.

"She said she needed to use the restroom. She's disappeared back into the hospital."

"You're kidding?"

"No. She's inside."

"She didn't say you were under arrest or anything like that?"

"No, only that she had a subpoena signed by the judge."

"Did she hand it to you or touch you with it in any way?"

"No."

"Do you think she'd tell the truth about that on the stand?"

Rusty thought for a moment. "Yeah. I think she would."

"Well, I guess we can argue that you weren't properly served. Come on over. I'm at home."

"Now?"

"Right. One thing, Rusty, if she reappears before you're out of there, or catches up with you, don't resist. Give me a call and go with her."

Seeing no sign of Lieutenant Maria Lopez-Hogan, Rusty walked slowly to his truck for the five-minute drive to Henry Wilson's home.

Once more, Lieutenant Maria Lopez-Hogan left him befuddled over her actions.

CHAPTER TWELVE

D URING HIS TWENTY years as a civil servant, prosecutor Henry Wilson had lived modestly. After five years in private practice, he was head of his own firm and had grown rich on just two class action lawsuits.

He now lived in the older and most expensive section of Sun City, the county seat. His home was barely five minutes from his downtown office, which was just two blocks from the county court house.

Rusty pulled his faded pick-up to the four-car garage behind the tasteful six-bedroom Tudor house. Magnificent, century-old California Oak trees in front shaded the house from the afternoon sun.

The rear yard was a different story. Sunshine was more than welcome on the sizeable swimming pool where Henry and his wife Dolores swam hour-long laps every morning. The pool was heated during the cooler rainy months, November through February. An automatic cover opened and closed at the push of a button, allowing them to enjoy warm water year round.

Rusty, who could play softball or tennis all day, disdainfully skirted the pool. It kept Henry and Dolores looking slim and youthful, like one of those nauseating television commercials.

During summer pool parties at the Wilson's, he and Pablo, bored out their minds after five minutes of swimming, would hoist their bulked-up, muscular bodies out of the water and retreat into the shaded gazebo for cold beers. Henry and Dolores drank something disgustingly healthy like lemonade, occasionally going to hell with themselves, drinking a Bloody Mary.

Lucy had a beer with the guys, until she got sick. The last two get-togethers there, she had joined the lemonade crowd. It hadn't made any difference. She died from pancreatic cancer that Fall.

Dolores, a striking brunette, who must have been ten years younger than Henry, had also been a deputy D.A. She still did some work when it pleased her, or when his firm was temporarily in need of an experienced trial attorney. During the years when Lucy was healthy, they had played a lot of tennis together at the club with Pablo, Teresa, Henry, and Dolores and Doc and his wife.

About a year after Lucy's death, Rusty had quietly told the three women that if they continued to invite single women, "appropriate" for Rusty, to their dinners, he wouldn't be there. Only when he stopped coming did they believe him, although, occasionally, they still gave it a try.

Dolores, whose vivaciousness was in sharp contrast to the serious Henry, greeted the ex-sheriff with an affectionate hug.

"Rusty," she said, moving back a step, holding him by the shoulders, "you hanging in there, Champ?" She studied him closely, as Henry approached from the house.

"Unhand him, Dolores. I witnessed this whole sordid scene," Henry said.

"She still call you Champ?" Rusty asked. Several years ago, he and Henry had won the men's A double championship at the club.

"Just in bed," Henry said, with a sly wink at Rusty.

"Rusty, would you like a beer? And how about you, dear," Dolores said sweetly to Henry, "shall I put the Viagra in your lemonade as usual?"

Rusty declined the beer. Henry ignored her put-down. The artfully constructed house sat on three, beautifully landscaped, prime acres. The two men moved out to the gazebo.

They sat in comfortable chairs around the garden table, which, indeed, looked out upon a sumptuous rose garden. A trickling waterfall fountain attracted an amazing variety of noisily chirping birds. Buzzing loudly, a tiny red-throated hummingbird hovered over the two men. After a brief inspection, it decided that no nectar would be forthcoming, and zipped away.

"Sorry about your house, Rusty. Bring me up to date," his lawyer said.

Rusty did. Henry, an expert listener, didn't once interrupt. He sat silently for a few minutes, pondering Rusty's description of events.

"What do you make of the Lieutenant coming to Pablo's prepared for the dog?" Henry said.

"She obviously knew about Bruno."

"Very interesting. And she also knew that Herrera was convening a grand jury before I or any of the courthouse gang knew, or even Sheriff Sally."

JOSEPH D. MCNAMARA

Rusty nodded.

"Then she appears sympathetic about your house burning. A moment later, she whips out her notebook and gives you a detailed grilling, suggesting that you deliberately let the two gangbangers bleed out, a possible manslaughter charge. Was she angry because you patronized her with the advice not to drive home?"

"How the hell do I know, Henry? Women. Those mysterious, marvelous creatures without whom life isn't worth living."

"Undeniably. Then, too, she somehow knew about you going to the Children's Hospital every Thursday. I didn't even know that. And obviously, she let you off the hook on the order to appear. Why?"

"I'm not sure. I saw her silently praying when she looked in at those poor kids."

"I don't know. She comes across to me as a smart, hard as nails, cop. The kind I liked to have in cases I handled."

"At the same time, she and Sally are quiet on why the hell gang officers were around my house when the attack took place. And why they were apparently deployed around the tennis courts."

"Their silence may well be explained by their concern that D.A. Herrera could try to picture the Department giving you special treatment, as he has publicly implied. My question is, is the lieutenant out to nail you, or simply smitten with you?"

"Oh, for Christ's sake, Henry. Get real. She's an attractive, successful woman, almost young enough to be my daughter."

"Father figure, Rusty?"

"Don't go Freudian on me, Henry. I'm too tired."

"How much do we know about her? What about hubby, Mr. Hogan?"

"She doesn't wear a wedding ring."

Henry wore a cynical smile.

"Henry, I was a real cop before becoming sheriff, remember?"

"Right. Trained observer and all that crap. Just happened to notice no ring."

Seeing Rusty's annoyance, Henry changed the subject.

"O.K., let's talk a bit about your visits to the Padre and Jacko. I take it that you generally agree that this present generation of gangbangers is considerably more fatalistic and lethal."

"Hard to deny."

"Yes. And it's also true that some drug enforcement hysteria has resulted in destabilizing things between the Norteños and Sureños?"

"I have to go with Jacko on that one. The feds pay the bill for the task force. They set strategy. The golden rule. They, who have the gold, rule. And the feds have the magic touch. Remember how after 9/11 the FBI went to local mosques asking if anyone knew any Muslim jihad terrorists?"

"Um. It raised hell, all right, and probably destroyed any chances of getting reliable information. Our guardians in Washington never seem to think about the unintended consequences of heavy-handed enforcement."

"Well, I'm out of the business now, but I've always been underwhelmed by Fed enforcement."

"I have news for you, Rusty. You may wish you were out of enforcement, but recent events show that you're not."

"I have no more arrest powers than you."

"True. But our governor did get you in a photo-op for his own jihad against dope and gangs, which, of course, has no connection with his proposed run for the open United States Senate seat in the fall elections."

"How about sticking to legal advice, Henry? I ran for office four times. I can do the political analysis, myself."

"About as well as you'd do in a tennis doubles match playing by yourself, without me. Frankly, Rusty, I'm really concerned about Jacko's contention that someone in the Sheriff's Department is trying to sink you. Could it be our old friend, Captain Jeremiah Christian?"

"He'd be a favorite in the derby. But, naturally, there are plenty of others. Over fifteen years, it's impossible not to make enemies. Some people advance. Others don't. Some get suspended. Others seem to get leniency. You tell everyone not to take it personally. It's professional. Not personal. Sure."

"Fair enough. But it's a stretch to think that someone who didn't get an assignment or promotion that they thought they deserved would set up such an elaborate plot to get you whacked."

"Still . . ."

"Yes, but I focus on Captain Christian. You did your best to send him and his gang to prison for a long time for robbing drug dealers, keeping their cash, and selling the drugs back onto the streets, as well as flaking Jacko."

"My best wasn't good enough."

"I still don't understand how the jury hung. Ironically, it's why I can now afford to live here."

"All it takes for evil to triumph is for a few good men not to run and let trash like Herrera get elected."

"When Herrera got elected, he refused to let me refile the charges. Result, I retired and got rich."

You going to take him on in a recall?"

"I don't know, Rusty. Dolores is totally opposed. I'm not all that eager to have the job."

"Dolores is right, Henry."

"But Pablo is convincing. I think we can do it. Herrera's outrageous. It's not just his politics and the abuse of power. The stories about his ties to drug dealers both before and after his election are very believable, and he's gotten a pass from any scrutiny."

"If you declare, you'll be even more in their sights."

"Even more? I just happened to be there at the tennis courts."

"Don't kid yourself, Henry. You stood next to Pablo when he did the press conference announcing the recall, as did Doc. And those three gangbangers were out to execute everyone on the court."

Henry waved it away. "You're stressed out, Rusty."

"Really? Well, Pablo and his family are gone. I think that it might be a good idea for you and Dolores to take a nice summer vacation someplace far away."

"I kind of think it would be a good idea for you to have me stick around, and for you to travel."

Rusty stood to leave. He changed his mind and sat. Placing his elbows on the table, he leaned closer.

"Henry, I never told you this because you had already resigned and were in private practice. I do have some close friends in the FBI. One of them took me for a beer one night. Told me they had a tap on someone's phone. A conversation was overheard indicating that two jurors in Christian's trial were gotten to."

"Damn! Rusty, even though I retired, you should have told me. I wouldn't have wasted my time going to Herrera, but I do have friends in the state A.G.'s office. It could have been a case."

Rusty took a breath. He leaned back in his chair. Without emphasis, he said, "Henry, You've heard of fusion centers?"

"The Homeland Security gimmick by which feds give secret clearance to some local cops so they can share secret information that really isn't that important, but makes the locals think, they are?"

Rusty inclined his head.

"So, you're telling me that you had secret clearance and he told you under that umbrella and that if you had told me you'd have violated federal law?"

"Ah, you didn't sleep through Harvard Law School."

"And you didn't sleep through your government studies program at Stanford. Why didn't the feds want to make their own case of jury tampering?"

Rusty didn't answer.

"My God! Christian is still in a police uniform. Tell me it isn't possible that they turned Christian, gave him immunity, and are using him?"

"They gave Sammy, the Bull, immunity for nineteen hits, just to get Gotti. As far as we know, Christian and his crooked cops didn't kill anyone. Sally forced three of them out, by the way, and assigned Christian to jail duty."

"And the jails are just about run by the gangs. So, he'd have all the access he needed if he wanted to play footsy with them."

"Possibly, although one would hope that the other deputies assigned would report on it."

"Report a captain, just on suspicion? I wonder."

"Don't go overboard, Henry. The deputies' code of silence doesn't cover rampant felonies."

"Maybe they weren't that obvious. Christian and his crooked buddies still on the force could have gotten Doc killed. You, using a bread knife, narrowly escaped a similar fate. At least, so far."

"Christian may hate me enough, but I'm not sure the gangs they were ripping off are fond enough of him to go partners."

"Dope money makes strange bedfellows. The gangs would be able to make the contract with the Phantom Brothers if Christian tied it in to some deal and convinced them you were behind the governor's anti-gang task force. The Sheriff's Department hasn't said a word about the Phantom Brothers, but you learn of their assignment from an abdicating gang leader?"

"True. It's strange."

"Should I meet with Sally in confidence to give her this information on the flyer so she can find out whether or not it came out of the Department?"

"I don't think so, Henry. It would be tough to discover who was responsible, and if she looked into it, word would spread."

"That could lead to more information."

"I doubt it, and Herrera could put her and other investigators on the stand. Like you said, it wouldn't look good for the sheriff to have secret meetings with the former sheriff's lawyer. Herrera is a master of feeding innuendoes to the media."

Dolores called through the screen door. "Henry, it's your office. They say it's urgent."

"Urgent. Everything's urgent nowadays," Henry mumbled. "I'll be right back, Rusty."

Sitting in tranquil shade, Rusty thought it over. Two hit attempts on him. His house burned down. His friend, Doc, killed.

His other close pals, Pablo and Henry, almost taken down in a machine gun attack on the tennis courts. Pablo, recognizing the danger, now in hiding with his family, but Henry in denial, sitting out there like low hanging fruit on the tree.

Then too, the fifty grand price on Rusty's head. The Phantom Brothers, who had plenty of notches on their belts for whacking judges, police chiefs, generals, and some top politicians, south of the border.

All of this, combined with a sheriff's department unable to stop the local slaughter, or worse still, complicit in it.

Not to be forgotten, the very sexy, but hard as nails, Lieutenant Maria Lopez-Hogan. A tough cop one minute, and the next, with moist eyes, silently praying for dying children.

His lawyer's advice? Run and hide. Where? If Lucy were alive, he would have considered it for her safety. But what little life he had lived after her passing was here with his friends. All of whom were now in jeopardy because of him.

He had never backed down to these thugs before. It would be a cold day in hell before he let bastards like Herrera, traitor cops, and gangbangers send him running.

Henry was still on the phone. Rusty walked through the lovely backyard and got into his faded truck.

It was time to cash in some chips. Time to get some outside help.

CHAPTER THIRTEEN

RUSTY MADE A long phone call from a public phone booth to Manny Diaz, the Mercedes-Benz dealer. Ending the call, he dialed a direct number for Benny Cabrillo, a long time friend, who had recently been transferred back to the San Francisco FBI office on Golden Gate Avenue.

Benny had spent years there, assigned to organized crime. He had leaned on Rusty to learn the major players in the Bay area, especially those hiding in elected office. Now, newly promoted to ASAC, Assistant Special Agent in Charge, Benny was number two guy in the office that covered all of the FBI subunits in this part of Northern California.

"Benny, Rusty, how are you?"

"Never mind me. How the hell are you?"

"I'd like to buy you dinner tonight and tell you."

"Tonight?"

"It's kind of urgent, Benny."

"When a laid back guy like you admits something is urgent, I guess I can fit it in. How about The Hayes Street Grill? It's close, and since you're buying . . . ."

"Hayes Street Grill is good. Six O.K.?"

"Yeah. I'll use some juice to get a reservation. One thing, Rusty."

"What?"

"Don't let any of those gangbangers follow you. I don't want a big shoot-out to screw up my welcome to the good restaurants in town."

"Anything for you, Benny."

Rusty dialed again. This time to the Daryl Foley, head man in the federal Drug Enforcement Agency's Silicon County's office.

"Rusty. I've been waiting for your call, Man. What can I do for you?"

"How about coffee in Sweet's Diner in half an hour or so."

"I'll be there, Man. Can't wait to hear all the latest."

The former sheriff then visited his bank ATM and withdrew two hundred dollars in twenties.

Five minutes later, Rusty pulled into Manny Diaz's Mercedes dealership. He buried his truck in the crowded rear lot filled with trade-ins for the lucky few moving up to the Mercedes class.

"Manny, you make me feel old," Rusty said.

He remembered Manny as an angry sixteen year-old. One of Jacko's selections for the special education program. Nowadays, Manny, a cool thirty-five, looked, well, like a Mercedes-Benz dealer. He apparently watched his diet, played a lot of golf, and led a quiet life with his wife and four children.

"Sheriff, what the hell is going on? People trying to kill, you? You were the one who made it possible for me and a bunch of other guys to escape gangs, make it in life. I hated to see you retire, but I can understand. What I don't get is why those fucking morons are trying to cap you?"

"It's good to see you again, Manny. I've caught you on the TV commercials. Looks like everything's going well. Family O.K.?"

Manny beamed. "I've got three boys and one girl in Little League. My wife's a saint. She knows the hours I've got to put in, but she makes sure I spend time with her and the kids. No sleeping on the couch, you know what I mean, Sheriff?"

"You bet. They let us feel important, but there's no doubt who's the real boss."

Manny laughed. "Look, I know you're probably in a hurry and can't take the time to tell me what's going on. But, as you asked me on the phone, I have a guy right now taking the plates off your truck, although I doubt anyone would look for it back in the lot. I also have your new wheels ready to go."

"Thanks, Manny. You have my promise. If I ever buy a new car, you're the guy. What do I owe you for this loan?"

"Nothing if you bring it back. And, any new car, you get it at my cost, Sheriff. I mean it. You saved a lot of lives. I'm not just talking about our program. I know how hard you worked to keep the shootings down. And the icing on the cake was the educational program."

Manny's face clouded with a frown. "It's a shame to see it closed down. I've tried to reach Jacko. Nada. I wanted to ask you. Could you get the governor interested? I've got the Chamber of Commerce, the Rotary, Pablo, and a whole bunch of donors lined up. I think we could get it going again."

Rusty tried to focus, push the present violence out of the way. Here in front of him was proof that all wasn't hopeless. If done right, they could salvage some kids.

"Manny, I promise, when this is over, I'll work with you. See what we can do."

"Great. Come see what I've got for you."

Manny led him back to the rear lot. The car dealer patted a faded Mercedes.

"She's ten years old, Sheriff, dents and all. I've had the engine and tires replaced. I was just starting to have the exterior stripped refinished when you called. As you can see, it doesn't look like much on the outside. Needs a paint job, but that's what you told me you wanted.

"It's terrific, Manny," Rusty said, looking at the beat up gray Mercedes. It wouldn't attract attention.

"And," Manny said, "Under the hood, you've got enough horses in this baby to outpace anything the gangbangers drive." He winked, "Even outrun everything the CHP has on the road, but I know you don't do stuff like that."

"What about the plates?"

"Belong to a dead man," Manny grinned. "A cousin down in Salinas. I gave him a deal on it when it was just a year old. He was a retired mechanic. Didn't care much about appearances, but treated the guts of the car like the children he never had. Left it to me. He checked out with colon cancer last month. I haven't replaced the plates. Of course, if cops stop you, you're not going to look Mexican."

"I'll do my best, Manny."

Manny was doubtful. "To look Mexican?"

"No. Not to get stopped."

Rusty was about to get into the car when he glanced through the showroom windows facing the avenue. A fast food burger joint was across the street. Two sheriff's department cruisers were parked in front. Cops on coffee break. He turned back to the car dealer.

"Manny, tell me a little about the special education program. Jacko boasted that nineteen out of twenty students went on to college and straight jobs."

Manny chuckled.

"Well, you know Jacko. Don't get me wrong. He really did kick ass to keep the program straight. But he did exaggerate about the numbers."

"So, it wasn't nineteen out of twenty?"

"No way. I don't know the actual numbers, but the success rate was pretty high. A lot of us still keep in touch. But I can remember one day when Jacko came over. He really lost it. He found out that three guys were leaning on the rest of us. Trying to say the program was white. Not for cholos like us."

"How was that going over?"

"Actually, they were older, bigger, and tougher. The peer pressure on us was terrific until one of the teachers ratted them out to Jacko."

"Remember who they were?"

"You bet. Jacko and the Indian showed up. Jacko took off his belt and beat the three to a pulp right in front of the rest of us. They were out of the program. No one who saw that ever forgot."

"I never heard about it."

"For good reason. Jacko was embarrassed. He had picked the three, and one was his son, Ralph. The others were Spanish Raymundo and Ricardo Campos. I doubt if any of them ever forgot or forgave."

"I can believe it. A beating like that in front of a crowd."

"Yeah. And the weird thing. They blamed you as much as Jacko."

"Me?"

"You have to remember, Rusty, how much you were on TV and in the newspaper in those days. Also, every chance you got, you boosted the education program as a way to combat gangs. Everyone identified you and Jacko as equally pushing the program. Word was, you sent Jacko to do what you couldn't do as sheriff."

Rusty tried to absorb what he had just heard. Did it explain Ralph's plan to kill him as a peace offering to the Sureños? Also, Jacko had implied that Ricardo was planning a coup against Jacko. In addition, it could explain why Spanish Ramundo had fled the gang to head up the rival Sureños.

How the hell was he going to unravel all this intrigue, let alone resolve it?

CHAPTER FOURTEEN

RUSTY WAS A few minutes late meeting Daryl Foley. Not that Foley was troubled. The diner had hired two new young shapely waitresses. The DEA man's eyes followed them with the same intensity as if they had been major coke dealers.

Rusty slipped into the booth.

"Got them under surveillance, Daryl?"

"You bet. Eternal vigilance and all that stuff. What's happening with you? Or I should say to you."

"I was hoping that you'd know something."

"Damn. Here, I thought I was getting some great intelligence and you're pumping me?"

"Right."

"I swear, Rusty. I don't know. I've heard some wild rumors, but that's all."

"Tell me what you've heard and I'll add anything I know."

Well, word is that the Sureños think you're setting them up for a big bust and that they've put a contract out on you."

"That's the same as I hear. But you know, and, I know, that it's bullshit. Since I've retired, I haven't paid any attention to them or anything else to do with law enforcement."

Foley looked skeptical. "You're not a consultant to the governor?"

"For God's sake, Daryl. Is DEA intelligence gathering as bad as when I was in office?"

"Worse. We're all task force stuff now. You remember how well that worked with all the different agencies hiding everything from each other. Trying to hog the media. Cops' careers depend upon their own agencies' success, not some task force that will dissolve in a few months. In fact, it's already pretty much a thing of the past."

Rusty scratched his head.

"Still, the task force managed to put a big dent in the Norteños operation, Daryl. I thought they were going to hit the Sureños, next."

"Yeah. It only took four years to nail some of the Norteños. And, we missed Jacko. In the first place, we really should have been on the Sureños who are the major meth dealers. Meth was supposed to be the focus, but," he shrugged, "the Feebies were in charge. Need I say more?"

"I really don't give a shit about the schemes between DEA and the Bureau, anymore, Daryl. I just want to know why the Sureños came after me."

"That's why I came. I thought you'd enlighten me. Who's your next stop? Consult Benny?"

Rusty laughed. "You're a piece of work, Daryl."

"Sure. But, I can save you a trip to San Francisco. Benny's going to tell you to ask me. By the way, I bet you're taking him to dinner, not coffee."

"I didn't say I was paying for coffee, Daryl."

"Well, you are. One thing, I can give you, Rusty. We hear the Phantom brothers have arrived in town. If you want my advice, which, of course, you locals never do, I'd tell you to take a trip, a nice cruise or something. What the hell, you don't have to stick around like us working stiffs."

In San Francisco, Rusty parked on the second floor of the symphony garage. No shortage of parking on a non-performance night for the symphony. He walked a couple of blocks to the Hayes Street Grill on Van Ness.

The symphony was on its night off. San Francisco being a cool, late dining city, the trendy bistro was half empty this early. The FBI agent was halfway through a large Gibson.

Benny smiled. "You don't look any worse for wear, Rusty. Taking out two punks with AK-47's using a bread knife, you kidding me? You never even shot anyone as a deputy. Suddenly, you're Jim Bowie, a knife fighter."

"Closest I ever came to shooting anyone was two Feebies who screwed up our stakeout. It would have been more than justified homicide. We'd been sitting on the bastard for a week, waiting for him to come out. Your two guys marched up, with their credentials in hand. A series killer went out the back window."

"Before my time, Rusty," Benny smiled. "You know nothing like that would have happened on my watch?"

"Right."

The waitress approached.

"How about a martini, Rusty," Benny asked.

"It's a Gibson, you Asshole." Rusty turned to the waitress.

"I'll have a Heinekens."

Benny said, "You can do this to me again, Darling."

The waitress didn't even look at him. She turned and walked to the bar.

"Ah, you still have your way with women, Benny."

"Exactly; it's a shame they now hire girls instead of women."

"Of course."

"So how come the Sureños want a prince of a guy like you dead, Rusty?"

Benny knocked down the last of his drink, before the refill arrived.

"I have a question for you Benny. How come the Sureños want a docile retired sheriff, dead?"

Benny laughed.

"No doubt you've already asked the useless DEA exactly that question, and since they don't know their ass from their elbow, you are now seeking sensitive information from the Federal Bureau of Investigation."

"Relax, Benny, I didn't expect you guys to know either. I'm still buying dinner."

"Good. I didn't want to write you into my expenses as a confidential informant."

"You did it often enough when I was in office."

"That was different. You were somebody then."

"Thanks."

They were silent when the waitress put down the beer and Benny's Gibson.

She smiled at Rusty, "Let me know when you're ready to order."

She deliberately avoided looking at Benny.

"Now I get it, a father fixation. I'm too young for her. No shit, Rusty. You mean neither your old Department or DEA has a clue as to why you're a target?"

"You left out our esteemed FBI, designated by Congress to be the primary counter-intelligence agency in the war against terror. You guys ever get a computer up and working?"

"No hurry on that. We hack into the CIA's stuff whenever we need information."

Benny Cabrillo was having a fine time, enjoying his drinks in a good restaurant just a couple of blocks from city hall, and eyeballing the political movers and shakers, especially the female shakers. The political army was beginning to arrive after a tough day squandering taxpayer money.

Rusty ordered a crab dish and Benny had the special pan-fried lamb chops in a reduced Madeira sauce.

"No wonder you look like you lost weight, Rusty. Is it true that those bastards who busted into your house had gags and shackles with them?"

"Yeah."

"Lucky they didn't snatch you. It would have been a major pain in the ass. We would have had to mobilize a lot of manpower to rescue you."

"True. And you would have done the same fine job as at Waco where all the people you were supposed to rescue got burned to death by a madman."

"Hey, Justice cleared us on that one. It was all on ATF."

"I remember. ATF was under Treasury and the Bureau under the same Justice Department doing the investigation."

"You've gotten cynical, Rusty. The Attorney General took full responsibility."

"I remember. What was the result?"

"They punished us. She stayed in office. We were still working for her."

Finishing everything on his plate, Benny pushed it aside.

"What did you really want to ask, Rusty?"

"You guys headed the task force that took down the Norteños. The next step was to take down the Sureños. I'd like to see some pressure on those bastards so they can't devote their full attention to me. Are you going after them?"

Benny sighed, "this is strictly off the record?"

Rusty nodded.

"We were all set to go. Unexpectedly, orders came down from Washington. Two senators from Nevada are about to butcher our budget. Supposed to be a big meth market in Law Vegas. Surprise, surprise. Like the locals there haven't invited it. I'm sorry, Rusty, but the Sureños are on hold for now. They took all of our guys for Las Vegas operation"

"I hope you told them not to gamble."

"Agents of the Federal Bureau of Investigation are too wise to the ways of the world to gamble in Vegas."

"I guess I forgot their wisdom."

Benny's face grew serious outside the restaurant.

"Rusty, my friend, why don't you travel a bit. You're retired. You're not impoverished. Travel to see all those exotic places that you've dreamed about."

Driving back to the county, Rusty brooded. He had done everything he could to get action from the Sheriff's Department, the DEA, and the FBI. The result, zero.

It was time for the self-help approach.

CHAPTER FIFTEEN

PROFESSOR RICHARD BIRD was now emeritus at State University. At one time, he had been regarded as the preeminent expert on California gangs. Sheriff Rusty, relying on a casual recommendation from a police chief, had invited the scholar to address his monthly gang unit training session.

Rusty had been appalled when he met the professor and led him into the conference room where the meetings were held. The narcs had stared at the university lecturer in disbelief.

At six-one, he was so stooped over that he appeared no more than a frail five-eight. He wore thick milk bottle eyeglasses, and his kinky, unruly head of hair had won him the nickname of "Bird's Nest."

As bizarre as the narcs were themselves, with phony tattoos, all sorts of facial hair, a couple of bushy Afro-haircuts, shaved heads, and more than a few extremely emaciated looking kids who passed for glass-eyed hypes, Bird stood out.

The cops looked in dismay. The sheriff had herded them together to listen to this asshole?

Rusty lamely introduced Bird as a gang expert who had lived for a decade with L.A. gangs and written four books regarded as the bibles on gang behavior before retreating to the classroom to teach about them.

Bird ignored the faint rebellious mumbling and looked out at his audience. This geek was going to tell narcs about the street?

Professor Bird flipped on his laptop projector for a power point presentation. The first image showed him more or less as he now appeared. Battered wrinkled clothes, looking lost and pathetically helpless in the Rampart section of L.A. Three or four vicious looking gang members stood glowering at the camera.

Bird's voice was surprisingly strong and confident as he told Rusty's narcs, "They called me 'Bird's Nest," you know, because of my hair."

He pressed the remote button on the projector. A new picture flashed on the screen. After a moment of stunned silence, the narcs guffawed. The screen showed Bird deadpanning with a large pigeon sitting calmly on his tangled hair. Even the gangbangers in the slide were doubled over with laughter.

Within a few minutes, the odd looking professor had the narcs spellbound as he spoke with the authority that only someone who lived with gangs possesses. He added nuances and structure and new insights to what the cops had learned about gangs.

Rusty now looked around Professor Bird's surprisingly small office. There was no window. All four walls were composed of floor-to-ceiling bookshelves, and all were jam-packed with books and manuscripts. Several waist-high piles of books were stacked on the floor.

"Ah, Sheriff, it must be six or seven years since you invited me to meet with your narcotics officers."

It had been fifteen, but Rusty merely smiled.

"Yes, as I recall," the professor said, "I used your group as guinea pigs to present a draft of my forthcoming book, 'The Epidemiological Foundings of Deviant Urban Subgroup Behavior.'"

"I remember."

"It turned out to be quite academically successful at the time, even though it's antediluvian history now. The young academics, 'quanto heads' look down on ethnographic hands-on field research such as I did as quaint, primitive, anecdotal, sociological history."

"Why?"

"Because we ancient scholars dismiss their computerized macro studies as, 'garbage in, garbage out.' As if a scientist can measure complicated human behavior on spurious, questionable, numerical data alone."

Rusty felt a dull ache in his stomach. He hadn't come for a Sociology 101 lecture. Frustrated, he headed the old man off by seizing a piece of chalk and moving to a small blackboard barely visible among the stacks of books.

"Professor," Rusty said, "I recall how you started your presentation." Rusty drew a large circle on the blackboard. "You asked the narcs to hypothetically imagine a gang of one hundred."

Rusty pointed at the circle. He drew a small bull's eye in the middle. "You said the leadership typically was made up of one or two extremely violent sociopaths here in the middle."

"Correct."

Rusty continued, "There was a more or less tenuous hierarchical leadership, subject to abrupt violent change. The next circle," Rusty drew a larger circle, "was made up of roughly thirty crime prone youth, some of whom were so violent that they almost matched the leaders."

Bird nodded in agreement.

"The remainder of the gang was quasi-interns. Many simply adopted gang colors and flashed signals for protection in their neighborhoods. Of course, most gangs were, and are, much larger."

"Indeed."

"Then, if I remember correctly," Rusty searched his memory, "you used an acronym ROBS, that stuck in the narcs' minds, to describe how gang membership fulfilled our human needs as herd animals. R—for recognition, O—for opportunity, B—for belonging, S—for security."

"We're herd animals," Bird said.

"You then startled us cops by pointing out that many of us satisfied the same basic human needs by membership in religious, racial, ethnic, and social groups, not the least of which was the camaraderie provided by being members of the sheriff's department."

"Yes. They were dismayed to hear that courage, loyalty, esprit de corps, ambition, elitism, and other characteristics were as prevalent in gangs as in law enforcement organizations."

"Right."

"You have excellent recollection, Sheriff. Pity you didn't continue as a graduate student instead of wasting your time on politics. Nonetheless, I must admit that gang phenomena have changed considerably, although the basic structure is similar."

The question floating around in Rusty's mind was beginning to crystallize. Still, he temporized, "How so? Professor?"

"Despite the efforts of the quanto heads to quantify every nuance or perceived nuance in gang behavior, there are an infinite number of intervening variables to explain the changes. For example, technological improvements in the firepower and lethality of easily available firearms combined with the lucrativeness that prohibition assures to drug dealing."

"A violent black market."

"Yes, along with demographic changes, the emergence of a negative 'Don't snitch,' 'Gangsta Rap' thug, drug subculture coalesced. In addition, an expanded embrace of illegitimacy, illiteracy, and dysfunctional unemployment among low income groups, and increased tendencies toward instant gratification on the part of young people are all factors."

Rusty nodded his agreement. Professor Bird wasn't looking. He sailed on.

"Furthermore, here in California, a number of sociologists have linked changes in immigration policies with social disintegration. Then too, we've learned that the Mexican Mafia and various other gangs serving long mandatory sentences in maximum security institutions, are, nevertheless, able to surreptitiously communicate and direct street gangs."

Rusty tried to absorb the professor's rapid-fire speech and focus on what he had come for.

"Let me ask you this, professor, I agree with your thesis that it's impossible to eliminate gangs, but is it possible to alter the goals promulgated by the leader or the inner core of leaders, the so called shot-callers?"

"Well, we suffer from the archetypal weakness of attempting to apply rational reasoning to the actions of sociopathic leaders who, by definition, are irrational."

"That's a no?"

"Not necessarily. The larger society in its quintessential quest for stability, proclaims norms denying the utility of violence in bringing change. Yet history shows that, at times, extreme violence does change group and cultural behavior."

"How so?"

"War is an obvious macro example. But with gangs, consider the admittedly crude example of the earth worm."

Rusty looked at him blankly.

"You cut the head off the worm. The organism usually doesn't die, but wiggles off in a different direction."

Leaving the campus, Rusty reflected that Professor Bird hadn't once mentioned the current gang violence surging through the area, or the attempts on Rusty's life. He wasn't with it, anymore. The old man was reliving his decades old memories of gang behavior in the Los Angeles barrios of yesteryear.

The professor hadn't come close to providing Rusty with a blueprint for saving his own life, or had he?.

CHAPTER SIXTEEN

B ACK AT PABLO'S, Rusty nodded to Antonio. The lean man in his thirties with an M 4 slung over his shoulder held Bruno straining on a chain leash. Antonio whispered, "Sheriff's cops here three times looking for you."

"If they come now, tell them I'm not here. I'm leaving in five minutes."

Rusty moved quickly to his room and picked up his large, empty canvas bag. Going through the patio door, he went directly to the arsenal building. He pressed his palm against the reader.

Nothing happened. He held his breath for a minute. How much time did he have before a sheriff's department vehicle came back to the house with the subpoena?

Rusty dried his hand on his pants and tried again. The solid door squealed open. Rapidly, he made his way down the aisle. He fit one of the sniper rifles with a night scope into his travel case.

Next, he tucked a pair of night vision binoculars underneath the rifle. Then, he grabbed a five round, street-sweeper repeating shotgun, and an M 4 carbine.

He stuffed a good supply of ammunition into the bottom of the bag. He turned to leave, with the now heavy bag. He halted.

Slowly, he walked back down the aisle to the open box containing the two grenades. A hand-tossed explosive would fit his questionable plans. All the same, had he become capable of this?

Military grenades were different now than years ago in his army days, of course. These were MK II a's. Much more deadly. Six seconds after the pin was pulled and the hand lever released, the projectile would explode into hundreds of razor sharp pieces of steel.

The fragments, traveling at more than a hundred miles an hour, would tear apart anything they hit. Especially, human flesh.

In Pablo's arsenal, Rusty placed the two grenades in the bag. He zipped it shut. He hustled back to his car. He had just broken the law. As a retired peace officer, he was authorized to carry the firearms. But illegal explosive devices were another matter.

Finally, he picked up a delighted Itsy Bitsy and deposited him and a large bag of dog food in the car.

He waved to the guard at the gatehouse and drove four blocks. A sheriff department's patrol car was pulling up to the guard shack. Timing was everything.

It had been more than five years since he traversed the neighborhood where the Fourth Street Sureños meeting place was located. But Rusty knew exactly where he wanted to go in Sun City.

Hoods changed, though. It would be a bummer if the old storage facility two blocks from the Sureños' Fourth Street joint had been urban-renewed out of existence. Turning onto Fifth Street, just two blocks from the tiny storefront meeting place on Fourth Street, he breathed a sigh of relief.

The storage garage rented individually locked spaces large enough to fit SUV sized vehicles. In this neighborhood, you paid $160 bucks a month, cash in advance, if you expected to see your car in the morning.

The storage facility didn't take credit cards or ask questions about what you were storing. Rusty wasn't ready to face the clerk just yet. He had some shopping to do, first.

He withdrew another two hundred bucks, the daily max from his ATM machine, and drove several miles to a down and out shopping center where he could keep one eye on his car while making purchases.

First stop was a chain drug store. He secured the most beat-up cart available and parked the tiny dog in it. They walked up and down the aisles. Rusty tried on a cheap pair of sunglasses that took up most of his face. Purchase number one. He dropped the glasses into the cart.

In the next aisle, a garden section, he found a ridiculously sloppy, floppy sun hat that could have belonged to the straw man in the Wizard of Oz. He also added a pair of workman's gloves, and hedge clippers to the cart.

He put cans of outdoor roach and bug killing spray and another of mosquito repellant guaranteed to ward off the pests without giving the user cancer, on top of the other purchases. He tossed a large comb and a tube of men's brown hair coloring goo into the basket, along with a powerful penlight with batteries installed. Carefully, he placed a case of bottled water on top of the pile that was beginning to crowd Itsy Bitsy.

Heading to the check-out line, he spotted a stack of cheap, but warm, looking blankets, going for $9.99 each. He grabbed two of them.

In the bin next to the hats, he spotted a half dozen garishly colored, junky looking, diminutive opera glasses. Using the attached silly, short, pink wood rod, he held a pair to his eyes. Surprisingly, the glasses provided good magnification throughout the length of the store. Unlike real binoculars, the piece of junk wouldn't raise suspicion if found in a homeless guy's cart. An eight-dollar bargain.

At the counter, he increased his bill another ten bucks, adding a Mickey Mouse battery-run child's watch. The dull-eyed teen-ager manning the register didn't even look up as she checked him out with his strange, varied purchases. He paid in cash. No paper trail on this shopping trip.

In an adjacent Goodwill donated clothing store, he came up with a weathered, but clean, work shirt, jeans, sneakers, and a full length gray raincoat, and a pair of cheap galoshes that would fit over the sneakers.

An elderly male cashier fumbled with Rusty's purchases and money, apparently not even noticing the rain gear, strange for an area that was lucky to get a rain shower or two during these hot summer months.

A mile away, he found the old theatrical goods store that catered to high school and local amateur theatre groups. Lucy had persuaded a reluctant Rusty to comb men's coloring goo that she purchased at her hair salon onto his graying, wavy locks. Her reminders had helped him to comb it into his full head of hair, keeping it a reasonably colored brown with streaks of gray.

With all of the recent occurrences, Rusty hadn't bothered to shave for almost a week, and was way overdue for a haircut. His hair had not only lengthened, but also, for the first time, begun to match the newly grown natural salt and pepper beard of a forty-three year-old.

Still, he wasn't quite satisfied with his appearance. After ten minutes of browsing in the theatrical store, he found what he wanted. He paid with a twenty and two singles for an attachable ponytail. It plausibly resembled his present hair color and cascaded down over his shoulders.

Covered by his floppy hat, it still looked phony to him. But it would have to do.

Returning to the storage center, he parked in front of an empty, half demolished rooming house a block away. Few people lived in the area. Even fewer were brave enough to walk the streets. No one wanted to witness anything that might be happening.

Certain that no one was watching, he quickly changed into his newly purchased duds and sneakers covered with waterproof rubbers. He put on the full-length rain coat. The outfit was absurd in terrain that hadn't seen rain in three months.

He attached the ponytail, covered it with the hat, put on the sunglasses and decided that something was wrong. He still looked too clean to pass as a homeless person.

Rusty, bent and shuffling, wheeled his cart down the street. Just another of the growing army of homeless ones. Cautiously, he entered the partially demolished building.

Finding it empty, he explored. In a corner, he spotted a rusting piece of sharp metal. Carefully, he cut a number of holes in his pants, shirt, and coat.

He prowled further and found an evacuated spot with loose soil. After checking for spiders and other vermin, he dirtied his pants, shirt, and the ridiculously long raincoat. He even spread some grime on his thickening gray beard.

Rusty picked up the dog and placed him in the front seat. He put the cart in the trunk and locked it. He was ready for the first test of his disguise.

CHAPTER SEVENTEEN

T HE TRICKY PART was presenting a photo I.D. that wouldn't get him tossed out of the storage facility. In his last year as sheriff, someone in The Department of Homeland Security, or as the deputies had quickly labeled it, The Department of Homeland Insecurity, had decided that a few "Key" local cops be provided with phony I.D.'s. The larger police agencies, like the Silicon Valley Sheriff's Department, were to establish a number of "safe" houses.

Rusty thought of it as typical Beltway funding madness, and a really stupid invitation for deputies to get into all kinds of trouble. But to be critical was to be soft on terrorism and unpatriotic.

Naturally, as head honcho in the Silicon Valley's Department, Rusty had to have a phony I.D. so that he could supervise various "safe" pads. By his last year, he was simply going through the motions until the time was right for him to retire and let Sally take over. He never visited a "safe" pad. He stuck the phony I.D. in his wallet and forgot it. Until now.

The elderly woman sitting on a stool behind the counter of the storage business must have been supplementing her social security checks for at least a decade. She was without makeup, and wore a dress that advertised her obesity more than camouflaged it.

Vigorously smoking a cigarette, she was engrossed in a worn edition of People Magazine. The woman tore her eyes away from stories of Hollywood madness. She carefully counted the eight twenties Rusty placed in front of her, barely glancing at the registration card he had printed out and placed next to his phony I.D., which hadn't looked anything like him five years ago, let alone now.

"You're paid for a month," she said, handing him a key card. "This card will open the front gate twenty-four hours a day. Be careful it doesn't hit you in the ass, because the gate automatically slams right behind you so no one can sneak in. Swipe the card the same way on your space, number

142. You don't have to come in here except to pay for next month, if you still want the space."

She hadn't been hired to charm customers. Turning the page to read about the insanity of another celebrity, she ignored Rusty's feigned limping from the office, followed by his little dog. He drove to the storage space and found that the card swipe did indeed open the automatic door.

A musty smell mingled with the lingering scent of pot left by previous renters. After a moment's thought, he put on his work gloves and backed the car into the space, leaving enough room to open the trunk.

He removed the cart he had "borrowed" from the drugstore, containing the blankets, bug spray, sun lotion, and childlike opera glasses. He wheeled the cart to just inside the exit from the Mercedes' storage space.

Cautiously, he stepped outside and peered around. His space was ideally located in the inner section of the facility, where it wasn't visible from street traffic. He saw no activity from other renters.

Quickly, he wheeled the cart outside the garage, with Itsy Bitsy quite comfortably lodged on top of one of the blankets. He slipped behind the wheel of the Mercedes and backed it fully into the parking spot, leaving the trunk flush against the rear wall. It would make it slightly more difficult to break into the trunk, and the car's alarm system was functional.

Rusty pressed the button closing the door. He hunched over the cart and headed toward the gated exit from the facility. He was quite uneasy about leaving the vehicle with all that military hardware in the trunk.

Yet, he had no choice about storing the weapons. He was about to reconnoiter the hood, posing as an aged, and addled, homeless man. He couldn't afford to be found by either cops or gangbangers in possession of any of the arsenal concealed in the car's trunk.

The casual sleaziness of the storage facility, and questionable clientele it attracted, made it useful to him, but also led to doubts about just how secure it was. On the other hand, if all went according to plan, he wouldn't be using the space very long.

And if things didn't work out, none of it would matter, anyhow.

CHAPTER EIGHTEEN

HUNCHED OVER, RUSTY hobbled toward the Fourth Street headquarters of the Sureños. The Sureños gathering place was a small store, flush in the middle of a block of single story mundane businesses. The stores on each side of the gang meeting place had been deliberately left vacant for as long as he could remember.

The other small businesses on that side of the narrow street, a shoe repair store, a sparsely stocked bodega, a cheaply priced clothing store, a discount mattress store, a miscellaneous brick-a-back store, advertising merchandise for $.99 cents as a come-on, were all struggling, signs of a long-declining neighborhood.

The whole block had long been recorded as owned by a shady legal group, which sometimes had represented members of the Sureños charged with crimes. The opposite side of the treeless, Fourth Street shopping block was a similar mix of vacant stores and marginal shops. Even at noontime, foot traffic was minimal.

The unusually narrow two-lane street, for unknown reasons allowed free parking on both sides, further squeezing car traffic. No bicycle lanes in this hood. The shopping strip didn't contain a single residence. Nevertheless, it attracted more than its share of drifters for whom even a modest handout from generous, but low income, shoppers was welcome.

The shoppers, from nearby low rent housing, represented every racial and ethnic group residing in California. But they did have one thing in common: an intense fear and silent hatred of the Sureños.

This sleepy time of day was exactly when Rusty wanted a closer look at the Sureños meeting center, and the block itself. Slowly, he pushed his cart, to which he had added empty bottles, rags, and other worthless accoutrements toted in pilfered shopping baskets serving as baggage carriers for the homeless.

Occasionally, Rusty stopped, looked skyward, and mumbled incoherently. The few people he passed ignored him, avoiding eye contact when he babbled aloud or held out a battered metal pot for coins.

He stopped in front of the small store where, according to Jacko, three or four of the Sureños gang leaders met every couple of days. It was as he remembered it.

The narrow glass entrance door was centered between two tinted large plate glass windows, offering only a dim view of the small single room. The space was dominated by a round table circled by four chairs.

Although the storefront bore no identification, its purpose was well known. No graffiti or vandalism had ever marred the location, even though the premise was never occupied unless the head honchos were gathering.

Since there wasn't a single surveillance camera on the entire block, and no gang lookouts or guards in evidence, Rusty took time to gaze through the glass door. The same oversized propane tank, which provided heat and hot water during the winter months, sat next to the floor heater standing a few feet behind the table. Two large ceiling fans for summer cooling had been placed in opposite ends of the modest sized room.

An unmarked door led to the small restroom. There was no rear access. A solid, gray back wall added to the grimness of the place.

It appeared exactly the same as years ago, when Rusty and a couple of other deputies had gone through the store after obtaining a search warrant based on reliable information that ten kilos of cocaine had been stored behind, and under, the conference table. A leak, later determined to have come from an unidentified court clerk, had alerted the gang.

The cops had come up empty, but Rusty had never forgotten the scantiness of space and sterile, bland furniture where the gang leaders planned their crimes.

He turned and sluggishly pushed his cart along the sidewalk. From the corner of his eye he spotted a sheriff's department cruiser creeping along behind him. Damn!

He had lingered too long. He felt his pulse quicken. Sweat begin to form and drip behind his neck. The two uniformed officers had watched him inspect the store.

Rusty fought an irresistible urge to scratch an itch under his phony ponytail. He turned his face skyward and began his mumbling act.

"Hey, Pops. Come over here," the deputy, on the passenger side, called to him as his partner pulled the car to the curb.

JOSEPH D. MCNAMARA

Rusty, stooped and mumbling, shuffled slowly to the car.

Both cops stared at him. The one who had summoned him said, "You're new here, Pops. What's your name?"

Slowly, Rusty made a priest's sign of the cross blessing of the two cops.

"I am the Arch-Angel Michael." He again looked skyward. "Our Father from above has sent me."

The police radio crackled. The cop jotted down the call and confirmed the assignment.

The driver laughed. "Hey, listen, Pop. That store you were thinking of ripping off. It's not only empty. It belongs to gangbangers. If they catch you looking into it, you're going to be rapping with the Father above a lot sooner than you think."

The police car pulled away. Rusty moved along. This time, his legs were genuinely shaking. If the cops hadn't gotten the assignment, they would have frisked him.

Anything more than a casual inspection, would have led to his recognition. His careful plan would have been in vain. Who knows what other complications might have arisen when they found the storage key card tucked into his shoe?

At the end of the block, he came to the street overpass allowing traffic on Fourth Street to travel over the creek. During the rainy months, the creek was vulnerable to flooding. When rainstorms abruptly sent an excess of water rushing down toward its final destination, San Francisco Bay, frequent overflows halted pedestrian and vehicular traffic on Fourth Street.

Rusty was a young deputy, during a time when the affluent residents had raised hell with the flood control people, demanding correction of the problem. A long-term study plan had been commissioned, but as increasing gang violence sent the middle class fleeing to the burbs, complaints from their lower income replacements fell on suddenly deaf political ears. The proposed flood control planning never even began.

As the neighborhood transformed into a barrio, homeless people increasingly began to inhabit the banks along the creek. Storms during the rainy season sent torrents of water downstream.

The deluges uprooted trees, creating mini-dams, propelling surging waters over the banks of the creek bed, flooding homes and stores. Failure to maintain creek-clearing efforts resulted in the homeless and their meager possessions being swept away every winter.

Now, in July, the creek had been dry for months. It wouldn't see flowing water again until late October, making it a convenient summer lodging place for those with no place else to go.

Rusty made his way through thick foliage surrounding the pillars of the petite, but ugly, roadway bridge over the creek. He tightly clung to his shopping cart while descending the steep slope to an incongruously beautiful and peaceful nether-land below the ominously dangerous streets above.

Hiding his cart under a bush, he carried Itsy Bitsy in search of the bedding place where, in his rookie patrol years, he had first met Bummy. When cops asked who he was, Bummy had simply replied, "a bum," thus creating his own moniker.

Rusty had been impressed to see how Bummy had dug out a level space for himself under foliage on the steep bank adjacent to the concrete bridge pillar footing. Other transients inhabited lower, more level, sleeping areas closer to the creek bed. These locations, consequently, were more threatened than Bummy's upper hideaway by flash floods and equally dangerous, sadistic two-legged male predators.

What piqued Rusty's curiosity back then was how Bummy had somehow dragged abandoned railroad ties to the spot and created a brush-covered, kind of retaining wall that gave him space to stretch out. It was also high enough to be ideal for peering unseen out into the street to spot approaching cops or other people to be avoided.

Periodically, deputies had been ordered to lurch on foot along the banks to urge the homeless to move to shelters, or, in some cases, to summon ambulances for those who had become too feeble to survive. He had almost missed spotting Bummy's resting place, cleverly hidden by surrounding undergrowth.

"How you doing, Man?" Rusty had asked the disheveled hobo.

"Fine, Officer," Bummy had replied, warily watching to see if Rusty was going to attack.

Rusty gradually convinced the frail man that he was no threat. He urged him to go to a nearby shelter where he could clean up and get wholesome food.

"Not interested. Much nicer and safer here," Bummy told him.

"That's an interesting set-up you've got, creating a little space here. You do that yourself?"

Bummy nodded cautiously.

"You can relax. I'm not going to make you move. Most of the folks along the creek couldn't do that. Where'd you learn?"

"Used to be an engineer."

"What happened?"

"Happened?" Bummy looked blankly at Rusty.

"You know, why'd you end up here?"

Bummy just shrugged. Rusty never did find out his story. But a couple of years later, as a patrol supervisor, Rusty had responded to a call of a DOA further up the creek.

The first deputy responding had found Bummy face down in the brush. The back of his skull had been crushed. The murder weapon, a brick, had been casually discarded a few feet away. Bummy had wandered too far from his "safe" spot.

The case had never been solved. It hadn't been high priority for the homicide guys. But Rusty had never stopped wondering about the man whose life, like so many of the homeless, had prematurely ended in his early forties.

Now, using the hedge clippers, he eventually found Bummy's dugout. Despite being overgrown with bramble, the retaining wall was surprisingly intact. With a little work, Rusty was able to restore its former secure position. Whatever else he had been, Bummy had been a competent engineer.

If all went well, Bummy's handiwork might well turn out to be Rusty's only chance of preventing his murder by gangbangers.

CHAPTER NINETEEN

RUSTY LAY PRONE and unseen in Bummy's former hideaway, his eyes fixed on the Sureños headquarters. Itsy Bitsy happily snored against his leg. But around 1300 hours, the dog's ears pointed forward and a low growl alerted Rusty to two gangbangers being dropped off across the street, by a dingy-looking Honda sedan.

The widespread and mistaken conventional wisdom was that gang members were mostly teenage kids. But these two were the more usual pattern. A slight young wannabe, perhaps eighteen or nineteen, accompanied the older, muscular, gangbanger wearing numerous prison tattoos visible under his gang clothing.

The older man opened the door with a key and entered. The younger one outside folded his arms, not yet heavily developed by pumping iron while doing a long jolt in the joint. He glared up and down the street, just daring anyone to have the effrontery to approach the shrine.

The other man emerged after a brief inspection of the interior. Crossing his burly arms, he took up the sentry position on the other side of the door. If Jacko's information was correct, the two would stand watch for a couple of hours until the shot-callers arrived. Rusty decided it was time to test the quality of the store's security.

He slithered down from his enclosure to where his shopping cart of junk was stored. Tucking the docile Itsy Bitsy into his blanket, Rusty wheeled the cart upstream to where he would be well out of sight of the two lookouts. He pushed the cart up the creek bank and tottered toward Fourth Street.

Stumbling across Fourth Street, he pretended not to see an oncoming vehicle as he wandered toward the Sureños meeting place. The auto screeched to a halt, horn blasting. The motorist yelled an obscenity at Rusty before driving on.

Rusty stopped in the middle of the street and gave his hand blessing to the departing vehicle. The driver, looking in the rear view mirror, responded by reaching out the window and giving Rusty the finger.

As Rusty hoped, the encounter attracted the attention of the two lookouts. They glowered contemptuously at Rusty as he looked heavenward and muttered incomprehensibly.

Walking unsteadily toward the two watchers, Rusty paused at a wire trash receptacle and searched through it. He retrieved an empty glass deposit bottle, put it in his basket, and continued toward the two gangbangers.

A few steps from them, he pathetically held out his metal donation bowl. The younger man charged forward, grasping Rusty by the shirt collar. Itsy Bitsy went from a growl into noisy barking.

Rusty quickly stumbled backward before the youth could detect the hard muscles under the bum's clothing Rusty had adopted.

"Mother Fucker, I'm going to break your fucking leg. How's that for a handout?"

"Luis, Luis," the older man quickly grabbed his accomplice's arm, "no fuss in front of the store. Remember what Ramundo said. He'll stuff your balls in your mouth if he finds out you gave the cops any reason to pay attention to us, here."

The younger man immediately calmed down.

"You old piece of shit," he said, "if you bother us any more I'll follow you for a few blocks and make sure you'll never mess with anyone again."

He turned to the older man. "We better check his basket to make sure."

The older guy shrugged. "Make it quick. We don't want anyone to see."

The young man, keeping his hand well away from the snapping dog, disgustedly rifled through the worthless junk in the cart.

"Bless you. I am the Arch-Angel Michael sent by the Lord, God," Rusty stuttered, starting to bless them.

The younger man roughly slapped his hand. "You're nothing. Trash. I'm warning you, you'll be dead trash if you bother us."

Rusty wandered away. The young man went into the store to wash his hands after touching Rusty and his grubby possessions. The older one, already ignoring Rusty, looked up and down the street. Rusty was satisfied. They had categorized him and would pay him no mind if he didn't approach the store.

He went directly to the storage unit. After making sure that he was unobserved, he entered the garage and let Itsy Bitsy out on a long leash to sniff whatever dogs sniff, and to answer a call of nature. While the dog prowled, Rusty opened the Mercedes' trunk.

He put the cheap, but effective, opera glasses and the night vision glasses into the cart. He had anticipated it being searched and hadn't dared carry the glasses earlier. But now, they were safe. He would keep a respectful distance from the lookouts. They'd give him dirty looks, but wouldn't leave their posts to hassle him.

The memory of Bummy's demise came back to him. After a moment's hesitation, he reached into the trunk and took the Glock from its holster. He ejected the magazine and carefully replaced the top two rounds with blanks. He slipped the magazine back into the weapon and reholstered the gun. He strapped it to his belt in the middle of his back. There wasn't even a slight bulge under his soiled, full-length, outer coat.

Just fifteen minutes after his encounter with the two gangbangers, Rusty worked his way down the opposite sidewalk back toward the creek. He pawed through waste containers, held out his cup, and actually received a few coins. He gave an elaborate blessing to the elderly woman who had tossed a quarter into his cup.

The two guards outside the gang storefront saw Rusty, but otherwise ignored him, alert for any drive-by or pedestrian danger. A few minutes later, Rusty and his faithful watchdog were again prone in their hidden niche. The former lawman, using the magnifying glasses, eyed both sentries through a small opening he had cut through the shrubbery.

The watch for the shot-callers had begun.

CHAPTER TWENTY

AT 1510 HOURS, a black Lincoln slowly cruised down Fourth Street. It paused in front of the lookouts. The older man gave the driver a nod that all was well. The Lincoln drove away.

About ten minutes later, the Lincoln was back. Apparently, it had cruised the hood and found all quiet. Once more, it halted, facing the older lookout. He repeated the O.K. signal.

The Lincoln turned the corner and circled the block. This time it was the lead car, followed by a gray stretch limo and a blue Caddy. All three cars pulled to the curb.

The limo stopped a few feet from the store entrance. Two bodyguards emerged from both the front and two from the rear car. The four men positioned themselves around the limo, constantly inspecting the surroundings.

A minute later, Rusty, looking through the opera magnifying glasses, saw Spanish Ramundo, Ricardo Campas, and, to Rusty's surprise, Ralph, get out of the limo and stride past the guards into the store.

Spanish Ramundo, of course, as head of the Sureños, was to be expected. Ricardo Campas' presence, as the number two shot-caller for the Sureños, and in Jacko's view, planning a coup against him and the Norteños, was no surprise. In addition, Manny Diaz's vivid recount of Jacko including Ricardo in the beating at the East Side Education Center also explained his closeness to Ramundo.

But Ralph? Rusty had last seen him apparently fleeing with his father, Jacko, and his mentor, the Indian. Rusty had a gut feeling that maybe a double cross by Ralph meant the Indian and Jacko hadn't made a getaway after all.

What had Manny said? That "Anyone who saw Jacko beating the three of them would never forget it." Ralph, too, had been one of those publicly flogged. Apparently, not only the spectators remembered the event, the three experiencing the thrashing had never forgotten, either.

The vehicles pulled away. They would be nearby in case a threat surfaced, to be recalled when the brain trust ended. Rusty kept the glasses focused on the storefront, but his mind wandered to the question of what the hell Ralph was doing with the supposed enemy? The former sheriff had a hunch that Ralph, unsuspected by the Indian or Jacko, had been in league with Ricardo in the planned coup.

Now, with Jacko and the Indian out of the picture, the three were probably hammering out an agreement for a merger of the two gangs. The dissolution of the Fourth Street neighborhood into its present condition was clear evidence of what happened to the quality of life when gangs got out of control.

And part of the control that Rusty had achieved as sheriff had been playing the two gangs against each other. The pending formation of a united large organization of violent gangsters was indeed ominous for the rate of bloodshed in Silicon Valley County.

An hour later, the meeting ended. The motorcade was summoned, the three gang kingpins, whisked away. Fifteen minutes passed. The older of the two sentries locked the door. The same undistinguished Honda that had dropped them off came by to pick them up.

Rusty ate a power bar and washed it down with a bottle of water. Dinner. Jacko's intelligence on the functioning of the meeting place had been right on target so far, but Rusty had to be sure. He couldn't afford any surprises. He would continue his scrutiny.

He placed a blanket on the hard ground and sprayed ant and bug killer in a circumference around his makeshift mattress for the night. He then thoroughly applied mosquito and insect protection to his skin and clothing. He let Itsy Bitsy briefly explore the vicinity on a long leash.

Periodically, he checked the meeting place. Gradually, he grew accustomed to the rhythm of the street, the sound of people coming and going, the noise of traffic. He also became aware that the world of the creek bed had its own cadence.

Jays angrily scolded other feathered intruders. A chorus of birds sounded alarms when the intermittent feral cat stalked the scene. Squirrels dashed to and fro, noisily communicating in their own language, sometimes dashing up trees, crashing from one branch to another or simply freezing in place, blending into the background.

Most of the time, Itsy Bitsy snored slightly and twitched during dog dreams. Once in awhile, the little guy came fully awake, bringing Rusty's attention to a homeless person heading toward the creek bed to settle down in his or her night spot before darkness set in.

Dusk gave way to darkness. He covered himself against the post-sunset chill with the second blanket. The tiny dog crawled under the blanket. With only its head sticking out, it resumed its slumber, briefly coming alert when nocturnal raccoons rambled by. Apparently sensing that the coons would avoid Rusty, the dog went back to sleep.

Rusty, lying flat on his back, unintentionally fell sound asleep. Awakening a couple of hours later, he stared up at the brilliant stars of a moonless night. The brisk day wind had cleared the valley of its typical sickly yellow automobile smog drifting from the heavily traveled north and south freeways serving the peninsula.

The silence struck him. He checked the luminous Mickey Mouse timepiece. 2230 hours. No law-abiding pedestrians would dare walk Fourth Street at this time of night. And passing cars were few and far between. The deceptive peacefulness of the night enveloped him.

Birds were silent except for an infrequent hooting owl. A bold group of raccoons foraged the creek. Confident that they had no natural enemies in this terrain, they made as much noise as they pleased.

Rusty gazed up at the spectacular star show. His mind drifted back to the days before Lucy became ill, when she sometimes mischievously lured him onto the smooth cut grass of their small but sheltered back yard. Spreading a blanket, much more comfortable than the one he presently rested on, Lucy had slipped off her midnight blue bathrobe.

"All right, you beast of a sheriff," she whispered, her voice full of schoolgirl naughtiness, "ravish me. Have your way with me, you brute."

And her passion had ignited him. Both of them furiously fucking in the dark. He felt himself getting hard now for the first time in a long while, remembering the delicious agony of them fighting to stifle their cries of ecstasy that probably would have been smothered by their adjacent neighbors' televisions, anyway.

He sighed. The other side of Lucy, the sweet, demure, very lady-like teacher, and do-gooder volunteer who no one would picture franticly screwing his brains out in the backyard. There were times during some of the endless, boring black tie fundraisers they attended when she sensed him looking at her.

The hidden wisp of a smile would cross her lips. That look would come into her eyes, her mouth open slightly to let a little gasp to emerge, as she read his thoughts and saw his face color, and breath quicken.

Then, she would sneak a wink and turn her attention back to the dinner speaker, like she was hearing the Gettysburg Address for the first time. His loss had been so deep.

He couldn't remember when he had last even thought of sex. The irony of it coming now. When it was entirely possible that he was living his own last few hours on this mortal coil, as Lucy had every so often referred to the planet.

An hour later, he rolled on his stomach, pulling on the night vision glasses and checking the store and the street. Nothing.

He was about to remove the glasses when Itsy Bitsy gave a low growl. Rusty saw the two silhouettes moving silently through the darkness. They were headed toward the same rough pathway he had used to descend, while looking for Bummy's former nest.

The leader was a huge, heavy shouldered black man. His white buddy was shorter, but with equally powerful shoulders. He carried a small baseball bat as a club. These weren't gangbangers. They belonged to the same sadistic predatory species, white and black, who preyed upon the homeless, sometimes to steal anything of minor value, sometimes simply to inflict pain.

Rusty hoped they wouldn't spot him. But remembering Bummy's demise, he slipped the Glock from its holster, and cast off the top blanket.

"Shit!" The first man had stumbled in the rough ground. His companion behind him held out a hand, pulling him to his feet.

At an awkward angle, trying to regain his balance, his eyes happened to spy Rusty's feet.

"Hey. What we got here, Bro? An old timer, and maybe a little treasure trove. Come on out of your burrow, Pop. We won't hurt you. Just want to rap a little," he unconvincingly coaxed, like he was talking to a child.

The dog barked. Rusty eased the safety off the gun.

"Shut that mutt up or I'll bash his skull in," the guy with the bat, said.

Rusty held up the Glock, pointing it at him in the dim light.

"I'll be damned," the big man said to his partner. "Looks like the old bum has a nice looking piece. "Let me see it, Pop. If it works, we'll give you a few bucks for it," he lied. "Get some good booze to warm your stomach."

Rusty trained the gun on him.

"Now, Pop. Believe me, you don't know how to use that thing. And you better not make me crawl in there to pull you out.

Precariously, he stood upright and took a step forward.

Rusty came up to his knees. He moved into a firing position, bracing the Glock with his left hand.

"One more step, and I'll blow your motherfucking head off," Rusty said, firmly.

The guy laughed and started to move forward. Rusty shifted his aim so that the barrel was aimed over the man's left shoulder. Blank or not, this close, stippling residue would pickle the guy's face if the weapon were pointed directly at him.

"Just take it easy . . ."

Rusty fired. The explosive flash lit up the darkness. The sound of the shot was deafening in the confined space.

The shorter man was already scrambling away. Rusty had to hold the dog to keep him from charging the fleeing man.

"That slug went right past my ear," he yelled of the imaginary bullet to his buddy, as he stumbled away.

The big guy was paralyzed with fright. Rusty fired the second blank. He brought the weapon down to bear on the middle of intruder's chest.

This round was for real. Rusty didn't want to fire it. But he was trapped in the hideaway, and in no position to defend himself.

He didn't have to shoot. The second blank shot sent the big man fleeing after his partner. The dog hadn't winced. His tail wagged triumphantly. Pablo had apparently trained him well.

Rusty listened carefully. Other than the two men crashing through the brush, the creek bed had resumed its silence. Rusty knew the two would-be tough guys wouldn't be back in this area for a long time, if ever. They had only enough balls to pick on the frail homeless, not on anyone who could fight back.

He turned again to the street. But as loud as the shots had been in his little nook, the sound probably hadn't been that audible on the street itself. Then again, frequent gunshots were part of life in the area. People were well aware that if they called 911, the call would be traced to their phone. It was better not to hear or see anything. Rusty settled back to wait.

Soon enough, it would be over, one way or another.

CHAPTER TWENTY-ONE

R USTY, CONFIDENT THAT his four-legged companion would signal any human activity, dozed off and on during the night. Based on Jacko's information, he didn't really expect any action. He had to stay somewhere. His shrub bed hiding place was preferable to holing up in the locked garage all night.

Besides, Ralph showing up in a limo with Spanish Ramundo and Ricardo Campas demonstrated that a new ball game was underway. It was impossible to guess what might happen. It was worthwhile to keep an eye on the meeting place during the night, just in case.

At 0400, Rusty again pondered the stars. Once more, he thought about whether he was capable of carrying out the extreme and irreversible plan. Itsy Bitsy growled. A noise from the street had startled him. Rusty swung over onto his stomach and peered at the storefront through the night glasses.

A deep green Mazda stopped in front of the Sureños store. Ralph parked and got out. He walked directly to the store, opened the door with a key, and entered. A dim light went on right where the table would be, but Rusty couldn't see anything inside.

Rusty was stunned. Ralph arriving in one car. No guards. No Ramundo. No Ricardo. Just Ralph, all alone in the meeting place. Rusty kept his eyes riveted on the storefront.

Within minutes, an official-looking dark blue sedan pulled to the curb. The driver pulled to the curb. He emerged, not bothering to lock the car. The new arrival wore a San Francisco Giants' baseball cap, incongruous dark glasses for nighttime, a three-quarter length light jacket, dark slacks and black shoes.

He casually glanced around as if not much concerned about security. He swaggered up to the door and knocked three times. Ralph opened the door and the two men gave each other a gang-hand greeting. The stranger entered. Ralph locked the front door.

The guy's attire, a three-quarter-length jacket, was common among cops to cover their handguns. The overconfident glance around, and the swaggering walk could also easily have spelled cop. But the gang handshake? What the hell could that have been?

Rusty cursed silently. The night vision glasses had no magnifying function, but there had been something familiar about the last arrival that eluded Rusty in the poor light.

Still, he might be able to get the plate number. He whipped off the night glasses and fumbled for the cheap magnifiers. It took awhile, but there was just enough light to read the license plate. He jotted it down.

The last guy to arrive was out of there in twenty minutes. Rusty was still frustrated. He hadn't gotten a clear enough look at him.

Almost immediately, Ralph quickly locked the store and retreated into the Mazda and drove away. Rusty grunted. This highly unusual meeting had to mean something, but it was beyond him.

Just before ten in the morning, Rusty decided that despite the mysterious night rendezvous he had witnessed, and the possibility that the shot-callers might not return that soon, he had to be ready.

He recovered his shopping cart, parking the content, tiny dog on the blanket. Obviously, the mutt was enjoying Rusty's company after being abandoned by the Garcia family.

Staying across the street from the Sureños storefront meeting place, Rusty swayed down the street, maintaining his repertoire now familiar to anyone who had paid him attention. He entered the storage area and parking garage without incident, closing the garage door behind him.

Rusty provided the dog with a bowl of dog food and another of water. While Itsy Bitsy was busy feeding, Rusty indulged himself with the luxury of sitting in the comfortable rear seat of the Mercedes and slowly consuming another power bar and bottle of drinking water.

Taking a deep breath, he opened the garage door. Seeing no one in sight, he allowed the dog to roam as far as the leash permitted. Quickly, Rusty drove the car slightly forward.

He moved to the trunk and picked up the two hand grenades. Gingerly, he placed them in his cart, wrapping them each in one of the blankets. Getting behind the wheel, he once more parked the car flush against the rear wall. He set the alarm system and locked the car. Rusty closed the door to the storage space, placing the dog in his now accustomed spot on top of the blanket.

Somewhat wearily, Rusty began what he hoped would be his last journey back to his creek bed hiding nook.

CHAPTER TWENTY-TWO

I T WAS NOONTIME when Rusty meandered back down Fourth Street. Shopping was a little heavier at this time of day, especially around the Bodega at the far end of the block away from the creek.

Rusty bumbled along, but skipped flashing his tin cup for donations. He still felt a little guilty over the two quarters donated by the elderly woman who could ill afford the half-buck.

After carefully removing the grenades and placing one in each pocket of his trench coat, he secreted his shopping cart beneath the bushes.

Leading the dog back to the observation point, Rusty and his faithful companion made themselves comfortable in their hiding place. Rusty watched as the street slowly settled down into siesta mode.

But Rusty was wired. He cautioned himself. Ups and downs could be self-defeating. Just cool it.

If Jacko's supposition were right, the gang leaders wouldn't be back until tomorrow. But something curious was happening. Ramundo, Ricardo, and Ralph putting their heads together yesterday.

Then, the four a.m. meeting between Ralph and the mysterious stranger. It wouldn't do to count on previous patterns. Rusty had to be ready.

Sure enough, at 1300 hours, the old Honda deposited the same two guards. They took their positions on each side of the store door. Jacko had said the leaders met every other day. But it looked like they were coming two days in a row.

And they did. The same routine was followed at 1500 hours. Rusty's pulse beat faster when he saw Ramundo and Ricardo enter the meeting place.

Right on cue, the three-car motorcade pulled away. Without delay, Rusty removed all traces of his and the dog's presence from the hideaway.

He had worn the work gloves and the overly large galoshes so his footprints wouldn't be identifiable. He raked over the area as best he could.

Luckily, a light rain had begun to fall. A prelude to an unusual summer shower. It would wash away any trace of DNA they had left in the highly unlikely circumstances that the police would ever inspect the area.

Carrying the dog, Rusty descended to his trusty cart. Depositing Itsy in his usual spot, he smiled grimly at the canine's tail wagging. The animal was totally unsuspecting of what was about to happen.

Rusty pushed the cart up the incline, and walked to the corner of the overpass. He was just about to wander along the sidewalk when he spotted a sheriff's department cruiser crawling down Fourth Street. Rusty, heart racing, ducked with his cart behind the concrete bridge pillar, hoping that the cops hadn't seen him.

Clearly they hadn't. They did momentarily halt in the traffic lane opposite the Sureños store to engage in some brief eye fucking with the two guards matching their hard looks.

It had been close. The cops had almost spotted Rusty. The police car pulled away.

Rusty stayed hidden until it was long out of sight, giving his hands a chance to stop trembling. He pushed the cart up onto the sidewalk.

Making sure that no one was watching, he lowered the metal bars on the cart enabling parents to seat their infants. He placed the two grenades into the space where a child might have sat, and firmly wedged a blanket over them.

He soon abandoned the sidewalk and lurched into the empty traffic lanes, gradually drifting close to the cars parked along the curb in front of the Sureños meeting place. Rusty had carefully thought out his mission, which, given the presence of two armed guards in front of the store, was perilous.

As he drew close, he realized that he had gotten an unanticipated good break. The two guards were still pissed at the cops, as well as concerned that they might be making a U-turn down the road and coming back.

The gangbangers probably wouldn't have paid mind to Rusty anyway, given their previous encounter, but both men continued staring in the opposite direction. Rusty was able to crouch unseen behind a parked car that would hide him from the guard's sight until it was too late.

Rusty tossed the blanket into the cart, uncovering the grenades. He picked one up. Staying bent over, he pulled the pin and released the handle.

Six seconds! He counted one thousand and one, one thousand and two, one thousand and three.

Rusty stood erect and made a perfect throw, hurling the grenade through the plate glass window in front of the metal meeting table.

As he turned to release the pin on the second grenade, he noticed that the two sentries were still staring after the departed police car. They hadn't seen Rusty at all.

The plate glass shattered. The two lookouts in front, startled, turned to see what had happened inside the store. They never saw the second grenade following the same trajectory as the first.

Rusty hunkered down behind his shopping cart and the cover of the parked auto at the curb. He tossed a blanket over the dog. Shrapnel could fly a long, deadly way.

The first grenade exploded with a flash. Seconds before the second grenade detonated, there was a huge explosion and a ball of fire burst through the front of the store and its roof.

The force knocked Rusty off his feet, even though the parked auto and cart protected him somewhat from the force of the explosion. Reaching out with his hand, he was just able to keep the cart from tumbling over, dumping Itsy Bitsy and all kinds of forensic evidence that might link him to the scene.

Shakily, he pushed his cart hurriedly away from the raging fire, wondering what the hell kind of new grenade behaved more like a bomb than a device that sprayed lethal, but minute, fragments of steel? Rusty hurried, murmuring soothing assurances to the whimpering dog.

He didn't totally abandon his act, but he knew it was unnecessary. People were all running, fleeing at top speed, screaming. No one noticed him.

He traveled unobserved into his storage space. Closing the garage door behind him, Rusty stripped naked. He divided all of the clothing into two plastic garbage bags.

He put on the sports shirt, slacks, and loafers he had stored in the trunk. Just as he was about to get behind the wheel, he remembered the ponytail and stuck it into one of the bags.

He drove away from the blaring fire and police sirens staying well within the speed limit. It was time to clear up some loose ends and disappear with his four-legged accomplice.

CHAPTER TWENTY-THREE

R USTY HEADED EAST and entered the northbound lane of the 101 Freeway. Five minutes later, he took an exit he knew well. Rusty was quite careful not to speed or run lights. The Bay area had any number of cameras to catch unwary motorists violating the traffic laws, presumably to increase safety, but more certainly increasing revenue. The last thing he wanted was his presence to be recorded in the Bay Area on this fateful day.

A few streets off the freeway, he entered a shopping center and pulled up to two dumpsters in the rear of a full size drug store that sold everything from toothpaste to household appliances.

He placed the now empty cart and two full plastic garbage bags in the dumpsters, viewing their fullness as a positive signal that they would soon be emptied and their contents on the way to a landfill.

The former sheriff was confident that all evidence of his presence in the creek bed, the storage facility, and most important, in the proximity of the Fourth Street Sureños meeting place was gone.

The final deposit in the waste bins was the pair of work gloves which had assured that no fingerprints or traces of his DNA from his hands had touched the cart or its contents.

He could think of no reason why anyone would have searched the creek area, but the surprisingly hard rain shower right after the explosion would have taken care of dog hair or fiber from the blankets, anyway.

He was now prepared to take the next step in restoring his pre-homeless appearance. Reaching into the glove compartment, he took out a package of wet wipes.

As best he could, he washed the grime from his face, throat, neck and hands. He doused himself with a cheap, sweetish smelling after-shave lotion in the hope that it would mitigate the odor of almost a week of roughing it.

Driving back to the freeway, he continued northbound, crossing The Bay Bridge. He weaved through the maze of intersecting freeways until he was heading north on highway 80.

He pulled into a mini-mall hosting a "Super Cut" hair emporium. It was a no reservations place, first come, first clipped.

As he had anticipated, the shop was almost empty that late in the afternoon. Tying the remarkably well-behaved Itsy Bitsy to an outside pole where he could keep his eye on him, Rusty slipped into an empty chair and had his overly long hair restored to its former length. He left a moderate tip that wouldn't be remembered as too generous or too cheap. Twenty minutes later, he was on his way again. Just another easily forgettable customer.

He was still ahead of rush hour traffic. He settled into the long drive, listening to the San Francisco Bay Area radio news stations located in San Francisco, but with an audience of over five million listeners within range. He was only a few miles from his exit when the news first mentioned a three-alarm fire in Sun City in the south bay.

The delay of the news and paucity of details were puzzling. The announcement by the news anchors meant that there were no reporters yet on the scene.

The brief commentary indicated only that it had been a powerful explosion, cause unknown, and that neither the police nor fire departments had announced whether or not there had been any casualties. There was a promise, however, that the traffic helicopters were now aloft and would soon be over the area and reporting on the event.

The two-bedroom cabin was just off Highway 80, some ten miles south of the county seat. The remote, rustic cottage bordered on Eldorado National Forest. It was the sole dwelling in the area and reachable only by a mile long dirt road accessible from Highway 80.

One of its great appeals for Rusty and Lucy had been its very remoteness. Any vehicle leaving the highway to travel the mile-long dirt road to the cabin would leave a trail of dust that was visible even before the car appeared.

Rusty was on the dirt cutoff when a news station's helicopter gave a considerably more dramatic report on the Fourth Street fire in Sun City.

The chopper announced that the smoke was still soaring high into the sky. It must have made great TV, but the aircraft really couldn't add much to the original report. By now, however, a reporter was on the ground and hyping up the event.

According to the reporter, fire officials said that the blaze was almost completely contained. The storefront that had been the source of the explosion was totally destroyed, as were the two adjacent empty stores.

JOSEPH D. MCNAMARA

Firefighters were attempting to ensure that the flames spread no further. Neither fire nor police would speculate on the cause of the explosion or whether there were casualties or injuries.

The reporter said, without explanation, that curiously, no spectators had gathered, despite the spectacle. The neighborhood was known to the police for people refusing to admit that they had seen, heard, or knew anything about events that occurred there.

Rusty pulled his car behind the cottage. He opened the spacious garage and pulled in. After the long drive, Itsy Bitsy was as anxious to get out as Rusty.

Still, this was wild country. Rusty kept the dog on a long leash. Dogs and other small animals venturing into the national forest, a thousand yards to the rear and sides of the house, were rarely seen again.

He carried the dog food and case of water to the cabin and unlocked the door. Rusty returned to the car and brought the various weapons into the living room.

He placed the scoped rifle and the Glock on the glider located in the screened area on the front porch. Next, he provided a hungry Itsy Bitsy with a bowl of dog food and another of water.

He sat on the glider, sipping a cold beer. He looked out at the wide-open space in front of the house that stretched all the way to the highway in the far distance. He was never sure whether it belonged to the federal or state government, but the most important thing was that the cabin had been grandfathered into the designated open space. No other dwelling could be erected within sight. But now, something was missing.

The tranquility that he and Lucy had enjoyed in the quiet countryside just wasn't there, anymore. And given the recent events in his life, maybe it never again would be.

In the shower stall, he shampooed and scrubbed himself thoroughly, but his pleasurable thought of a lengthy hot shower suddenly vanished. He couldn't afford to be absent that long from his surveillance point on the front porch.

Still drying himself with a towel, he joined Itsy Bitsy on the glider long enough to sense that everything was still peaceful. He went back inside, shaved his heavy beard, and applied enough coloring to restore his hair to its former appearance before he had let it go gray.

He took a frozen steak and package of broccoli from the freezer and started the propane grill in the side yard. Searching the kitchen cabinet, he selected a bottle of barbeque sauce. He washed both sides of the steak, drying it with a paper towel.

Opening the bottle, Rusty brushed a generous amount of sauce on the steak. Securing the barbeque tools from the kitchen, he placed the still frozen steak on the grill, searing each side on high heat for two minutes. He then turned off the middle burner of the grill and set the front and rear burners at low.

Slowly cooking the beef with indirect heat enhanced its flavor and tenderness. When the smell of the cooking meat began to float through the yard, Itsy Bitsy quickly returned from his sniffing wandering, never taking his eyes off Rusty.

Rusty added the broccoli to the grill area for indirect cooking. He opened another beer, placing it on the small table in front of the glider. Sitting down to eat, he made the mistake of feeding Itsy Bitsy a small sliver of the steak, guaranteeing that the animal would continue begging until the meat was gone.

He finished his dinner as darkness settled in. He left the cottage lights unlit, so they wouldn't be spotted from the highway.

The day had been stressful. Even the long drive that usually relaxed him had been tense. He felt fatigue and thought longingly of the wonderfully comfortable bed that Lucy had installed. But the more he considered it, he realized that it wouldn't be safe to fall into a deep sleep.

Itsy Bitsy's keen ears, eyes, and nose would provide early warning of any visitors if he and Rusty spent the night on the screened porch. He located an old blanket for the dog and placed it at the foot of the glider.

He then brought out a comfortable pillow, a thick blanket to serve as a mattress for the glider, and a warm top blanket. Nighttime temperatures could drop quite a bit this far north.

Stretching fully out on the glider, Rusty was dropping into a deep sleep when Itsy Bitsy leaped up on his chest and snuggled down alongside him. It turned out to be a dreadful night's sleep.

The dog was simply too good a watchdog. Every unseen animal, and it seemed that there was a virtual parade of them through the night, led to growling, and Rusty staring sleepily through the night goggles.

Come dawn, he took the dog by its leash and jogged a few miles at a leisurely pace. Once Itsy Bitsy got it into his head that he couldn't stop to sniff every few yards, he seemed to enjoy the exercise. They returned to the cabin, and Rusty did his daily stretches and calisthenics in the outside-screened area.

He took a quick shower while the coffee was brewing. Once he was dressed, he toasted the English muffins that he had removed from the freezer to thaw before he'd gone jogging. The cottage was well supplied with a variety of books. He and Lucy had decided that this was to be their reading refuge and had never added a TV or radio.

It turned out that he did more dozing than reading. Daytime produced less animal traffic, as far as he could tell from the number of Itsy Bitsy's warnings. By the third day, he was somewhat more relaxed and much more into reading, although the nights were still hell with the dog's frequent awakenings.

Rusty spent a good deal of time peering through the night vision glasses and the rifle's night scope, only to spot small game and a number of deer.

He remained haunted by his foreboding that two legged predators would soon enough mar the landscape.

CHAPTER TWENTY-FOUR

A T 1400 HOURS on the fourth day, Itsy Bitsy was up on his legs bristling, and uttering a loud, full growl. Rusty looked into the distance without sighting anything.

Then, a minute later, he spotted a trail of dust. A car had left Highway 80 and was heading down the dirt road toward the cottage.

Rusty looked through the binoculars, but the car's windshield, in the distance, was clouded with dust. He put down the glasses and picked up the scoped rifle. He knelt on one knee, propping the rifle barrel on the porch rail.

He sighted in on the driver. After another minute, he spotted Lieutenant Maria Lopez-Hogan behind the wheel. He placed the rifle behind him and unclipped the Glock and its holster from his belt. He slipped them under the glider's seat cushion.

She pulled up in front of the porch, turned off the ignition, and unhooked her seatbelt. Slowly, she got out of the car, stretching her legs. She walked up to the screen door and entered the porch area.

"Good Afternoon, Sheriff," she said.

Rusty nodded. She was wearing a pale blue pants suit, white silk blouse and an unbuttoned jacket matching the pants. A modicum of makeup, nevertheless, looked freshly applied.

"Once again, Lieutenant, I have to ask how you found me?"

"I engaged in brilliant detective work, Sheriff." There was a twinkle in her eyes. "I remembered that you never took vacations, but you and your wife used to sometimes sneak up to the Gold Country for three-day weekends. I simply called the County Record clerks in three counties checking your name against property owners."

"The cottage isn't in my name."

"True. So I checked on under your wife's maiden name as well. Bingo!"

Rusty watched Itsy Bitsy, the disloyal little scamp, energetically wagging his rear end in an overly friendly greeting to Maria Lopez-Hogan.

"Got yourself a watchdog, Sheriff?"

"That's Itsy Bitsy."

She turned her head sharply toward Rusty, her brown eyes quite serious. "Don't call him that. They understand, you know."

She bent over, her face quite close to the dog's.

"Your name is Itsy, isn't that right, little guy?" she said, as if talking to an eight-year-old child.

The delighted mutt actually rubbed noses with her. She scratched behind his ear. She smiled and straightened up.

"Uh, Sheriff, it's been a long drive. O.K. if I use your rest room?"

Rusty waved toward the screened door to the house.

"Second door on the left, down the hallway."

She had a brown manila envelope under her arm, which she carried inside with her. Rusty wondered if it contained another grand jury subpoena.

The Lieutenant took her time. Rusty sat looking out toward the highway. It may have been a long drive, but there were plenty of fast food chain eateries with spotless restrooms along the way. And he was pretty sure her makeup had been recently applied. Finally, she returned and sat in the comfortable lounge chair facing him.

"Find any clues inside?" he said.

"A few. Your freezer is heavy on protein and light on fresh veggies and fruit. All those steaks and chops. No farmers' markets around?"

"I haven't left since I got here."

"Right. I noticed all the books. No TV. No radio. No phone. No contact with the outside world?"

"I've had more than enough contact with the outside world this month."

She looked out toward the surrounding forest, then toward the horizon.

"Peaceful here, Sheriff. Very cozy. It must have been tranquil for you and Lucy to escape from all the politics, media, and bureaucracy once in awhile."

He waited.

"Still, the world doesn't stop while you're up here, does it?" she said.

"What's on your mind, Lieutenant? You didn't drive all the way up here to comment on my seclusion. Got another subpoena in there?" He pointed toward the envelope.

"No. The term of the grand jury expired. D.A. Herrera is pissed that we didn't serve you, but it will be at least a month before he can convene a new jury. Sheriff Sally sent me to talk to you."

"So maybe you should, instead of nagging about veggies and what I call my dog."

She grinned.

"I guess I deserve that for intruding. But you did give us fits for a couple of days."

She took an eight by ten glossy black and white photo from the envelope and pushed it toward him on the coffee table, carefully watching his reaction.

Rusty barely managed to keep a straight face as he stared at a clear picture of him being led from the Norteños headquarters at the point of Jacko's shotgun. Ralph, the Indian, and the angry crowd of gangbangers stood out just as vividly.

"H'm," he said, "this is my bad side. I photograph better on the other side."

She stood, considering the picture. She touched the other side of his cheek. He flinched from the shock of feeling her cool palm. She took her hand away.

"I don't know, Sheriff. I think I like this side better," she nodded toward his cheek, which still tingled with the electricity of her touch.

She sat back with a slight smile, totally relaxed.

"So what do you think of the picture, Sheriff?"

"Well, outside of the angle that's unfavorable to me, it occurs to me that the photo lacks a time and date, which would make it inadmissible in any legal proceeding."

Her smile grew.

"I like that. Even though you're retired, sloppy police work annoys you as much as when you were boss."

"It bothered me even when I was a deputy."

"Ah, yes. The super sheriff. Well, you'll be happy to hear that we can lay the blame on the Feebies. In their rush to move their task force to Nevada, they left the automatic remote motion camera they had hidden across from the Norteños gathering place. It was a full week before they asked us to retrieve it. The automatic clock and calendar function had malfunctioned, but there was no one there to notice. Things hit the fan when one of our intelligence guys was curious enough to take a look at what was on film."

"I bet. Sorry to be a bother. I would have let you know that rumors of my demise were exaggerated."

"You and Mark Twain. Intelligence wanted to put out an APB and an Amber Alert."

"I thought Amber Alerts were only for missing kids."

"Yeah. Intelligence thought that if you were childish enough to visit Norteños headquarters, you qualified."

He laughed.

"But Sally and I went over and over the photographs." She jabbed her index finger on the envelope. "There were ten in all. The two of us decided that there was something phony in Jacko's, Ralph's and your expressions. The Indian, of course, never has an expression."

"Women's intuition?"

"Something like that, but more the ability to read male behavior."

Rusty smiled. "Well, you turned out to be right. I spoke to the Padre who informed me that Jacko had told him that the Sureños had put out a contract on me. It didn't make sense. I wanted to hear it from Jacko, himself. Turned out to be true, and Jacko was under siege by his own gangbangers as a result of the task force decimating them while letting the Sureños get stronger. We staged the whole thing just to get out of there alive."

"And?"

"I'm alive."

"So I've detected. And the others?"

"I dropped them in the Supreme Super Market Mall."

"And decided to hide here?"

"Not right away. I talked to DEA and the FBI who agreed with Jacko about the contract. They, as well as my lawyer and friends, all advised me to get invisible the next day."

She inclined her head in acceptance of his version.

"Still, despite the peacefulness up here, you look haggard, Sheriff."

"Yeah. Well, my loyal little four-legged friend who appears to want to leave with you is so alert at night that each time one of the eight hundred or so small animals wanders by, he wakes me up."

She again leaned over and said softly to the dog, "But it's not your fault, is it, Itsy? It's simply a bad plan."

Rusty scowled at her.

"If I could find you so easy, what makes you think the Phantom brothers can't? Even if half of what Interpol says about them is bullshit, they're still top pros. You have your scope rifle, the Glock, and a Street Sweeper repeating shotgun leaning against the couch inside, but you have no idea how they would come at you, or how many there would be."

"I'm not really in the mood for a Home Alert lecture, Lieutenant."

"Oh, excuse me. I really didn't think you'd take advice from a mere female lieutenant, but one has to try."

"Cool. You've been itching to unload something else on me since you arrived. What is it?"

"Well, first," she opened her purse, "Sheriff Sally ordered me to give you this cell phone and tell you, no ifs or buts about it, keep it within reach. The Phantom brothers are rumored to be in Silicon Valley, so we would like to be able to reach you if we get more info."

She tossed the cell phone on the glider. Rusty glanced at it without touching it. It sure as hell contained GPS chips somewhere in it. The lieutenant, watching him ignore the phone, sighed.

"One other thing, since you've imposed a news blackout on yourself, the Sureños meeting place was mysteriously bombed a few nights ago."

Rusty adopted a thoughtful frown. "The little place on East Fourth Street."

"That's the one. It is no more."

"What happened?"

"Ah, that's unresolved among the fire marshal, the medical examiner, and the sheriff's bomb squad."

"I don't get it."

"Neither does the media or the public. All hell is going on in formerly quiet little River City. The fire marshal will only certify that the cause was a huge explosion of a three hundred gallon propane tank used to heat the building. The M.E. says the heat was so intense that he cannot determine from bones that didn't melt the number of deceased and causes of death. The sheriff's bomb squad says that, although the fire marshal will not permit them or the department's crime scene unit to analyze the site, tiny scraps of steel were found in the street."

"Meaning?"

"Well, our people believe that a RPG—rifle propelled grenade or home-made bomb exploded and penetrated the steel-skinned propane tank. Maybe it was a drive-by with the RPG or an inside job with a planted bomb. Anyway, it took out three stores and almost the entire block. The violent explosion probably sent steel particles of the propane tank cover flying. And surprise, surprise! No one around there heard, saw, or will say anything."

"And what does the head of the sheriff's department homicide unit think?"

"Oh, I suspect foul play. Gang intelligence indicates that Spanish Ramundo and some of his top guys are in the habit of meeting there at that time of day. People in my squad are calling them public service homicides."

"Any suspects?"

"Sure. First of all, none of your three escorts from the Norteños headquarters have been seen before or since the explosion. Then, there's your angry friend, former Special Forces Captain Garcia, an expert on explosives. Whatcha think, Sheriff?"

"Pablo? Forget it. He's a successful family guy and devoted do-gooder. He talks like he's still in the Army, but—,"

"Sure. Also, it happens that he has an almost too airtight an alibi. He was in Mexico City meeting with Mexico's chief prosecutor. But, you know, Mexico? Integrity in government? We've asked the Feebies for their help, but . . . How do you feel about your three companions in the photo?"

"Anything is possible, I suppose, but they seemed to be in a hurry to get out of town. Anyone else? You've been questioning me, the subject of a Sureños contract. That's motive. On the other hand, you haven't Mirandized me, so I guess I'm not a suspect. Am I what is now known as "A Person of Interest?"

The lieutenant stood and moved quite close to him. She leaned over. Her face was only inches away. He caught a slight whiff of a delicate rose-like perfume. She unleashed a smile. Her teeth were dazzling white. Her skin was light brown, and smooth. She had brushed her short hair in a more attractive style than the normal cop mode she adopted. Her eyes, shining with pure delight, sent him reeling back away from her.

This woman who had lowballed her femininity and sexuality had suddenly unleashed it. Her beauty crashed through the wall he had built against other women over twenty years ago when he met Lucy.

He had treated women with respect and courtesy, but there had been room for only one in his life, Lucy. He remembered hearing of a female Deputy D.A. who had expressed interest to a colleague about Sheriff Rusty. "Married. Very, very, married," her girlfriend had replied.

Maria Lopez-Hogan had deliberately hurtled through that wall a moment ago. And she knew exactly what she had done.

"Yes, definitely. I find you a most interesting subject of interest!" she said, still close and beaming.

Then, she backed away. He let out a deep breath. She bent down and scratched the dog's head.

"Itsy, you take good care of your Daddy. Keep him safe, you hear me?"

And with that, Lieutenant Maria Lopez-Hogan swayed back to her car to drive home to Silicon Valley County.

Within twenty short minutes, she had destroyed his smugness over covering his tracks. And, almost as casually, she had also obliterated his inner confidence of being able to survive within his own fortress of solitude.

Lieutenant Maria Lopez-Hogan had something in mind and Rusty had no idea what it was.

CHAPTER TWENTY-FIVE

RUSTY WASN'T SURE whether his mood had upset the dog or the pooch was simply more restless than usual. But he was increasingly haggard because Itsy seemed to wake him every half hour or so during the night. He didn't let himself get casual about the alerts, however, peering intently through the darkness. As a result, he came fully alert time after time, and had trouble going back to sleep.

It was well after midnight when the dog's growl got considerably louder and his body tensed up. The mutt tried to jump off the porch in pursuit of something or other. Half asleep, Rusty looked into the distance and was suddenly wide-awake. A vehicle with only its parking lights lit was moving slowly on the dirt road, in the distance.

As he watched through the night goggles, he saw that it was a good-sized SUV. It pulled off the road and came to a stop. Its lights went off. Rusty patted the dog, calming it down. Total quiet swept over the terrain.

Quietly, he picked up Itsy and brought him inside the cabin. He placed the dog's blanket on the living room couch and provided the dog with a small bowl of food to occupy him while Rusty explored the scene outside.

After a moments thought, he placed the sniper rifle in the corner, trading it for the semi-automatic shotgun which carried five rounds. He clipped the Glock to his belt and silently let himself out the front door. Itsy's attention was focused on the dog food.

It was an ink black night. Rusty hugged the tree line, moving slowly and carefully toward the van parked about a hundred yards away. He left the dirt road, and traveled along a narrow parallel path he and the dog had discovered during their morning jogs.

He stopped some twenty yards from the van, straining to see any movement though the night glasses. Maria Lopez-Hogan's warnings echoed through his mind. "You don't know how they'll come at you, or how many they'll bring."

There was no sound from the van. No sight or movement in the surrounding woods. Sighing to himself, he slipped the shotgun safety off. Step by step, he moved closer and closer to the van.

Suddenly, the springs began to squeak. Rusty dropped to one knee and sighted the shotgun on the van. The up and down movement increased. A decoy operation to gain his attention? He peered intensely around him, but all else was quiet.

He made a decision. He dashed the last few yards to the van, gazing into the rear window ready to fire. At this point, he saw a heavy-set, naked woman with pendulous breasts bouncing vigorously up and down on top of a slender guy flat on his back. He was squeezing her overly large breasts.

"Come on, son-of-a bitch, squeeze harder, harder." She yelled, then, "You bastard. You slipped out." The woman, who plainly had had a lot to drink then said, "I'll strangle you if you come now!"

She moved back into position, and they began all over again. Rusty closed his eyes and leaned back against the tree, drained. Sluggishly, he started walking back to the cabin. He had stalked a lover's lane.

When dawn came, the van was gone. He let Itsy roam on the leash. Rusty sat on the glider too tired to even think about a morning run. He did manage to get some sleep off and on during the morning.

More for something to do than hunger, he cooked himself a boneless, skinless filet of chicken on the grill. He knifed a slash of Dijon mustard onto a piece of toast, and downed half a pot of coffee along with the chicken sandwich. Itsy demanded, and got, his chunk of the chicken, not the slightest bit turned off by the spot of mustard residue on it.

Around 1430 hours, his watch dog again stiffened and growled loudly. Sure enough, dust was yet again rising on the dirt road. Rusty, unable to make out the vehicle in the cloud of earth enveloping it, sighted the powerful scope of the rifle on the car. As it drew nearer, he saw that it was a marked police vehicle. He quickly lowered the rifle, but kept it loose on his lap. It wouldn't be the first time the Phantom Brothers killed, disguised as cops. Then too, maybe he was getting a little paranoid in his hideaway.

The police car pulled to a halt. The local sheriff, and his long time friend, Pat Kelly got out, wearing a Stetson, with his neatly pressed uniform, and highly polished boots which he was careful to keep above the dirt path. Lean as a cowboy, the wrinkled faced, tall man approached.

Rusty was surprised to see that the sheriff was loosely carrying a scoped rifle in his left hand. His semi-automatic pistol was tightly holstered on his

JOSEPH D. MCNAMARA

right hip. In his right hand he carried an envelope very much like the one Lieutenant Hogan had carried.

"How y'all, Rusty. Mighty unfriendly of you not to drop into town and say hello. Haven't seen you in a coon's age."

"Pat, we both know you were born in the Bronx. When are you gonna drop the good ole boy stuff?"

"Heck, that was seventy-five years ago. Y'all never gonna let a fella live that down, are you?"

Rusty smiled. "Was it that long? When the hell, you going to retire, Pat?"

"Been married to Martha for fifty years. She says me retiring means more me around the house and less money. Neither of which she's looking forward to. Besides, can't get anyone else to run for the darn job."

"Carrying a rifle on patrol, now, Pat? Things getting that wild up here in the boonies?"

"Well, got a call from that lady lieutenant in your old department early this morning."

"What'd she say?"

"Called you an asshole. You give me a cup of coffee and I'll tell you all about it. How you doing, little pit bull?" he bent over patting Itsy on the head, who was sniffing the rifle suspiciously.

Rusty brought two mugs of black coffee out to the coffee table in front of the glider. Sheriff Pat Kelly was sprawled in the corner of the glider, his long booted legs stretched almost to the porch rail.

"Thanks, Pardna," he said.

"So what's up in your bustling metropolis, Pat?"

"You, mostly, Rusty. That lady lieutenant is a whiz, ain't she? Took all of five minutes on the phone to rat-a-tat-tat fill me in on everything happening, including these so called Phantom fellas. Gotta admit she's convincing."

"Um. You've been sheriff twenty-five years Pat. Long enough to remember what insubordination is."

"Hell. Even long enough to remember what civility was. Though I gotta admit that she was quite respectful to me. Was only when she got around to you not answering the phone she drove all the way here to give you, that she got kinda blunt. Called you an asshole. But I gotta admit my best deputy, Gloria Bell ain't much more tactful with me sometimes, to say nothing of Martha."

"The lieutenant tried to call me, Pat? I honestly didn't hear the phone."

"I can believe it. You look like you been on a week's bender. Tho, given what she told me I can understand why you might not be sleeping much."

"What was so urgent that she had to phone me after just talking to me yesterday?"

"Intelligence unit told Sheriff Sally, who, by the way, is spitting mad at you for the same reasons, that the Phantom Brothers were on the way up here."

"You know about them?"

"Just what she told me from Interpol. Not the kind of guys to go camping with. Well, as you know, I've got one of the largest county jurisdictions in the state with the fewest deputies. We don't like to pay taxes up here. And frankly people don't like a lot of enforcement either. So I'm not able to surround you with Secret Service like coverage."

"Still, even with low staffing, you've managed to stay in office all these years, with your brand of leadership—just let things be until you absolutely have to do something."

"Now, that ain't exactly accurate, Rusty. When I do spy something getting out of hand—"

"Like a criminal homicide?"

"Right. Sometimes, even when I spot it as about to happen, I assign a deputy. Tell 'em what the problem is and to go handle it. Give authority commensurate with responsibility like the textbooks say."

"The books also say the boss can't designate responsibility."

"Really? Guess, I didn't read that far. Anyway, I passed on to Gloria everything that your lieutenant said."

"I remember Gloria. Wasn't she the one who blew away the robber who shot the teller in the bank on Main Street?"

"You bet. Drilled him right between the eyes. I only winged his partner twice in the chest. He lived. She could have run and knocked me right out of office. But she just laughed. 'Who the hell wants to sit behind a desk filling out papers?' she said."

"So you assigned me to her?"

"Not exactly. Assigned the Phantom Brothers to her. She agreed with your lieutenant, no one can tell a stubborn, male asshole like you what to do."

"She dispatch you out here with your scope rifle to watch over me?"

JOSEPH D. MCNAMARA

"Hell, no. I'm not staying. Just brought the rifle along to protect myself in case they arrive while I'm telling you that I agree with your lieutenant. No way, you're safe out here, Rusty, once they find out where you are. Them two boys got more ways of whacking people than anyone can prevent against."

Rusty sipped his coffee.

"You don't have to be polite and stay to finish your coffee, Pat."

"I know. But we got a little time. That sure is a beauty you got there, Rusty," he nodded toward the rifle Rusty held on his lap. "Custom job?"

"Yeah. Borrowed from a friend."

"Mind if I look?"

Rusty handed him the weapon. Pat Kelly sighted it out toward the open field.

"See that little gopher sticking its head up out of the hole? I figure it's about a thousand yards."

"About that."

"This baby ain't been fired yet. Mind if I try?"

"Help yourself, Pat."

Almost as if it had heard them, the gopher disappeared down into the hole. But Pat patiently kept the rifle on target. After a minute, the animal's head reappeared. Ever so slowly, the sheriff squeezed off the shot. The gopher's head shattered into pieces.

"Beautiful, weapon, Rusty. Think you could have made that shot?"

"Probably not."

"So you say, but I remember one year at the California Sheriff's Associations annual conference, you won the marksmanship gold medal. Only time you ever even entered."

"It was just to shut those guys up from talking so much about guns every year. So has Gloria Bell knocked off the Phantom Brothers after following the strategy you set for her?"

"My only strategy was to tell her to work on them. Gloria would have done it her way no matter what I said." He held up the envelope. "Hell, I got to admit that she surprised even me to come up with this stuff so soon."

Rusty just sat, knowing Pat had to set the stage for this story his own way.

"You remember one of my deputies, Hank Nordstrom?"

"Yeah. An old timer. Didn't he retire?"

"Yep. But has a wife like Martha. Don't appreciate husbands who retire. So he bought that gas station. The one you gotta pass when you get off 80 to come into town. Everyone seems to stop there for gas or directions, or to take a leak. So Gloria went out to talk to Hank. He still likes to keep a hand in our reserve posse, which as you well know, is a royal pain in the ass for me, but a political necessity."

"Everyone of us in the sheriff's association felt the same way, but we all had them."

"Have to. But sometimes, they come in handy. Hank went along with Gloria's scheme. She and her long time girlfriend went and got one of them same-sex marriages in San Francisco. Conservative county. No one up here really gives a shit about what other people do as long as they don't bother someone. Anyway, Gloria's now spouse, Rita, is a professional photographer and does real good work."

Rusty poured them another cup of coffee. Pat knew how to tell a story.

Pat took a sip and continued, "Well, with Hank's help, the three of them set up an old Lexus in the garage bay so that its grill was pointed at the first gas pump. Rita hooked up a terrific digital camera behind the grill so that it couldn't be seen. Gloria and Hank disconnected the other pumps and put up signs that they were out of order. In other words, the only way you could get gas was to position yourself right in front of that long distance camera lens."

Rusty pictured the scene. "Gloria was that sure that a Phantom Brother would stop if they came?"

"Well, she had contingency plans, but we don't have to go into them. Anyway, Hank put an old Ford that he doing a lube and oil change on up on the other hoist. Every time a car approached, Hank got under the Ford. He had that corner of the garage loaded with as many weapons as the armory in town."

"Where was Gloria?"

"Behind the cash register with all the oil, junk food, water, and other stuff for sale. Now, Gloria's kinda plump, middle-aged, and likes to read all those crap magazines about Hollywood nuts. She's dressed in plain coveralls. Not carrying because she figures there's no way they get made. No one make her for a cop in a million years. Besides, if something surprising goes down, Hank's well covered and equipped. The pump's credit card hookup's been disconnected, so she knows anyone who gets gas is coming in to see her. Meantime, Rita hooked a little remote shutter bug on the side of the cash register, and went back to her studio in town. The gadget she used can take one picture at a time or go on full automatic."

Rusty was coffeed out, but he filled Pat's cup again.

"Couple of hours later," Pat's eyes alternated between looking at Rusty and scouring the horizon, "up pulls a big black Lincoln. Guy gets out. Suspicious. Disregards the out of order signs and tries all the pumps. Gloria makes him right away. Slips a wink to Hank, who moves even further under the Ford. Anyway, the guy tries the credit card slot. Naturally doesn't work. Meanwhile, Gloria hits the camera gizmo and it silently starts snapping away. The stranger fills up, and goes in to give Gloria a real looking over. Then, turns and sees Hank messing around under the Ford."

"Gloria nervous?"

"She's been cool as they come during her ten years in the Department. I didn't think she'd admit it. But she said there was something so evil about this guy that she almost pissed her drawers, her words. Still, she played the dumb, friendly hick. He signed the credit card bill, and gave her a friendly smile. He was half way back to his car when he stopped and came back. She watched him out of the corner of her eye, pretending to look at the pictures in the dumb magazine."

"Oh, boy!"

"Oh, boy! You better believe it. It made her even more nervous to see Hank in the corner aiming an M 4 at her and the guy. She was about to hit the deck, but they really didn't have enough for Hank to start blasting. So she raised her eyebrows at the stranger."

"What'd he want?"

"Just a friendly question about whether there were any rustic cabins in the area for rent. She gave him directions to a real estate office. The one on Main Street run by one of her friends. Guy in the Lincoln was real gracious to Gloria. Gave her a friendly wave and was on his way. Gloria got her friend in the real estate place on the phone and told him to send the guy looking north of town if he stopped in, and to no way mention your place."

"She did a hell of a job, Pat."

"You ain't seen nothing, yet Rusty," he crowed, holding up the envelope. "This little middle-aged lady from the hick sheriff's department got what all the police forces, FBI, DEA and Interpol couldn't get over the past fifteen years."

Carefully, he opened the envelope. There must have been twenty-five pictures from all different angles of the guy from the Lincoln. Facial close-ups, angle shots, and full body pictures. Someone that you'd pass twenty times a day, Rusty thought, without noticing. Except, he was way too coolly dressed for this area, in expensive sports shirt, slacks and loafers. About as inconspicuous as someone wearing a tux up here. And the Lincoln was too large and expensive for the Gold Country, even for the endless stream of tourists who favored big SUV's.

"Now, Gloria is also a whiz at crime scene forensic stuff." Pat held out a glassine evidence envelope containing three photos of finger and palm prints from the glass counter the Phantom had leaned on to sign the credit card slip.

"Also," Pat held up another evidence envelope containing the credit slip itself, "you not only got his handwriting here, although the name is sure to be phony, but Gloria thinks you probably got DNA traces from his sweaty hand when he leaned down to sign the slip."

"I'm truly awed, Pat."

"Damn. So am I, Rusty. Think of it. All those years when we kept women out of the ranks, too delicate, couldn't handle it, not strong enough, too gory."

"And a lot of that nonsense is still going on, Pat."

The old sheriff shook his head.

"Anyway Rusty, Gloria suggested that you bring this right down to Sheriff Sally. We identified one of the Phantom Brothers for the first time as sure as hell. But it will take a big county sheriff like Sally to light a fire under the Feebie's ass so that this doesn't end up in a desk basket like the pre-9/11 intelligence form their own agents sent to D.C. on the Islam terrorists taking jet flying lessons on everything except how to land."

The two men stood and shook hands.

"I can't thank you enough, Pat. Tell Gloria, her partner, and Hank that they're true all stars."

"I already called Sally. You just get that stuff down to her office by tonight. We'll make sure the Lincoln doesn't go anywhere until tomorrow. You take care of yourself, young man," Pat strode toward his car.

"Pat," Rusty called, stopping him.

He came back.

Rusty said, "Maybe you can do me another favor." He handed him the slip of paper from the creek bed, on which he had jotted down the license plate of the car Ralph's mysterious four a.m. visitor had used.

Pat glanced at it, then looked up at Rusty.

"Probably nothing," Rusty said, "but I thought I saw this car following me a couple of times. Can you check the ownership on your car computer monitor?"

"We're loaded with IT stuff. Just give me a sec."

Pat returned to his car and punched the plate number into his monitor. He frowned at the reply and punched the keys a couple more times. Finally, he got out and sauntered back to the porch, still frowning.

"You wouldn't be gaming me, would you, Rusty?"

"Gaming you?"

"Yeah. I had to override the system to get the registration information. You know what that means. Government owned. That car belongs to the Silicon County Sheriff's Department, Jail Division! You saw it up here?"

"No. Actually, it was down in Sun City."

"Then it's your problem. Not mine. About time for you to get going, isn't it?"

"Yeah, having me take it down tonight also gets me out of your jurisdiction, doesn't it."

"You bet. You think I want to listen to all the bullshit at the Cal Sheriff's conferences if anything happens to you up here? One other thing. You notice that the credit card bill for the Lincoln is sixty-four dollars? Hank wants to be reimbursed."

"Hell, Pat. I never said anything about expenses. You ought to cover it, or bill Lieutenant Hogan."

CHAPTER TWENTY-SIX

THAT EVENING, RUSTY sat in Sheriff Sally Henson's office. Little Itsy, proving to be a regular Lothario with the ladies, had Sally smiling and petting him at her desk. Her attitude was considerably less cordial with Rusty.

"As much as I admired you, and as much as you did for me, Rusty, I never thought I'd be saying this. But you are a complete asshole. Have you gone Loco?"

Rusty patiently waited.

"Of course, you're sitting there now, the classic leader. Stay calm, set the example. Let other people lose it while you remain cool, no matter how they castigate you."

"You look terrific, Sally," he said.

And she did. She was a tall, slender blondish fifty, dressed in a pinstripe suit, every bit the exec of a Fortune Five Hundred company.

"And you look like hell. When was the last time you had any sleep, Rusty? You've got some of the top assassins in the world tracking you down, but no, you're James Bond. Go it alone. Don't use the cell phone I sent you. Instead, when you arrive here an hour ago, you send the phone in an envelope to Maria Lopez. Cute. She was so ready to toss you in a cell that I had to send her out to a DOA they just found by the roadside in east county."

"Well, Sally, if you, or she, had had the courtesy to tell me that the device contained a GPS chip, I might have gone along. But when you treat me like a doddering old citizen . . ."

"Hence, when you see Maria rush out, you meander in here with the key information that you want me to get the FBI so they can drop everything to identify one of the Phantoms."

"You might say thanks. It's a major coup for law enforcement."

"Law enforcement. Exactly. Not you. Maria got to Pat Kelly and he gave it to his best deputy, Gloria Bell, who put the I.D. info together, in spite of you two good ole boy sheriffs."

Rusty grinned. He pointed to the envelope from Sheriff Kelly on her desk.

"But it got delivered. And you're all prettied up for a big meeting with the FBI."

"Prettied up? Next thing, you'll be calling me Honey. A pity that it didn't occur to either of you two experienced sheriffs to keep the chain of possession in the hands of law enforcement personnel before getting me to kick the Bureau's butt to get it analyzed."

"Sally, both Pat and I know that I'm an active member of the Silicon Valley Sheriff's Department reserve and have active duty status when you activate me."

"Yeah. We'll see how that holds up in court."

"What court? You don't have any evidence of a crime, just intelligence information."

"Well, you're lucky. The director of the FBI tapped me to chair his Feminine Leadership Council last year. I did a lot of traveling and spent a lot of time for the feds. He owes me one. In half an hour, the FBI jet is flying me to Dulles, then by helicopter into Quantico where their criminal profiling unit is headquartered in the FBI Academy."

"You'll be safe among all those marines on base. Don't let them talk you into enlisting."

"Seriously, Rusty, the FBI profile people have been alerted and are raring to go. The Phantoms haven't just been working for the drug cartels; they freelance some terrorist stuff, too. I'm going to have to run. But before I do, promise me to stay out of the case and let us protect you. Don't make it a do it yourself project."

The phone rang. Sally frowned.

"I told them hold the calls. This must be important."

She picked up the phone and listened for a minute.

"Yes Maria, I understand. I'll tell him. I'm off to Quantico, but you have my cell number."

Sally placed the phone back on its cradle. Her brow puckered in thought, she slowly said to Rusty, "That was Maria. The DOA tossed on the side of the road from a moving car was the Indian. One slug through the back of the head. Maria will be here within an hour. She wants you to wait and go over in detail your last meeting with the Indian, Jacko, and Ralph."

"The Indian executed, and no sign of Jacko or Ralph?" Rusty said.

Sally didn't hear. She was rushing out the door, carrying the information Rusty had delivered. Within hours she would arrive at the Marine Base in Quantico, Virginia, which housed the FBI academy.

One Phantom brother would be I.d.', the other anonymous. But both on the loose, and still two of the world's most highly skilled predators were out to kill Rusty.

CHAPTER TWENTY-SEVEN

RUSTY HAD NO intention of waiting around for Maria Lopez-Hogan to go through a repeat of Sally's ass chewing. He left headquarters and drove, twisting and turning, through Sun City. Convinced that he wasn't being followed, he made his way toward St. Sebastian's.

Nightfall had engulfed the deserted area and darkened church with a kind of Fall of the House of Usher eeriness. He tried the back door of the church, expecting it to be locked, surprised when it opened easily.

Inside, he melded into the gloom. The only lights came from some flickering candles on a metal stand at the altar rail, before which supplicants could kneel and drop coins as an offering.

Then they would light a candle to pray for sick or deceased relatives, or a winning lottery number, or whatever else constituted a fashionable request from heaven nowadays. The uninhabited emptiness of the large space with its faded statues of long forgotten saints added to his exhausted depression.

He froze. Watching the slow movement from the area near the dull gray marble altar rail, Rusty became conscious that he wasn't alone. Here, in this dead church, a stooped figure, clothed in a hooded, dark priest's cloak moved lethargically along the rail.

Studying the figure, Rusty knew his hunch had been right. The man was unenergetically moving a broom along the floor.

Soundlessly, Rusty approached and sat in the front pew. When the sweeper was right in front of him, facing the altar, Rusty said quietly, "Hello, Jacko."

The stooped-over Jacko turned instantly, the broom raised above his head as if it could be used as a club if needed.

"Sheriff! Did the old Padre once more forget to lock the back door?"

"I'm afraid so, Jacko. But I didn't." He gestured toward the pew he rested on. "Sit, so we can have a word."

Jacko did. He peered at Rusty in the dimness.

"Sheriff, you look almost as bad as I do. How did you know I was here?"

"Just a guess. I heard the Indian's body was found, but no sign of you or Ralph. I knew your bodies would be with him if you had been killed, and, if you hadn't, where else could you hide?"

"The Indian shot?"

"Executed. One through the back of his head."

Unexpectedly, Jacko made the sign of the cross.

"Forty loyal years. He seemed indestructible."

"Tell me what happened, Jacko."

"As you may have guessed, reserve funds were in safe deposit boxes. I didn't want Ralph or the Indian's pictures on the bank's security cameras, so they stayed in the car. I left the bank with the two bags. Only when I got close to the SUV did I notice the Indian in the passenger seat looking straight ahead."

"He wasn't moving?"

"No. He should have been looking at me to make sure I wasn't being followed. Ralph was in the rear seat behind the Indian, not at the wheel where he belonged. I ran. Ralph and Ricardo jumped out, chasing me.

"Ricardo had been hiding on the floor in back of the van. I threw the two bags of money in opposite directions, knowing they would go after the cash, not after me. I ran through the department store and out the side entrance. A lady was leaving a taxi. I got in and came here."

"And the Padre gave you shelter?"

"In a way. He's in and out of it. Half the time, doesn't know me. He belongs in a home. Rome, the Eternal City, takes an eternity to do things. A woman comes five hours a day. She's in the rectory now. That's why I'm here. I don't want her to see me. But with the money gone, I have no place else to go."

"Perhaps I can help, Jacko."

Rusty reached into his pocket. He had always stored some cash under a brick hiding place in the cabin. He pulled out a roll of twenties, around eight hundred dollars. He handed the money to Jacko. But the man made no effort to take it.

"Thank you, Sheriff, but I'm afraid that wouldn't get me very far."

"No, but if you can help me, I can visit my bank and come up with about ten grand in cash for you."

Jacko frowned.

"You would give me your own money?"

"It won't do me very much good if the Phantom brothers catch up with me."

"True. But I don't know how I can help."

"Who bombed the Fourth Street meeting place?"

Rusty watched him closely for even a glimmer of suspicion. Jacko shrugged.

"I'm holed up here. Watch television, read the daily paper that's delivered. I know nothing."

"Jacko, you told me that you hired a former deputy who traced the hit notice on me to the sheriff's department. Did he ever tell you who he suspected?"

"No. I really wasn't that interested in who. By that time, I knew we had to get out."

"Suppose I told you that the police haven't released the information yet, but they're pretty sure the only ones killed in the Fourth Street bombing were Ramundo, Ricardo, and two bodyguards. That means the Sureños have no leaders. There's no one in a position to pay off the Phantom brothers. So why are they still around trying to kill me?"

Jacko sat deep in thought.

"Ralph," he hissed. "My own son. When I saw him and Ricardo at the bank, I thought they were only after the money."

He fell silent. The eight hundred dollars rested on the seat between them. Rusty realized Jacko wasn't about to volunteer more.

"Jacko, what's the name of the former deputy private eye you hired?"

"Ah, sheriff, he did what he was paid for. I see no reason to rat him out."

"I'm talking about ten thousand reasons, Jacko. Take this as the down payment. I only want information from the guy that might help against the Phantoms."

Jacko thought for a moment. He put the money in his pocket.

"You'll bring the rest here?"

"Tomorrow."

"Just you? No one else?"

Rusty nodded.

"The former deputy's name is Arnie Grime. His office is in downtown Sun City."

"Jacko, there's another thing I don't understand. How did Ricardo know exactly when to meet Ralph at the bank pick-up?"

"I just thought about that. Remember right before we left, Ralph went to take a leak and pick up a piece?"

"Yes?"

"Well, I recall now. Before you came, I noticed that he had a Glock holstered to his back, hidden under his shirt. He already had a gun. He simply went into the back room to use his cell phone to call and alert Ricardo to be at the mall."

Rusty frowned.

"Do you think Ramundo was in on Ralph's plan?"

Jacko stroked his chin.

"I kind of doubt it. Remember, I suspected Ricardo was trying to pull a coup to take me out and bring the Norteños under Ramundo. But I was too blind to see that maybe it was all Ralph's idea."

"Out of the blue?"

"There were some signs, I missed. He blamed me for you and the task force taking down the Norteños, and for who knows what else? Me, being in his way to take over on his own? I'd love to have the pleasure of asking him, if it turns out he wasn't in the blast that took the others out."

The two men sat silently for a minute, each contemplating how abruptly their lives had plunged into violence within a few short weeks.

"Jacko," Rusty wondered out loud, "I've been really out of it since I retired. Tell me about Ralph. Did he get into any more trouble with the law after I left?"

"Yes. He ignored my orders, and stupidly got involved with some Sureños, who knows, maybe even Ricardo, in a meth deal. It went bad. They got busted. It cost me a lot of money to get him out of the case. But I didn't go bail for him, let him sit in your jail for ninety days, hoping he'd start thinking straight."

The jail, ninety days to plot with Sureños, and maybe the cop who had driven to the four a.m. meeting with him?

Rusty let himself out the rear door. Looking back into the dark church, he saw Jacko still sitting in the front pew looking for all the world like a supplicant asking for a miracle.

It occurred to Rusty that maybe he was the one that needed the miracle.

CHAPTER TWENTY-EIGHT

RUSTY CRASHED AT Pablo's home that night. The family was still absent, the guards alert. He slept his first sound night's sleep in more than a week. Incredibly, he saw that it was 0900 hours when he finally was aroused by the smell of fresh coffee.

Mrs. Gladys Monahan had done her magic again. Rusty, still groggy with sleep, went to the kitchen table in his robe and pajamas. She greeted him as if he showed up for breakfast every morning. Smiling, she poured him a mug of hot coffee.

Without asking, she put a steaming plate of hotcakes and a pitcher of warm maple syrup in front of him. The stack of hotcakes was piled with six slices of very crisp bacon. Rusty put aside the ghostly memory of Doc Hoffman telling him that the number of occasions a year that he could sample bacon was zero. To compensate, he fed Itsy a whole slice of the bacon.

Full and content, he took a long, pleasurable shower, shaved, and dressed, making sure that the Glock holstered on his right hip was fully covered by his short-sleeved sports shirt.

Rusty visited his bank and withdrew nine thousand dollars in cash. The bank was busy with long lines. The teller didn't even have time to comment on the unusually large withdrawal from Rusty's account. Rusty had deliberately kept it under the ten thousand buck transaction threshold that the feds required banks to report.

He called St. Sebastian's, only mildly surprised to hear Jacko's voice answer.

"Jacko, I'll be there in ten minutes if it's O.K. with you," he said.

"Ten minutes is good. I'll unlock the back door and be sitting in the front pew."

Even in the daylight, the interior of the church was gloomy, Rusty observed. He stood in the rear entrance a couple of minutes to ensure that the church was indeed deserted, except for Jacko. He locked the rear door, walked to the front row, and sat next to Jacko, in his priest's hooded cloak.

Jacko looked at him. "You slept well last night. I envy you."

Rusty handed over the nine thousand dollars in cash.

"I had to stay under the ten thousand limit, Jacko."

"Of course, I understand."

The two men sat looking at each other. It didn't seem possible that it was only a few days ago that they had faced each other for what they thought would be the last time. Now, neither had any doubt about it.

"I appreciate this, Sheriff," Jacko said. "You didn't have to do it."

Rusty merely shrugged. There was nothing to say. He rose to leave.

Jacko spoke in a hoarse whisper. "The Padre mumbles a lot. Recently, he quoted scripture. Something about he who casts bread upon the waters for others shall see it returned."

Rusty left the church wondering what the hell Jacko had been talking about.

JOSEPH D. MCNAMARA

CHAPTER TWENTY-NINE

H E CAUTIOUSLY DROVE away from the grounds toward Arnie Grime's downtown office in Sun City, making sure he wasn't tailed.

Grime was an appropriate name for the P.I.'s office, Rusty concluded, looking at the single glass door to the small storefront, whose windows needed washing. "Arnold Grime—Discreet Private Investigation." was printed in small lettering on the front window.

The decrepit office was right out of an old Raymond Chandler tale. The business section had gone downhill more than a decade ago.

He entered the cluttered office that obviously didn't employ a cleaning service. The short, balding man behind the desk wore wide, garish, wine-colored suspenders that barely managed to support trousers fighting to contain his ample belly. A faded, gray shirt with the top button open, and a drooping blue tie completed his unimpressive attire. He looked up through thick glasses.

It would be anybody's last guess that his unimposing appearance and mannerisms had helped make Arnie one of the best detectives in the sheriff's department before he had gotten into trouble.

"Sheriff!" he said, surprised, looking up from a pile of records in front of him. After a moment, he opened the top right drawer of his desk and started to reach in.

"Don't even think about it, Arnie." Rusty had lifted his shirt and had the Glock half way out of his holster.

"What?" Arnie's mouth dropped open. He held his palms outward in a peace gesture. "You didn't think for one moment that I . . ."

"What I think Arnie, is that you have a piece in that drawer and that you were going to be dead before you got it out."

"Cripes, Sheriff! Of course, I was going for it. You're red hot. But I'm on your side. If they came at you in here, which is not all that unlikely, I'd be blasting away with you. Never in a million years against you."

"Just close the drawer, Arnie."

"No. With all due respect, Sheriff, you got to believe me. I'm with you. You want to talk, fine. But you've got to trust me. I'm not going to sit here unarmed while you're in the office."

"All right, but don't take it out. Just leave it where it is."

Arnie rose. Stepping around the desk, he went to the front and swung a "Closed" sign into place and locked the door.

"Don't sit, Sheriff. No way, do I want you to be seen in here. Come on. We'll go out back to a safe place."

Ignoring Rusty's warning, the short fat man took a holstered Beretta semi-automatic from the desk and hooked it to his belt. He slipped into a wrinkled suit jacket he had lifted from a coat rack, and led Rusty down a basement staircase.

They walked through a poorly illuminated corridor featuring only a single hanging bulb. The two men climbed four steps to a door. Actually, they had left Arnie's building and crossed into the one adjacent.

Arnie signaled Rusty to a stop. He peered out into an alley making sure that it was clear. Rusty followed him into the alley. Four doorways from the basement door they had left, Arnie led him into the rear entrance of a dingy bar.

He pointed to a back booth. Both men sat behind a rounded table with their backs to the wall, where they could watch both the front and back doors to the bar.

"Buy you a drink, Sheriff?"

It was eleven-thirty in the morning. Rusty declined.

"O.K., but I'll order you one, anyway. Don't want these people to get curious. Don't worry. I'll drink it if you don't."

The three people at the bar hovering over their drinks, staring aimlessly at the shelf of bottles, didn't look like they had been curious about anything for a long time. A rather slovenly, thin woman in a stained waitress dress, who wouldn't see fifty again, came to the table.

"We'll take two double bourbons on the rocks, Doris," Arnie said. It was the kind of a dump where customers didn't specify a brand.

When she left to get their drinks, Arnie looked at Rusty. "What can I do for you, Sheriff?"

"A little information, Arnie. Tell me about the flyer."

"The flyer? How'd you hear that I worked on it?"

Rusty smiled.

"Right," Arnie said. "Well, ain't much to tell, really. 'Course, I was surprised when Jacko wanted to hire me. But when he told me what he

JOSEPH D. MCNAMARA

wanted, I didn't see a problem. I knew you and him had been tight, so I didn't see him causing you any trouble. Besides, all he wanted to know was where they had been produced. Offered me good money to find out. Frankly, I thought it was bullshit when he told me that he knew they had come from the sheriff's department."

Arnie lapsed into silence until the waitress disappeared after serving the drinks. Arnie downed half of his in a swallow.

"Anyhow, he went on, "when I looked at the flyer I believed him."

"Why?"

"Well, since you retired, the department got in this outside management analysis firm. Reorganized all the administrative stuff. One of their innovations was that every copying machine and all the IT machines have an identifying symbol."

"Cool."

"Yeah. For example, something coming out of the uniformed bureau would automatically has SVSD U in the lower left margin. You know, Silicon Valley Sheriff's Department, and U being the designation for uniform. Each substation or other unit would also have a number, so just by looking you can tell where the form came from."

"And you found that on the flyer."

"Yep. Your flyer had SVSD D on it. It came from the Detective Bureau."

Rusty was shocked. He had pretty much expected that it had come from the jail bureau, given the license plate number that Pat Kelly had traced had been from the jail. Then too, the unknown person who had met with Ralph had seemed familiar, like, maybe, Captain Jeremiah Christian from the jail bureau.

"And you never thought of letting me in on this?"

Arnie didn't hide his surprise. "You mean the Department never told you? The flyers were all over the street."

Rusty rubbed his chin. "Arnie, did you ever find out which individual in the Department was responsible?"

"Hell, no. Jacko didn't care. Even if he did, I wouldn't have tried. I still have my contacts in the department, but you know cops. If they think you're after a particular cop, they'll freeze up. You become persona-non-grata."

"The Detective Bureau is huge. You didn't narrow it down?"

"Well, yeah, a little. Jacko was sure it was the anti-gang unit or intelligence unit. But I actually found out that it was also possible to trace stuff to the particular copying machine it came from. My source told me it came from the second floor in headquarters."

Rusty tried to picture where the various squads were located. Of course, there had almost certainly been some reorganization in his absence.

"And?" he asked Arnie.

"You know, Sheriff, I never got a chance to say this, but don't think for a moment that I'm not grateful for what you did for me. I don't deny what I did was wrong, but those bastards in I.A. were in a blood feud to get me for reasons having nothing to do with what I was accused of."

Rusty waved it away.

"No, Sheriff, I want you to know I'm aware that you personally let me retire, get my pension, kept me from a conviction. I would have lost my P.I. license. What I.A. said was wrong."

"It's history, Arnie. We all have to get over some really bad stuff."

"No. We shouldn't forget. I also remember how you kept me away from the perp for my own sake. He got whacked in prison anyway. You were right. I would just have thrown my own life away. So what I'm saying is anything I got, you got. And if you need some work just ask, no charge."

"You're O.K. with me, Arnie. But, if you can, tell me which unit of the detective bureau it came from."

"I don't know which unit. But Gangs and Intelligence are on the third floor. It didn't come from them. The second floor is all the Crimes Against Persons Units, you know, homicide, robbery, assaults, sex crimes. It could have been someone from any one of those units."

Arnie reached over and took the drink in front of Rusty. He downed it in one long gulp.

"What do you hear is going on with the gangs, Arnie?"

"Some kind of war, I guess. Tell you the truth, I stay away from gangbangers. It's not like it used to be. Today, they think someone looked at their ho, dissed them personally, or even eye-fucked them, and if they happen to be carrying, they cap people just like that."

"You've heard about the Phantom brothers?"

"Who hasn't? Don't know whether it's bullshit or to believe it, or what. Still, that flyer. It promised 50 big ones from the Sureños to take you out. That would be enough to draw the Phantoms if they really exist. Thing is, I heard from inside the Department that Ramundo and Ricardo were taken out in the Fourth Street blast. So now, who can speak for the gang? Guarantee the money?"

"And who made the hit on Fourth Street?"

"What I'm hearing from cops is, who knows? And who gives a shit? A few less bastards in the world. The Sureños are as scattered as the Norteños. It's going to be awhile before someone new kills their way to the top."

"Anything else you can tell me, Arnie?"

"Just watch your back. I'm going to have another, Sheriff. Do me a favor and leave by the front entrance. I'll sneak out the back in a few minutes."

Rusty left the bar. Heeding Arnie's warning, he scanned the vicinity. There was no doubt now that he was hunted prey.

CHAPTER THIRTY

RUSTY SAT IN his car, looking at the crummy street housing Arnie's office, remembering the detective's last days in the department. The events had almost ended Rusty's close relationship as well as his friendship with Henry Wilson.

Arnie's twenty-one year old daughter had been brutally raped and murdered in her apartment. Arnie hit the booze hard. He crashed. The department carried Arnie, looking the other way, as his work deteriorated.

But finally supervisors thought enough was enough. He was dangerous to himself and others.

Rusty compromised. He transferred Arnie to the records unit, and ordered him to attend an alcohol treatment program.

The homicide dicks pulled out all stops on the murder of Arnie's daughter. Within two months of the crime, they had identified the killer. He never should have been freed from prison, given his previous vicious crimes against women. But he had conned the parole board. He had found Jesus during his four years in prison.

Two months after his parole release, he had tortured, raped, and murdered Arnie's daughter. Detectives complained that Arnie, on his own, was pressuring informants, seeking the whereabouts of the elusive criminal.

When the killer was finally collared by detectives, Rusty had Arnie brought into his office. The man was still in bad shape. Clearly, his drinking was out of control. Rusty didn't berate him. He simply told Arnie that his drunken presence in the courtroom could give the defense an opening to talk trash about his daughter, play on the jury's sympathy for the accused. If Arnie could be there every day, clean, sober, and properly dressed, it would help get a conviction.

It worked. Arnie stopped drinking and attended every hearing for several months. The killer's conviction seemed to provide some solace to Arnie.

Rusty still wasn't ready to put him back on the street, but his work in records was excellent. Arnie, like a number of cops seeing their retirement dates down the road, had passed the California test and obtained a license to be a private investigator.

After word reached him that his daughter's killer had been killed in a prison shanking, he opened a one-man private detective agency. It was allowed under department regulations, and Arnie was meticulous in following the rules for off-duty work.

He seemed to have cleaned up his act. About a year later, Rusty was ready to assign him back to the detective bureau. Then the shit hit the fan.

A worried landlord had hired Arnie as a private eye to check out a tenant. Three women, each of whom lived alone, had complained to the building owner that the guy had tried to push his way into their apartments on a pretext.

It turned out that the women had good reason to be scared. The guy had two convictions of assaults on women and a long arrest sheet listing other attacks. The complaining witnesses in those cases had eventually refused to press charges out of fear.

Arnie had done a routine name check on the suspect through the records' unit computer. He made the mistake of giving the guy's sheet to the landlord, instead of just a verbal report.

The landlord promptly confronted the suspect and accused him of falsifying his rental application. He waved the sheet in the guy's face and told him that he'd better move or he'd have him arrested.

Trouble was, the criminal tenant had become something of a jailhouse lawyer during his two convictions. He knew that under California law, it wasn't a crime to lie on your rental application. But it was to disclose someone's criminal history.

He grabbed the sheriff department's sheet of his arrest record from the landlord, slammed the door in the landlord's face, and called his lawyer who complained to I.A., and sued the landlord, and the Sheriff's Department.

I.A. then checked the record unit's criminal history queries and found that Arnie had made fifty such enquiries on different people over the last six months.

Rusty received a legal notice from the D.A.'s office. They were going to indict Arnie. Rusty immediately called and set up a meeting with Henry Wilson, the assistant D.A.

Henry was behind his desk, cluttered with files and material from the murder trial he was trying. Rusty shook hands and sat.

"Henry, felony charges against Arnie? I know you're personally trying a murder case. I appreciate you meeting with me. I won't take up much of your time. But I wanted to talk about the indictment."

Henry pointed his finger at the file in front of him. "It seems the facts are pretty clear cut, Rusty."

"You really intend to indict a twenty-eight year veteran on sixteen felony counts that amount to an eighty year sentence?"

Henry had a brief afternoon recess in his murder case trial, which was all-consuming. He obviously didn't want to spend a lot of time with Rusty.

"We have to send a message to cops who refuse to answer I.A. questions. He and his lawyer will now understand that there's a cost to taking the Fifth Amendment."

"Funny, when I studied the Constitution and the Bill of Rights, I never read anything about a cost for invoking them."

Henry sighed and leaned back in his chair, resigned to the fact that this conversation wasn't about to end quickly.

"Look, Rusty, the deputies' union is constantly complaining about you being a disciplinarian. I don't get where you're coming from on this. The computer records show at least fifty unlawful queries of criminal records over a one year period."

"I know. But before you proceed with the indictment, I urge you to listen again to the tapes and reread the investigator's reports." Rusty was being diplomatic. In the middle of a murder trial, Henry hadn't done more than skim the case file and rely on the written and verbal summary of a newly appointed deputy D.A. fresh out of law school.

"O.K. I won't take it to the Grand Jury until this murder trial is over. Just briefly tell me what your problem is. You're usually over here explaining why we have to prosecute a dirty cop."

"Well, in the first place, you have to remember how Grimes' daughter was killed."

"I do remember, Rusty. It was terrible. But that doesn't give him a right to commit fifty crimes with premeditation over a year's time. The indictments will show him and his lawyer that we can play hardball, too. If they have any sense, they'll plead out. We could live with a single felony conviction, no jail time, and a couple of years probation."

"With a felony conviction, you'd take his pension and his private investigator's license. As a convicted felon, he'd never get a job. He's already lost his daughter. His wife divorced him when he hit the bottle. He's off the booze and has something to do. Your deal would take his life away. Within a year, he'd be living under a bridge with the other bums."

"It's a slam dunk conviction, Rusty. What do you think my staff would think of me for cutting a sweetheart deal for a cop?"

"Oh, some will probably bitch about you, the way the deputies' union does about me, no matter what I do. But those of your staff who take the time to go over the case will realize that you'd never get a jury to convict. I intend to fine him six months pay, sixty grand, and force him to retire. That's a real blow to a good cop and one of our best detectives for the last ten years."

Henry leaned forward, pissed. "Rusty, you're a good sheriff, an expert in police management, but you're not a lawyer. Don't start telling us what the law is or how to try cases. That's our job."

Rusty held up his palm in a peace gesture. "I respect that, but I do have an obligation to point out the police aspects of the case for your consideration."

Henry wasn't at all mollified.

"I listened to the interrogation tapes several times," Rusty said. "The lieutenant didn't inform him of his rights, denied him an attorney, and the other cops in the room describe the lieutenant assaulting Arnie, not the other way around."

"It sounds like your department screwed up."

"That's what I'm trying to tell you. It's why I'm here."

"You're playing me like a defense attorney, Rusty, and I don't like it."

"I know. But because the overzealous lieutenant messed up, we don't have any incriminating statements from Arnie. And if the "fruit of the poisoned tree" rule is still in effect, I don't see how you get the evidence in."

"That's what I mean about you making the mistake of trying to be a lawyer. We'll get in under the newer rule of "inevitable discovery.""

"I'm familiar with it, Henry, but what I have to tell you is what you'll be getting in. The computer files will only show that the queries were made from the records unit. Any number of people could have made them. The lieutenant blew his chance at getting Arnie to admit he did them."

Henry waved it away. "Juries aren't morons. We'll put Grime's clients on the stand."

"Good luck. If you look at their statements, they all refuse to talk. The guy who waved the arrest record in front of the con gave conflicting statements. But he's adamant. Arnie never billed him. We subpoenaed

Arnie's bank and office records; he apparently never charged anyone for checking records. It was all done because of his daughter being murdered by a guy who lied about his crimes against women on his rental application. Also, you may not even be able to get the complainant on the stand, since he's in jail in Ventura County awaiting trial on a new rape charge."

"Well, it seems to be my duty this morning to instruct you on the law. Neither the federal nor California statutes require a motive. Merely disclosing someone's criminal history or checking it for non-law enforcement purposes is a crime."

"I've talked to the feds about my intended discipline. They're not going to prosecute. And since when is it not a legitimate law enforcement purpose to warn potential victims of danger?"

Henry was openly sarcastic. "Yeah, I can just see you taking the stand and testifying that's it's O.K. for a cop to decide a woman is in danger because a guy living in the building has a record."

"I'd have no trouble saying that that was a reasonable frame of mind for a detective who went through what Arnie did with his daughter."

Henry's mouth dropped open. "I can't believe I'm hearing this. The legislature passes the laws, not us. We have a sworn duty to enforce them, not to decide what is justice. If every individual decides what is law, we have anarchy."

"Brandeis?"

"You really mean you'd take the stand and sabotage our case?"

"I'll answer the questions truthfully. But I remember another legal ruling from the Nuremberg trials. It does not excuse a person from violating human rights because he's following the orders of the government. At the end of the day, individuals have a conscience."

"Preposterous. They were talking about cold-blooded murder."

"Wasn't that what the perp in the death of Arnie's daughter was convicted of?"

Henry's face reddened. "Well, you'd certainly be a public hero. What's next, Rusty, a run for governor?"

Rusty stood and walked out. The two men didn't talk to each other for months. But three weeks later, the Sheriff's Department received notice from the D.A.'s office that after reviewing the Grime investigation, it had decided that there was insufficient evidence to prosecute.

The irony now, was that now Rusty's life might be resting on the work of a detective whom Rusty had forced to retire for misconduct.

CHAPTER THIRTY-ONE

STILL SITTING IN his car near Arnie's office, Rusty watched two gangbangers strut into a bodega across the street. The gangs may have been shaken up, but these two Sureños were still making their extortion stops at local merchants. This time, however, the Vietnamese owner shouted back at them.

They said something in return. The shorter one reached toward his pocket. The owner behind the cash register whipped out a forty-five semi-automatic. Rusty picked up his cell phone to dial 911.

The two gang members insolently walked toward the door, voicing what were undoubtedly threats to the owner, who kept his gun trained on them. Rusty put down his phone. But he knew the owner wouldn't be able to guard the store twenty-four hours a day.

Extortion, dope, robberies, burglaries and other crimes kept neighborhoods terrorized and the gangs flush with cash.

Rusty thought about Arnie, the short, bald, overweight man spending his life on this decaying street. He must be sixty-five or so, lonely, drinking cheap bourbon in a flophouse bar in the mornings. Formerly a highly thought-of professional detective, he now conscientiously did his investigations for peanuts.

Rusty pondered his own life, and the pile of ashes that had been his home. When he and Arnie were boys, Silicon Valley had been a beautiful mass of apple, pear and prune blossoms in the spring. The blooms, a harbinger of a lush produce crop that would help feed San Francisco, the ravenous metropolis to the north. The valley's fertile soil yielded ample harvests, a stable economy, and peaceful life.

Almost overnight, tiny chips of silicon had created IT, the Information Technology industry, great wealth, plentiful employment and a population explosion. Farmland disappeared to provide housing for a rapidly swelling work-force that led to widespread prosperity.

But it also led to too many streets like this, too many gangbangers, too many lives like his and Arnie's sliding downhill instead of easing into the good life of retirement.

He drove towards the hospital. He hid his weapon under the car seat. It was time for Sheriff Thursday to read happy fairy tales to very ill children.

But walking into the parking lot afterward, he didn't feel the usual lift that being with the kids gave him. He was down, wrestling with what Arnie had told him about the flyer.

Preoccupied, he made his way to the car, which he had parked in a shady spot on this relatively cool day for August. He had left the windows slightly open, and Itsy comfortably ensconced on his blanket in the front passenger seat.

He frowned at Lieutenant Maria Lopez-Hogan resting her backside against the front fender.

"How'd you know I had new wheels?" he asked.

"Brilliant detective work," she said, nodding her head slightly toward the dog. "I couldn't find your truck, so I simply worked my way through the lot until I found him."

Rusty grunted.

Her smile had been thin. Her eyes uncharacteristically not focused on his, but roaming the lot. She was on edge.

"You're not carrying, are you, Sheriff?"

"I never take a firearm into the children's ward."

"You think the people who want to kill you would hesitate to fire just because children were in the way?"

Rusty was in no mood for her this afternoon. He was about to tell her so when she turned and watched a mail truck slowly approaching. It stopped, and a uniformed mailman got out.

Maria suddenly drew her gun and squatted into a firing position. Rusty stared in amazement.

The mailman lifted a heavy looking, large, leather mailbag and slung it over his shoulder. He started toward them. Seeing Maria, he dropped it and bent over the bag.

She fired two shots. The first hit his forehead, jerking his head backwards. The second, the middle of his throat as he fell.

"Jesus! You killed the mailman!" Rusty yelled.

"Get down behind the car, Russ." She pushed him roughly.

Three of her backup team raced up.

"Pete, drive the Sheriff's car down to headquarters, and park it in the secure area in the basement," the lieutenant told an older, gray haired detective. Turning to Rusty, she said, "I'm sorry. Pete will take you to headquarters. I'm going to be on the scene for a while. I'll see you downtown."

Dazed, Rusty gave the keys to the detective and sat in the front seat with Itsy on his lap. The lieutenant snapped, he thought. A psychotic break. All these killings. All these cases. The enormous pressure on her, a woman, commanding the most elite squad in the department.

His mind was still trying to cope with what he had seen. The driver didn't say anything until they got off the headquarters' elevator.

"The boss will be stuck at the shooting scene for at least an hour, Sheriff. Can I get you some coffee while you're waiting to give your statement?"

"Statement?"

The detective looked at him strangely. "You were right next to her. An eyewitness. We'll need a statement."

To what? That I saw a police lieutenant for no reason gun down a postman?

"I'm not making any statement until my lawyer gets here," Rusty said.

The detective frowned; he was about to say something. Sheriff Sally Henson rushed up. She took both of Rusty's hands.

"Rusty, are you all right? I just heard."

"I'm O.K., Sally."

"Come into my office, we'll have some coffee while we wait for Maria."

The detective tried unsuccessfully to get Sally's attention, but she had turned and led Rusty by the hand into her office.

Rusty calmed down while they were being served coffee that he didn't want.

"Rusty, I know that you've had your doubts about Maria, but while we're waiting I want to show you how good she is."

They sat behind a modest sized conference table across the room from her desk. Sally pushed a button on the table. A small screen unrolled from the blank wall opposite them.

"One of our uniformed patrol guys spotted a gangbanger looking dirty. He frisked him and came up with a loaded Colt revolver. Tough guy wouldn't say a word when they brought him in. They took him to the temporary holding cell for a body search before taking him over to the jail.

"Once the search was complete, the uniform called in gang intelligence. The Intelligence dick recognized the suspect as Ralph's driver. He saw what the search had yielded and called Maria."

Sally dimmed the room lights. "Suspect clammed in the interview room until Maria chased the cops and talked to him alone. The kid, José Torado, is nineteen, but he's been a Sureños for four years. And to qualify to be Ralph's driver, we can bet that he's been a shooter."

"That's for sure."

"He struggled against the required body search. Here's what he was wearing under his gang outfit."

Sally reached into a paper bag and brought out a lacy black bra and a pair of delicate silk panties with frills.

"Straight out of Victoria's Secret," Sally said.

"Oh! Oh!"

"Right. Now here's Maria's video-taped interview."

She started the video. The tape showed Maria entering the room. The prisoner looked tough and sullen.

"José, I'm Lieutenant Maria Lopez-Hogan. Have you been advised of your rights?" She spoke softly.

He nodded.

"José, you've been told this is being recorded," she pointed to the recorder on the table. So I have to ask you to speak out loud, O.K.?"

"They told me the usual bullshit about rights to say shit, call lawyers. But that pig had no right to stop me just because I'm a Spic."

"José, believe me, I'm not here to argue with you or accuse you of anything. Would you like anything to eat or drink?"

"A cold cervaza."

She laughed. "Me, too. But it's not allowed. Have the officers treated you O.K. since you're here?"

He flushed. "The motherfuckers took all my clothes off."

She nodded. "I know. That's why I'm here. Let me explain. We're required to do that. You're a smart hombre, you know some people hide stuff everywhere. We don't want people getting shot or cut in the jail."

"Nobody going to bother me. I'm Sureños."

"Yes, I know that, José. You've got status in the family. It's another reason I've come, to see if I can help."

"You know how long a bitch lasts in our clubhouse if she acts out like you?"

"I've been doing this work a long time, José. I know how the gangs feel about women."

"So why don't you get out of my face?"

Maria took Polaroid shots of him wearing the lingerie out of a paper bag. Tears of humiliation were running down his face in the pictures.

"I don't want to see you go into the jail population wearing what you're wearing."

The boy was pale now, his lower lip and his hands were trembling slightly.

"So I stopped at a store on the way in," she pulled out a very white T-shirt and dark blue briefs.

He stared hungrily at them.

"What you want from me? You know we don't talk. We look out for each other."

Maria sat there, not saying anything.

"Man, I don't call no shots. I just drive where the main man tells me."

"Yes. But they picked you to drive because you're smart. You moved up because you watch, listen, and learn."

"And they know I got heart. You think I'm a rat?"

"Of course not. I think you're smart. Maybe some of the other cops don't like you, but I've got nothing against you."

"Lady," he said, with considerably more respect than he'd shown, "I never did anything against you. Don't even know you."

She smiled. Still speaking softly, she said, "But we know each other now. As far as I'm concerned, no one else has to know what we say to each other."

"I ain't said nothing."

"Do you drive Ralph?"

He nodded. Maria didn't press him to say it out loud.

"When was the last time you drove Ralph?"

He didn't say anything. Maria looked at her watch. Then she put the new underclothes back in the bag. José got the message.

"I drove him last night."

"Last night? We heard he went down in the Fourth Street blast."

"No, Man, er, Miss, that was Ramundo and Ricardo. Ralph's the main man, now. And I'm his driver. You'll see, a lawyer be in court in the morning, get me out."

"I'm not sure, José. You told me how a woman is treated in the gang house."

"That underwear stuff don't mean nothing. Just a joke. I'm no maricone."

"It doesn't make any difference to me what anyone is, José. I don't care. But those guys you'll be in a cell with . . ."

"I'll stay here, by myself until court."

"I'm sorry, José, but it's like the beer. You know, against the rules. The courts say we got to treat everyone the same. Book them. Take them from here to jail. Then in the wagon with the other prisoners to the court jail until the judge calls them."

He was very pale now.

"So you think Ralph will stay the main man?"

"Yeah. He's been tight for months with the two R's, just pretending to suck up to Jacko and the Indian. He got the Indian, but not Jacko. Ralph and Ricardo brought back a ton of money. Gave all us assistants a taste. No one gonna take Ralph on."

"You think he's the one who took out the two R's on Fourth Street?"

"No. They were real tight, Lady. Ralph was gonna bring all the Norteños in with us. But, you know, at the bottom. I heard Ralph rapping, he thinks Jacko did it."

"What about these Phantom brothers and Sheriff Carter."

"Phantom brothers," he shuddered. "No one knows them except Ralph. That sheriff. He's the one gonna get the governor and feds to go against us."

"How do you know that?"

"Shit. Ralph knows. Says he got it taken care of. You know, the Phantoms. You gonna help me, Lady? I'm dead if you don't."

"I'll help you a lot, José, maybe even make the gun go away, if you give me one thing."

"I told you what I know."

"I just need one more little thing. I'm not going to ask you rat out any of your brothers. Just tell me what Ralph meant when he said he had the sheriff taken care of."

"No one know we talked, and you give me those?" His eyes flickered to the new underwear.

"You have my word."

"I heard Ralph tell Ricardo last week, he found out that this sheriff goes to the hospital every Thursday to visit his kid or somebody. So it's today. No one knows I hear that."

JOSEPH D. MCNAMARA

"So that's why she was at the hospital today," Rusty said.

"Right," Sally said, turning up the room lights, and pressing another button that rolled up the screen and turned off the tape. "We were assembling the SWAT team. In the meantime, Maria took four of her people who were here, and raced to the hospital. They've been there since noon."

"Lucky for me."

"More than you know. The weirdest thing happened. We get a mail truck robbery over on the east side. We've never had a mail robbery."

"I don't remember any in California."

"Two gangbangers with shotguns stop a postal worker while he's delivering mail on a side street. They take him back to his truck make him take his uniform off. Another guy gets in and drives away with the truck."

"That brazen?"

"Yes. The two gangbangers are leading the poor mailman in his skivvies to their car. He panics and breaks for it. Used to run high school track, outraces them to the avenue, and we get lucky. A cruiser is coming by. The gangbangers beat it. It's so unusual with the mail truck and kidnapping the cops let me know. It screams Phantom M.O. I got Maria on her cell. You've been damn fortunate again, Rusty."

Rusty gave his statement. He took the elevator down to his car. Lieutenant Maria Lopez-Hogan was sitting in the front seat having a big conversation with Itsy. She put him down and got out to greet Rusty.

"Thanks Lieutenant. I owe you big."

She gazed at Rusty with a look in her eyes he had never seen before. "Pete told me that you refused to give a statement. But then sought him out after Sally briefed you." She smiled at him, differently. "It couldn't be that you thought I went postal and killed a mailman and just didn't want to tell what you saw?"

His voice was gruff. "Of course not. But I meant what I said. You put yourself between me and the shooter. If there's anything I can ever do for you, just ask."

"You mean that?"

"Absolutely."

"How can I ask if I don't have your working cell phone number?"

He opened the glove compartment and saw that his cell was still there. "Lieutenant, I would bet my life that you already have that number."

She smiled. "I wouldn't let that persuade you to buy green bananas, Sheriff"

CHAPTER THIRTY-TWO

THE NEXT MORNING at Pablo's, Rusty was finishing his coffee and skimming the Sun City Daily Newspaper. Itsy leapt from Rusty's feet and ran barking to the front door. Noisily, the Garcia family arrived home.

"Uncle Rusty!" Sonia charged forward for a hug. "We were at Grandma's. I went swimming in the ocean every day. He ducked me under the water." She pointed at her brother, Enrique, who was happily smiling to see Rusty.

The little girl aimed an impressive right cross at her brother's stomach. He blocked it, and slid to the side. Before he could retaliate, his mother, Teresa, expertly moved to grab him.

"Hey, you two go into the kitchen to see what Mrs. Monahan made for lunch," Teresa ordered.

The kids rushed off. Pablo gave Rusty a high-five. "So, we heard Rusty, the cat, lives on."

Teresa gave Rusty a long embrace. Her face reflected sadness and worry. "Why, Rusty? I don't understand."

He shook his head. "Neither do I, Teresa."

She held Rusty by the shoulders. Her eyes were moist. "Rusty, you reading to the children all these years made them so happy. Also, I know it inspired you. Now, I have to say something very hard. You must stay away, Rusty, until this is over. We can't endanger the children."

Rusty looked at her tears. He didn't know what to say.

"I know it was very brave of you to continue. The kids will miss you terribly, but Pablo and I will try to make it up to them. We can't make it up to you, but . . ." her voice faltered. Teresa walked toward the kitchen, dabbing at her eyes.

Rusty felt terrible, thinking that the children would feel he abandoned them. He shrugged at Pablo, who looked disappointed in Rusty. He had made Teresa cry. He started to follow his wife to the kitchen. He stopped.

"I called Henry. He's coming over in an hour. You can bring us up to date. Meantime, let's you and I talk in the den, after I check on the kids."

Rusty looked down. Itsy was rubbing against his pants leg like a cat. The whole family had returned and no one had made a fuss over him.

Rusty picked him up and went into the den. A couple of minutes later, Pablo came into the den, closing the door behind him. Itsy ran over and got an absent-minded pat on the head from Pablo, whose face was uncharacteristically hard.

"Pablo, before Henry gets here, I want to say something he doesn't need to hear. I was hiding out up in the cabin, when Lieutenant Hogan broke the news to me about the Fourth Street bombing. I kind of casually asked her if there were any suspects. She mentioned you as a possibility along with me, and Jacko, Ralph, and the Indian. I didn't know how serious she was, but I was afraid she might get a search warrant for here. I took the grenades and got rid of them. You know mere possession of an explosive device violates both federal and state law."

Pablo stroked his chin for a moment. "We really need this Cobra stalking us?"

"Pablo! She put herself between me and a shooter yesterday. Blew away one of the Phantom brothers."

"Well, I never said she wasn't deadly."

Rusty gave up. Pablo was impossible when his mind was set.

"Look, Rusty, we both know what Henry doesn't want to talk about. Some bastards simply need killing."

"Pablo, you're my best friend, but I don't want to go there with you."

"Go there? Man you've been there since the two punks invaded your home on Rosebud Lane. If someone is trying to kill you and you don't kill them first, you're dead. It's called self-defense."

"Yeah? Well, I don't think D.A. Herrera would see it that way if he could even convince a grand jury of some doubt, let alone my guilt beyond a reasonable doubt."

"You don't have to worry about Herrera. He won't be around much longer."

Rusty frowned. He didn't like the sound of that. Neither did Henry Wilson, who had come in the door just in time to hear Pablo's ominous comment.

"What do you mean, Pablo? I actually had some good news about Herrera. Some vibes reached me from his staff. All of these gang killings have ended Herrera's implications that the gangs deserve sympathy for the way the sheriff's department is treating them. The D.A. doesn't even roll out on deputy shootings anymore."

"How nice. The county prosecutor is leaning toward protecting the victims and prosecuting the criminals."

There was nothing subtle about Pablo's derision, but Henry was used to it.

"What did you mean, Pablo, about him not being around much longer?"

"Well, you remember, Henry, I've been working two years on a project in Mexico City to build a thousand low cost housing units, and a school and a hospital to go with them. I'm sick and tired of everyone's hand out to be greased for a non-profit operation that will help the poor. So, I've cultivated Mexico's A.G. down there. This is a young guy. He's for real. Already survived two assassination attempts."

"I read about him," Henry said, "unfortunately we've heard it so many times previously."

"Yeah. But this A.G. has the president one hundred percent behind him. He's knocked out a couple of drug cartels already, and sent a cabinet member and two national politicians to prison for bribery. He guaranteed me that he'd send a message to the political crooks and the unions that the public housing project is off limits."

"What does that have to do with Herrera?" Henry said.

"Nothing. But this does." Pablo held up four tiny cassette-recording cartridges. "The A.G. mentioned as an aside, that in appreciation for what I was doing for no profit, he had some information for me as a gift. They'd been tapping a couple of drug cartels' phones for two years. Got some calls to and from our Silicon County D.A. discussing drug shipments."

"When he was a defense attorney, or since he's been in office?"

"Well, as shocking as it may be to you, Henry, this is both. And the most recent was right after he kind of hinted that Rusty's self defense of his home was actually criminal."

Pablo promised his two friends typed translations of the calls between D.A. Herrera and the cartels. Rusty then brought the two men up to date on what had happened since he had last talked with them, naturally leaving out his Fourth Street actions.

"So you gave Lieutenant Hogan an interview up at the cabin?"

"It wasn't really an interview, Henry. She came to warn me about intelligence that the two Phantom brothers were in Sun City looking for me, and to give me a cell phone from Sally."

Henry exhaled noisily. "I don't know what I have to say to get you to stop talking to cops without me being present. And you gave another statement on the shooting in the hospital parking lot."

"That was her shooting, not mine."

"Rusty, you're too good a cop to be fooled by that. How many times have you gotten incriminating statements from suspects during so called friendly conversations?"

"Often enough to know not to trap myself with exculpatory statements."

Henry threw up his hands in frustration. "All right, I warned you. What about this mystery of who's going to pay off the Phantom brothers if they whack you? If Ramundo and Ricardo were taken out on Fourth Street as you've heard, who's running the Sureños with enough clout that the Phantoms would continue the contract?"

"Hell, Henry," Pablo cut in, "this isn't a courtroom where we have to prove everything beyond a reasonable doubt. Rusty already hinted that it's probably Ralph and this mysterious guy, maybe a cop. After all, he drove a police car to meet with Ralph, the night before the blast. They probably put a bomb in the meeting place, using a timer or demolition fuse they could set off when they saw the top shooters gather."

"H'm," Henry said, thoughtfully, "does that mean that the remaining Phantom brother still plans to take Rusty out? And, he probably has added Lieutenant Hogan to his list for killing his brother."

"My guess is yes on Rusty," Pablo said, "I'm not so sure on the Dragon Lady. These macho idiots wouldn't want to admit that a Phantom brother was taken out by a female cop. Whatcha think, Rusty?"

"All the possibilities are giving me a headache. We don't even know yet which brother was killed. If it's the one who didn't track me north up to the cabin, then we caught a break. We should be getting an I.D. today from Washington on the guy who came after me. We're one up on him. He won't even be aware that we know who he is. When will we get the translated transcript of those wire taps, Pablo?"

"Obviously, I need to be careful who I use. But I hope that by this evening I'll have them for you."

Rusty hoped that after they read them, it would lead them to the way out of this quagmire of violent death.

CHAPTER THIRTY-THREE

RUSTY'S CELL PHONE rang.

"Yeah?" he answered.

"Sheriff, I got some stuff for you. Can you meet me where we last talked?"

"Sure. It will be about forty-five minutes."

"That works for me."

Rusty disconnected the phone and headed for the shower, wondering what the hell Arnie could possibly have for him. He was just preparing to leave when the cell rang again.

"Hi Sheriff," he recognized Lieutenant Maria Lopez-Hogan's voice, "I have some disappointing news. You know, because of the headshots in the hospital parking lot, we were unable to immediately I.D. the phony mailman. By the way, he had a sawed-off Winchester shotgun loaded with double ought. At that range, we would both have been history."

"Yeah."

"Anyway, we were hoping that the DOA wasn't the cool dude who traced you up to the cabin. Regrettably, that's who he was. If it had been his brother, at least we'd know who we were looking for now. The FBI traced the dead guy through NCIC. He's Pedro Aurello, age forty-two, born in Juarez. Here's what weird, though. Pedro was an only child."

"No brother?"

"Nada. No siblings, both parents dead. So the Feebies and Interpol figure that he had a partner and that they were so tight that they were thought of as brothers. Bad news for us is that we have no idea who the partner is."

"Maria, that means you're a red hot target for blowing away his partner."

"Who knows? Sally authorized issuing a press release which, for security reasons, says that the bad guy attempting to kill former Sheriff Rusty Carter was brought down by a volley of police gunfire. No names of cops. For some reason, Herrera's team isn't rolling on our shootings anymore, and he doesn't seem that interested in the report. It looks like our internal report will stay internal."

"Good. For what it's worth, my friend Pablo thinks that the macho gangbangers won't want to admit that it was a female officer who took him down."

"For once, I think he may be right." She hesitated, "Uh, Sheriff, remember yesterday you offered to do me a favor if asked?"

"Of course."

"Well, I have a kind of strange request."

"Just ask."

"I was wondering if you'd take me on in singles at 0900 tomorrow at your club."

Rusty was stunned. He groaned inwardly. Of all the peculiar things. He had been thinking of something substantial like being a reference if she applied for a police chief's job.

But a tennis match? Rusty was one of the club's top singles player, although he now played mostly doubles with the guys, since his bypass. It was nice when they played mixed doubles with their wives, but it was an entirely different kind of tennis when there were four men on the court banging volleys and overheads directly at the net man.

In mixed doubles, it was an unspoken rule that the men didn't whack a ball right at one of the female players. And Maria was probably a beginner.

"Er, Maria, the club is closed for renovations."

"It reopened a week ago."

"Oh, I was unaware. But, you know, all of my gear went up in smoke with everything else at Rosebud Lane."

"Sure, but I bet you have a spare set in your locker at the club. I've played at the club a couple of times. It has a great tennis shop where you can pick up whatever else you need. Come on, Sheriff. I'm on automatic administrative leave because of the shooting, going crazy just sitting around. Tell you what. For fun, let's have a little wager. Loser buys dinner. Winner picks the location."

"You're that confident?"

"Actually, yes, although I haven't played for a while. All these bodies piling up, you know."

Rusty thought about it. This might be a good chance for a casual meeting in which she would disclose what they knew and didn't know about the Fourth Street blast.

"O.K. I'll see you there at ten to nine, tomorrow."

"Cool."

CHAPTER THIRTY-FOUR

A T THE TENNIS club, Rusty found Maria waiting for him in the comfortable lobby. She wore a light warm-up jacket over a sedate blue tennis blouse and skirt. Her eyes glistened, and she gave him a friendly smile. She looked like a high school girl.

Rusty felt foolish. At six-one, with a well developed body, he towered over her slender five foot nine figure. Roger, the club pro, manned the office. Rusty asked for a can of new balls to be added to his account.

"Got you down for court one, Sheriff," the pro said.

"The stadium court? How about one of the back courts, Roger?"

"Sorry. Looks like court one is the only one open."

Great! The sunken court was surrounded by stadium seating. People wandering by would automatically look down only to see the big sheriff picking on the little girl.

Descending down to the court, he was surprised to see any number of club members sitting in the stadium seats. When he was in office and first joined the club, this occasionally happened. After a while, he had gotten used to people being curious enough to sit and watch to see what kind of game the sheriff had. But that attention had faded a long time ago.

This morning, almost all of the audience was made up of women. They must have played early and were sitting in the shady stands to cool off. He was kind of surprised to see Roger join them. He was even more surprised when a number of them applauded as he and Maria made their way onto to the court.

Maria shed her jacket and they began the routine warm-up. Within a minute, he knew that Maria was no weekend hacker. She had beautiful strokes and a steady rhythm. Still, most of her ground shots were sailing long.

Toward the end of their warm-up drill, Rusty began to power his forehand. He had decided that Maria was a good enough player that he would have to out hit-her, wear her down, but she seemed to match his pace, shot for shot.

Normally, people playing each other for the first time explore their opponent's backhand. Rusty expected Maria to serve into his backhand, but she spun him wide to the other side, taking him off the court.

He was quick, driving a hard forehand return down the line into her backhand side. Maria had followed her serve to the net. Rusty's shot would have won the point against people he played with, but she had anticipated the return and volleyed a clean winner into the open court.

Applause came from the stands. He laughed. So, the female crowd would be cheering on the slender woman against the hulk. He moved to the ad court, pretty sure that this time she would try to take him wide to his backhand with a high kick serve, but her serve hopped into his forehand.

Once again, he hit a hard return in keeping with his game plan of using his greater strength to wear her down. This time, his return landed at her feet. She handled it deftly enough with a half volley, but her shot bounced a little high.

Rusty moved in quickly, pouncing on it. He smashed another forehand, this time, behind her, which was fortunate, because she was so quick that she had covered the open forehand court where he should have tried to hit.

And so it went. Not once did she serve into his backhand, although it was clear to him that she had the kind of racket control to do so.

They went to deuce to advantage, back to deuce, to ad, several times. Then, Rusty got a chance to hit a vicious slice into her backhand, and Maria finally hit a shot that sailed long. Rusty had broken her serve on his first try.

They changed sides. Rusty was known for a big serve. He wanted to overpower her, following the ball to the net, pressuring her to miss, or hit weak returns, giving him easy volleys.

Sure enough, his first serve to her backhand brought a fine return, but it sailed long. He tried for an ace down the T on his next serve. She was quick enough to get it back, but the return was a bit high and Rusty hit a solid volley for what should have been a winner into the open deuce corner.

Instead of it being an easy winner, Maria was there. On the full run, she hit a forehand cross-court. He lunged for it, barely getting his racket on it. The ball hit the top of the net and dribbled over to her side. They both laughed at the lucky shot. He got his next two first serves in. Maria hit hard returns that sailed a bit long. Rusty was up two games to love.

Maria continued to hit a variety of serves into his forehand. He got to all of them, but her quickness in getting to the net and fine volleys were beating him.

He decided to cross her up. Instead of banging a hard return, he hit a beautiful lob. Maria, charging the net, nimbly backtracked, attempting a tough overhead. Rusty looked for a weak shot, but she hit the ball firmly into the corner. He had no chance to reach it. He hadn't won a point on her serve. A round of applause came from the crowd.

Then she closed the door. Rusty served just as well as he had during the first game. However, Maria's shots now found the back and side lines.

When she served, mixing an occasional serve to his backhand, and jamming his body with a hard flat serve, she simply dominated.

She ended up taking the set at six to two. In the second and third sets, Rusty managed to win all of two games, losing each set at six-one. This time, some in the crowd were sympathetically cheering when he won an occasional point. He had lost three straight sets, winning only four games.

He came to the net to shake her hand and congratulate her. "You sandbagged me," he said with a grin. "I never had a chance."

"You played well, Russ. Walk with me to the side exit."

He wondered how she knew of the side exit to the parking lot. When they got to the gate, she looked around to make sure that no one was watching. She took her holstered service weapon from her bag, lifted her skirt slightly, and hooked it to a cloth belt circling her undergarment. He caught a full flash of thigh.

"Russ," she reached into her tennis bag once more and pulled out an index card, "here's my address. I'll look for you at 1830 hours. Don't pay any attention to the name on the doorbell. The place isn't in my name for security reasons. Please be sure that you aren't followed, O.K.?"

"Of course. Where do you want me to make reservations for dinner?"

"I'll do it. A surprise, but casual." She smiled for a moment. "Are you armed?"

"In my bag."

"Please take it out. I'd like us to watch each other's back when we go to our cars."

He frowned, but complied, hooking his holster to his tennis belt and putting on his warm-up jacket to cover it.

"No one knew we were playing here, Maria."

"Look, Russ," she was quite serious, "to be honest with you, I'm spooked by the hospital shootout. We got a big break when the gangbanger caved during questioning and gave us notice of the planned hit. We thought we had it taken care of. But if we hadn't been real lucky finding about the mailman dodge just in time, the Phantom would have taken both of us out, despite the coverage. We can't be too careful."

Rusty dutifully followed her into the parking lot. He had to admit she was right. Who could guess what they'd try next?

And she called him Russ. No one had ever done that. He had been Russell to his mother, Rusty to everyone else in his life. He wasn't sure how he felt about it.

JOSEPH D. MCNAMARA

CHAPTER THIRTY-FIVE

RUSTY RETURNED TO Pablo's place stiff and wet. He was pleased with his stamina and the absence of any hint of angina. Maria had run his legs off.

The house was quiet, empty except for the staff. Both kids were busy at different day camps. Teresa and Pablo were off on their own activities.

Rusty changed to his swim trunks and swam a few laps in the pool to cool off and stretch his muscles. He passed up the lunch Mrs. Monahan had prepared and enjoyed a relaxing shower.

Drying off, he slipped into a pair of shorts and went back to skimming the phone tap transcripts Pablo had given him. Going through the pages for half an hour, he found that he hadn't made any progress.

It usually wasn't clear who the participants in the conversations were, or what the encrypted chatter meant. This was going to be quite a job; maybe Henry would be more adept at it.

He felt as drowsy as he had the previous evening. By two in the afternoon, his attention was wandering. In addition, his legs were cramping.

He decided to stretch out, let his legs relax, and ponder what his next move against Ralph and the remaining Phantom brother would be. Clearly, what Maria had said in the tennis club parking lot indicated that the danger was still intense. The only defense against anyone as good as the Phantom was offense.

He awoke from a deep sleep, astounded that three hours had passed. Last night's Margaritas and Maria's superb tennis had taken their toll. Looking at the time, he hustled into the bathroom and shaved.

Minding her caution about being tailed, he was especially careful after leaving the gated community. Anyone hoping to follow him would be picking him up from here. He wound in and out of local streets, sometimes making a U-turn in mid-block. Finally, convinced that there was no tail, he headed for Maria's.

She lived in a quiet residential neighborhood. It was a rather sizeable complex of two story townhouses in a nicely landscaped setting. He parked in the numbered slot that she had indicated and walked along a long, paved path adjacent to a running brook edged by green grass and some blooming shrubs that he couldn't identify.

The brook emptied into a large pond. He stopped for a moment to gaze at some white swans gliding effortlessly through the water. Silent pumps hidden somewhere kept a gentle current of water sufficient to ensure that mosquitoes didn't breed. Lamp poles provided soft lights to illuminate the path. Lights were lit in most of the homes, but it was quiet, peaceful.

He wandered through the labyrinth of two story units and found her address. A private deck on the second story, with hanging red fuchsia plants, looked out on the pond. The drapes were drawn, but he could see subdued lights in her residence.

Rusty rang the bell for unit 2B. The nametag under the buzzer read simply, Schmidt. The entrance door buzzed and he pushed it inward and made his way to unit 2B.

Maria opened the door. She wore a red apron over a man's long sleeved white dress shirt open at the neck. Her short, dark green skirt was similar to the blue one she had worn on the tennis court. She was barefoot. Something delicious-smelling was cooking in her open-countered kitchen.

He stopped, confused. "I thought we were going out."

She smiled. "As much as I'd like to appear in public with such a handsome hulk, after consideration, I decided that we'd be safer and more relaxed here."

He was appalled. Trapped into this with no gracious way out. He forced a smile. "You should have told me. I would at least have supplied the wine."

"No problem. But it would help if you opened the bottle I have on the counter, and poured us a couple of glasses, while I serve the salads."

He moved to the counter and uncorked a chilled bottle of Chardonnay from Napa Valley. He filled two wine glasses and replaced the bottle in the round wine cooler.

"Come and relax for a minute before we eat," she said, leading him into the living room. Jazz music softly ebbed through the room from her entertainment center. They sat on the couch.

"Here's to less stressful times," she held out her glass and he clinked his against it.

"Amen," he said.

JOSEPH D. MCNAMARA

It was cozy, intimate. A kitchen, bathroom, bedroom, and comfortable living room made up the first floor. He guessed a master bedroom and bath took up the second floor, with a sliding door to the outdoor deck.

Maria's subdued femininity dominated the decorating. It always surprised him how so many women were able to create a sense of warmth and home that somehow was absent from male bachelor's pads.

Maria was a damned fine looking woman. He knew she hadn't given him a chance to bring the wine because, in a million years, he wouldn't have come. His unease grew. He fought off the awkwardness of being alone with her in this setting.

The wine was chilled perfectly, just cold enough to bring out the full flavor. Rusty had no idea what to say.

"Nice wine, Maria."

She smiled, watching him struggle to make conversation.

"So how come you let me win two games in the first set?" he asked.

"I didn't, really. You played well. I told you I hadn't played for a while. I needed to find my zone. And it was fun to get a good workout. Also, I knew you were the rare man who would remain a good sport after losing to a woman."

"Losing? You cleaned my clock. Totally out of my class. I've played varsity college players. I'm not saying that I always won, but I usually played close. You could easily have won all three sets at one or love. You played pro, didn't you?"

"Two years."

"How high did you get?"

"I was ranked 80 when I quit."

"80 in the whole world! Wow. Why'd you quit?"

"Probably had the same motivations that made you quit pro baseball. I saw you play in the California Police and Fire Games in San Diego one year. You were very good."

"Oh, our guys let me start just because they got a kick out of the old sheriff actually getting out on the field."

"You went three for four, including a home run that won the game. False modesty doesn't become you, Russ. I stopped playing tennis for a number of reasons. It got to be work. The sheer pleasure of playing wasn't there anymore, and the daily grind of the tour, training, practice, and rigid diet, made it a job. How about you?"

"Yeah," he said, "I guess when playing stopped being fun and turned into work, it was time to quit."

"And, for me," she said, "I don't know. It suddenly struck me as kind of a frivolous way to make a living."

Sipping the wine, he relaxed a little. The crowd at the club had come to see the famous Maria Lopez play. What had happened to Mister Hogan? Rusty had no idea what to talk about next.

Getting into the gang violence would clearly ruin the dinner atmosphere she had created. She dimmed the lights and lit two tall white candles on the table.

She brought their salad plates from the kitchen. It was a simple dish of butter lettuce, with tiny slices of tangerines, and a sprinkling of flavored roasted pecans topped with a delicately flavored dressing that he couldn't identify.

She watched as he sampled it. "Delicious," he said. And it was. He was also aware of not having eaten all day. He was ravenous.

They leisurely consumed the salad. The candlelight flickered, enhancing her good looks. Maria appeared to be basically a quiet person, but the silence wasn't uncomfortable, and she smiled pleasantly from time to time, observing his enjoyment of the salad.

She removed the plates. He refilled their wine glasses while she was in the kitchen. Maria returned with two steaming casseroles of Paella sitting on dinner serving plates.

"Very hot," she said, pointing to the casserole dishes. "I mean plate hot, not flavor hot."

When she sat, he gingerly took a steaming forkful of the dish and held it in the air, to cool, before tasting it. He savored a number of different flavors and textures of the entrée.

"God, this is great, Maria; what am I eating?"

"Let's see how well you do identifying the suspects," she teased.

"H'm, well, I think there's some chicken in the mix. Something from the sea, crab?"

"You got the chicken right, thighs sautéed slowly in olive oil before being added for baking. And actually, there are also some lobster medallions, diced white onions, boiled skinned tomatoes, mashed garlic, diced red peppers, plenty of rice, and chicken stock. All baked around four hundred degrees until the stock is absorbed. Then garnished with lemons."

"I have to admit the overall flavor is superb. This beats anything I could whip up on the grill up at the cabin. But I deserve some credit. If I had been able to give you some competition at tennis, you wouldn't have had the energy to do all this work."

She colored a little, pleased at the sincerity of his appreciation of the food. Rusty helped her clear the table. In the tiny kitchen, he brushed against her, and caught the fragrance of her delicate perfume. His face reddened. Fortunately, her back was turned. How the hell was he going to get out of here?

"Let's have our coffee on the couch," Maria said.

Rusty carried a silver pot she had filled with coffee and placed it on the coffee table. Maria brought cups and saucers. No cream or sugar. She went back into the kitchen and returned with a small plate of chocolate nut cookies that she had baked. If they were half as good as they smelled . . . he thought.

Rusty took a bite. "Um," he mumbled, the home baked cookie was delicious.

"Maria, you've turned out to be a super detective, an expert shot, a tennis champion, and a gourmet chef. I'm almost afraid to find out the next thing you excel in."

"You're not afraid, Russ," she said, slipping into his lap, "you're terrified."

And he was. He had noticed that the buttons on her white shirt had come undone except for the one on her neckline. The apron had vanished someplace in the kitchen and the remaining button was now open. Her firm young breasts were momentarily visible when the shirt flapped open and shut.

The only way of escape was to stand abruptly and dump her on her pretty bottom. But it would be a rejection that would make it impossible to ever face her again. He took a deep breath.

Just like that, the apartment lights went dark.

She leaped up. "Russ, take your gun out from under the couch cushion where you stashed it. And stay right where you are. I don't want to shoot you! And don't you go shooting me." Her whisper was urgent.

Maria moved swiftly to the dinner table. She blew out the candles. Rusty held his weapon, listening intensely for an intruder while trying to keep track of where she was. She moved silently in her bare feet. Finally, he caught sight of her shadow when she doused a battery-run night-light in the kitchen. He saw the faint glint of the Glock in her right hand.

A moment later, he noticed that she was using a small penlight flash to examine the alarm system near the front door. Her light went out. Where was she? He started when she gripped his arm.

Her lips lightly brushed his ear as she whispered, "The alarm kicks in with an emergency battery during power failures. There's no indication that the circuit has been broken anywhere. It may be just a regional power blackout. Stay put. I'm going to check through the drapes to see if the lights are out throughout the complex."

She came back shortly. Still speaking in a low voice, she said, "Everything is dark. But 911 will be flooded. No use calling to check it out. I have a direct number. I'll call on my house phone just to be sure."

If it hadn't been for the Phantom brother coolly tracing him up north, and the near success of the unlikely mailman assassination scheme, Rusty would have thought she was overreacting. Instead, he was impressed at how prepared she was, in contrast to his haphazard, but lucky, reaction to the Rosebud Lane and tennis court attacks.

Five minutes later, she relit the candles. "They told me that one of those huge eighteen-wheelers took a freeway exit too fast, mashed a transmitter, which in turn, blew out all of the safety relay switches within thirty miles, to prevent a burnout overload. There's no power for ten square miles around here, and no estimate of when it will be restored."

In the faint light, she poured coffee. Her hand was shaking so badly, the cup clattered. She put it down. She had been ice cool a minute ago during the emergency, but now she was trembling.

"Hold me, Russ," she said, putting her arms around him and burying her head on his shoulder.

Damn. Rusty felt her warm, tender young body next to his with misgiving. For a wild second, he wished bad guys would crash the door and Maria and he would turn into cops together, blasting away in a gun battle.

It was unthinkable to imagine leaving now.

CHAPTER THIRTY-SIX

A ND, SO RUSTY sat with Maria cradled under his arm. Her eyes were closed. He looked at her face, tranquil, and relaxed. Her lips were slightly parted, her breath soft upon his neck.

It took him a startled moment to realize that she was asleep. People reacted to shock and trauma in different ways. He had read someplace that this unexpected, slumbering escape from stress was rare, usually only accompanied by a sudden release from fear. She had dozed a minute after his right arm had wrapped securely around her shoulder.

She looked so peaceful that he almost held his breath, trying to remain completely still so as not to disturb her. Earlier in the evening when she had bent over to serve his salad, he had noticed that the white, long sleeved shirt she wore was fastened loosely enough to give a teasing glimpse of her full, firm breasts, unencumbered by a bra.

Now, in her sleep, her left breast protruded, fully exposed from under the shirt. He gently cupped it with his left hand, marveling at the full, soft warm texture. How long had it been? Twenty, twenty-five years without a woman other then Lucy?

She muttered quietly and unintelligibly in her slumber, almost imperceptibly sliding a little closer into his embrace. It must have been at least twenty minutes that he sat there motionless, holding her, gazing hypnotically at the candles casting shadows throughout the room.

Abruptly, he became conscious that she was awake, her large brown eyes fixed on him. He wondered how long she had been studying him. Reflexively, he started to remove his hand from her breast, but she covered it with her own hand, holding his, still. Minutes flashed by. The two of them sat, wordless, unmoving, their eyes locked.

Delicately, her index finger squeezed in between his grasp of her breast. Unhurriedly, she began to manipulate her nipple. He felt it harden. That, and her unblinking stare, combined to send desire surging so widely through his body that he felt a faint dizziness. All of which her large eyes absorbed with the intensity of a scientist conducting a break-through behavioral lab experiment.

"Er, Maria," he found his voice but it was hoarse, "I wasn't expecting this. I'm afraid I came unprepared."

His rather half-hearted attempt to escape failed. She smiled slightly, and continued using his and her hand to finger her breast.

"I'm a big girl, Russ. That's one thing you don't have to worry about."

Her breathing had also quickened, but she showed no inclination to escalate from the slow state of arousal that he was beginning to find agonizing. He leaned over and found her lips. At first, he was tenderly explorative, but quickly escalated into excited passion, his tongue frantically probing hers.

But then, she sat fully erect, deftly wrapping her legs around him. She leaned back, so that his hands and mouth could no longer reach her. But his eyes could, and she looked even more deeply into his, as she flipped her shirt off and began to softly caress both of her breasts, her own excitement increasing as she perceived the effect on him.

Alternately, he shifted his eyes from what her hands were doing, to her unblinking gaze fixated on his. Then, ever so slowly, she reached her right hand under her skirt, while her left now began rhythmically pinching her nipple.

Fascinated, his eyes followed her right hand. For the first time, he realized that she wasn't wearing panties under the short tennis-like skirt. He watched as she wet her middle finger in the mouth, and then leisurely inserted it into the bushy cushion between her legs. Her back and forth motions continued apace; gradually her hand motion quickened. She blushed, but her eyes never stopped drinking him in as he watched what she was doing.

Then she stopped. In slow motion, she raised the finger that had been between her legs and held it under his nose, the scent of her sex sent him wild.

So, Rusty thought, this is what's been going on out there during the twenty years, or so, he'd been out of the action. He pushed away her arms, and again sought her mouth.

"No, Russ. Not here on the couch. Take me up to the bedroom."

He stood, taking her hand, but she made no movement. Then he understood. She wanted him to carry her upstairs. It gave him pause. Rusty was two hundred pounds, but Maria, after all, was a well-muscled top athlete. He reached his arms under her knees and armpits, and lifted her.

JOSEPH D. MCNAMARA

Amazingly, he felt no strain. The refrain from an old song floated through his head, "I touch your hands, and my arms grow strong."

On the way up the stairs, she ran her hands over his biceps. "My God, Russ. You have such a beautiful body. I almost lost the first set, not because I was out of practice. I was watching you, wondering how I was going to keep my hands off you. If it hadn't been for the audience, I would have raped you right there."

"Damn them," he said.

CHAPTER THIRTY-SEVEN

WITHIN SECONDS, THEY had shed their clothes and were kissing each other in the big comfortable bed. Anticipating her slow pace after the experience on the couch, he was surprised when she abruptly pushed him onto his back. Her agile tongue tantalized his ears and throat as she lay on top of him.

Maria then pushed herself upright. Her tennis trained legs easily supported her crouch over him. The brown eyes that he didn't think could open any wider did. Very slowly, she lowered herself onto his erection. He took as deep a breath as he could, feeling her warm wetness and trying to maintain control. She sensed it immediately, and tightened her pelvic muscles preventing even his slightest movement deep inside her.

It worked. At least momentarily, he felt his orgasm recede. Without warning, she relaxed her pelvic muscles and just once or twice slid up and down on him. Before he could get into it, he was amazed to see a series of tremors course through her body.

"Oh, my God!" she gasped. Her eyes rolled back in her head.

Rusty was alarmed. "You, O.K.?" he said, but she didn't hear him.

Acutely conscious of this gorgeous, sexy woman on top of him, he was puzzled, his passion subsiding. For her part, Maria seemed unable, or unwilling to move. Her arms were grasping him as tightly as her pelvis. He found himself gently stroking her hair. He had always found women somewhat incomprehensible, but the mercurial shifts of mood of this woman were something else.

He attempted to push her onto her back and enter her.

"Simmer down, for a minute, Sheriff. We've got all night."

She was right, of course; he would have popped the moment he entered her.

"You taste and smell as delicious as you look, Russ."

"If you keep talking, you can have anything in the world I can get for you."

"Another promise?"

"You bet."

"I'm ordered on this stupid administrative leave for a week. Sally told me in no uncertain terms to get out of town, before the routine grand jury hearing. Will you take me up to the cabin for a few days?"

Rusty was still hot with excitement. But Maria's cold-bloodedness was like taking a cold shower.

"We can do that if you like."

"Russ, can I ask you something?"

"Like there's any stopping you."

She flashed her impish grin. "No. It's something I'd really like to know." Her face had grown serious. He knew part of this was that she was talking him down from a quickie ejaculation. But he sensed more.

"How come you're never scared? I didn't see you at Rosebud Lane with the bread knife, but I bet it was the same as at the tennis court, the hospital parking lot, and tonight when the lights went out."

"It doesn't do any good to be scared."

"Yeah, sure. But it's normal."

"Maria, you didn't get to be number eighty in the world of tennis because you choked in the clutch."

"Tennis is a game. Violence isn't."

"True. But fear inhibits performance. You put two shots in the Phantom brother's head. If you had panicked we'd have been dead."

"So, you're not really scared of these killers?"

"Not really, no."

Maria's hand had been busy on him, and they were ready to take up where they had left off. He was on top of her now, their eyes only inches apart.

"So, why is it that you're so scared of me?" Maria asked.

She quickly guided him inside her before he could react to the question. "All right, Big Russ," she said, "now, fuck my brains out."

CHAPTER THIRTY-EIGHT

THE DAWN LIGHT drifted through the blinds that they had forgotten to close completely. They hadn't really gotten much sleep, anyway. Maria's hair was tousled; she looked sleepily at him. Somehow, she was even more sexy.

"Thank you, Maria," he said, his hand on her smooth cheek.

"You know, you can be so silly some times. I think that's why you get to me so much. Did it ever occur to you that I should be thanking you? I didn't count, but it must have been like, girl fifteen, guy one."

Rusty grinned at her.

More awake now, Maria said, "You remind me of a short story I read a long time ago. A woman meets a guy and takes him home for the night. She finds out that he's been in prison for ten years without a woman. By morning, she can hardly walk. There's certainly nothing wrong with your heart, Russ."

"Is that why you ran me around the tennis court, to test me?"

"Well, after all, I didn't want the sheriff to die in the saddle, did I?" she said, unsmiling.

He wondered how true it was. "And here, all the time, I thought it was a stratagem to lure me into your web. Actually, I guess I couldn't have been easier."

"Are you kidding? I had to be so careful. You were like a deer frozen in the headlights. One false move on my part and you would have bounded into the woods and escaped."

She hadn't once smiled, but Rusty did.

She chased him out. She needed to pack, and if he were around she wouldn't get very far. She needed two hours at her desk in headquarters dictating the paperwork necessary for her grand jury appearance. He could pick her up at 1500 hours. That way, they would be ahead of the rush hour traffic heading north.

He returned to Pablo's to gather the few clothes he had there, and, once again, to borrow the super watchdog, Itsy. Rusty was surprised to see Pablo at home sipping coffee.

"What's with you? You look different this morning," Pablo said. "Anyway, I'm glad you're here. Henry is on his way over. We need to figure our next step. Here," he handed Rusty a small tape recording apparatus and several miniature cassettes that fit the device.

Rusty recognized them as mechanisms for typists to transcribe dictation. The device allowed the typist to adjust the speed and stop and start the recording at will. Rusty studied the recorder.

"What's this gadget?" he pointed to the right side of the mechanism that had separate controls and its own little mike, and cassette slot.

"The latest." Pablo inserted one of the tiny cassettes. "This is a blank one. See, if you want to record your own comment on what you're transcribing, or anything else, you push the play button and just press this red button to record. It will be good for half an hour on the separate cassette. It's so sensitive that you can record a fart from the next room."

"Farts are inadmissible without a Miranda warning," Henry said, coming through the door at the tail end of the conversation.

"Of course. What haven't you lawyers made inadmissible?" Pablo handed a duplicate device and cassettes to Henry. "Now you have the complete recordings to go with the typed transcripts of the Mexican intercepts I gave you. You both understand a little more Spanish than you let on, and you may recognize some of the codes these dudes are using. That damn transcript is over a thousand pages. No one is going to read all of it."

"I know," Henry said, "I started on it. I was about to delegate it to an intern who speaks fluent Spanish, but I'm leery since I don't know what's in there."

"Yeah, good," Pablo said, "but take a look at a few highlights I marked on my copy. You can make a note of the pages and read them when you have time. The thing is that the cartel called some interesting numbers here in this county."

He handed Henry and Rusty three pages of notations of the numbers called, and the date and time of the calls.

"Oh, oh, this is the county jail number," Rusty pointed to an entry on the first page.

"And this is the D.A.'s number," Henry fingered another notation. "We'll definitely have to take a detailed look at this stuff, Pablo, but you're right. Even with these specific indicators it's going to take time to see what we have."

"I'm going up to the cabin for a few days," Rusty said. "I'll bring the stuff along with me."

"Do you really think it's a good idea to do that after the first Phantom brother located you there?" Henry said.

"First of all, there's no indication that he ever learned for sure that I was in that county, let alone where the cabin was located. And even more important, in case you haven't heard, Washington I.D.'d him from the pictures, fingerprints, and DNA that the local sheriff gathered."

"Good."

"Yes and no. The Phantom that Maria Lopez-Hogan killed was an only child. And his M.O. was not to share information with clients, so even if he did know of the cabin, the information probably died with him. The bad thing is that we don't know the other Phantom or where he is."

"Just in case, Rusty, make sure you take what you need to defend yourself, Amigo."

"Right. I was hoping you'd lend me Itsy."

"Itsy-Bitsy? Shit. Take Bruno. He'd like nothing better than to eat one of those mothers alive."

"The idea, Pablo, is that the dog barks and I take out the bad guy with the scoped rifle."

"Point taken," Pablo said.

"I don't know, Rusty. You'd be on thin ice shooting someone a thousand yards away. Suppose you couldn't prove it was a would-be assassin," Henry said.

"Henry, it's still part of America up there. You're allowed to defend yourself, unlike this great county we live in." Pablo got up, ending the conversation.

Rusty was ready to go. He still had plenty of time before he had to pick up Maria. He brooded over the conversation with Henry and Pablo, the lights going out at Maria's the night before, and her fear.

She was a smart tough cop, her distress was not to be dismissed. Nor, despite Rusty's reassuring words, was Henry's concern about just how safe the cabin was as a sanctuary. On the whole, the situation was unsatisfactory. They were in a reactive mode, waiting to see what would happen next, instead of taking the initiative.

He called Arnie Grime and asked if he was available for a brief get-together. Arnie agreed to the usual meeting place. Rusty visited Kinko's and made a copy of the three pages of notes Pablo had provided. On the way, to The Last Stop Saloon, he tried to formulate the questions he wanted Arnie to pursue, but failed to come up with a script.

JOSEPH D. MCNAMARA

Arnie was waiting in the back booth, two bourbons already in place on the table.

"Arnie, I'm not really sure what I want you to do, so let me muddle through, thinking out loud."

The private detective shook his head in agreement.

Rusty briefly ran through the chronicle of events, mentioning doubts about how he had become a target in the first place. He also told Arnie of his bewilderment of learning the hard way in the hospital parking lot, that the Phantom brothers' contract was still on, when, supposedly, Ramundo and Ricardo who were to pay for the hit, had themselves been eliminated.

Arnie was a good listener, letting Rusty talk out his own thoughts without interrupting. Rusty decided the circumstances were dangerous enough to warrant taking a chance.

Cautiously, Rusty invented the fiction that he had grown suspicious of Ralph and had been shadowing him. Since he couldn't mention his hideaway under the bridge, he described an improbable scenario of tailing Ralph at four a.m. to the Fourth Street Sureños headquarters and observing a cop look-a-like, who could have been Jeremiah Christian, meet with Ralph.

Arnie made no comment on the unlikely situation of a four a.m. tail. Rusty passed the copy of Pablo's notes to the detective.

"To sum it up, I'm not sure just what the hell I'm asking you to look at. But one thing, Arnie, be very careful. Don't arouse any suspicions of who or what you're looking at. I don't have to tell you how easy these people kill."

"No. You sure don't. I'll use only my most trusted contacts. I'll give you a call on your cell and let you know what I come up with, if anything."

"Good. And I'll, of course, pay any expenses, so don't worry if you have to lay it out. Here, take this in advance, and this job I insist on paying for your time. So don't argue. Give me a bill when you're done." He handed Arnie three hundred dollar bills.

It was only when driving away that he realized that Arnie hadn't asked about his reaction to the envelope full of material that Rusty hadn't yet looked at. Just as well.

It would have been embarrassing to tell Arnie that he was asking for more probing and hadn't yet reviewed the previous material. But that damned transcript . . . and then twenty-four hours of Maria. Oh well, he had Arnie's package in the trunk. If he could keep his hands off Maria long enough, he'd go through it up in the cabin.

CHAPTER THIRTY-NINE

MARIA HAD TOLD him where her car was parked in the headquarters' parking lot. He drove past the high rise, county jail across from headquarters.

The depressing facade of solid, ugly brick walls was broken only by tall slits of heavily barred windows. Even a block away, he got a whiff of the acrid smell of penned up men, and heard the unending drone of inmate gangsta rap.

He remembered a long ago college course on penology. The original penitentiaries had been derived from a Quaker reform ideology. Instead of hanging most criminals, they would be confined to solitary cells and required to keep perpetual silence, contemplating their sins and repentance. It had sounded barbarous in the classroom, but given the non-stop gangsta-rap assault on inmates and staff, he wondered which was worse.

Rusty had called to alert Maria that he was on the way, and found her standing next to the car. Quickly, she transferred a small bag to his trunk and then a portable stereo with two small speakers.

It was between shifts and the lot was deserted, but Rusty got them out quickly. Neither of them wanted to be spotted together.

"I noticed that extensive collection of music cassettes up in the cabin, but no equipment," Maria was in a festive get-away mood.

"Right. We used to do just what you're doing, bring a player and speakers with us. The seclusion is nice, but teenage kids have broken in a couple of times and helped themselves to different things. It's worth the effort not to leave anything they might want."

"It says something about this generation of kids that the music you have there doesn't appeal. Classical, jazz, pop, Broadway musicals, soft rock, and no western? You guys would have been condemned as anti-Californian. But I bet I can guess who belonged to what."

"Really?" Rusty wound through the streets to a freeway entrance, keeping an eye on the rear view mirrors.

"Let's see. I bet Lucy leaned toward the classical. You were a jazz guy and you both enjoyed all of the rest."

He smiled. "Actually, Lucy really had an interest in, and an ear for music. I'm tone deaf. Lucky to recognize the tune of the national anthem. But I did love to listen to classical when we sat on the glider and watched the sun go down over the fields. It was almost a spiritual thing, to hear Mozart, Chopin or Beethoven floating out from the cottage."

"You weren't into the Count Basie and Louis Armstrong, Charlie Parker or Roy Hargrove, or the Blues?"

"Oh, sure. I enjoyed it all. Lucy had taught music and it was an education to listen to her explain the music."

They were making good time, ahead of the afternoon traffic. Maria moved closer to Rusty.

"You shouldn't have worn these shorts, Russ. How am I supposed to control myself looking at those thighs built like Johnny pumps?" She reached up under his shorts with the flat of her hand, and began to wiggle her fingers.

He tried to twist away from her. "You might control yourself if you think of me swerving across lanes and totaling out in an accident."

"Oh no," she laughed. "You're mister self control. How about a blow job, while all these people are driving past unaware?"

Before he could stop her she undid his zipper, and was running her tongue over his already erect penis.

"For God's sake, Maria!" He swerved into the left lane and got an angry horn which didn't slow Maria down at all.

Rusty frantically fought to pull into the right lane, trying to ignore what she was doing and stop on the shoulder of the road.

He finally pulled to the side. "Are you crazy? You almost got us killed!"

"Well, if you have to go, can you think of a better way?" She was openly laughing at him.

"I hope this Chippie shares your strange sense of humor." He watched as a female California Highway Patrol officer walked to his side of the car.

Rusty lowered the window.

"You folks O.K.?" the cop asked.

"This women molested me while I was driving, Officer. I had to pull off the freeway."

The Chippie bent over and looked at the grinning Maria. She straightened up, and eyed Rusty. "You wish, Sheriff," she said. "But you were in the business long enough to know how dangerous it is here on the shoulder. I suggest you get back into traffic. I'll light up my bars and slowly pull into the lane to let you get out of here without getting mashed."

Rusty carefully followed the CHP officer's directions. Maria was hysterical with laughter.

"Oh, Rusty. You got busted and unsuccessfully tried to rat me out. And she recognized you, you handsome devil."

"I think she was much more interested in looking at you."

"Wow! A politically incorrect statement. You never got caught at that while you were in office."

"Maybe you'd like to drive?"

"No way. I can read your dirty mind. You'd turn the tables on me right away."

Maria watched in the side view mirror as the California Highway Patrol car pulled off at the next exit. She again slid over next to Rusty.

"How about a truce, Maria?"

"What do you have to bargain with?" Her hand had slipped right back under his shorts.

"I'll keep heading north instead of getting off at the next exit and making a U-turn to take us back."

"But you promised."

"I was under duress. You had me pinned down, sitting on my face."

"I don't know. Would you really turn around?" Her hand move further up his thigh."

He spotted an exit coming up and put on the right turn signal.

She sighed and withdrew her hand. Suddenly, she was laughing again. "I wonder what would have happened if the Chippie had pulled up a couple of minutes earlier? I can see the headlines: Politically influential retired sheriff, adviser to the governor's gang task force, arrested speeding while engaging in oral sex."

"Anyone ever tell you that you have a bizarre sense of comedy?"

"It's you, Russ. You're so straight, I can get to you in thirty seconds."

"Fifteen," he said. But the words, "politically influential retired sheriff, adviser to the governor's gang task force," resonated, an echo of the contract flyer.

They reached the cabin in plenty of time to unload the car and prepare for dinner. Itsy had taken only a short walk. He smelled people food coming up. Rusty had picked up two Caesar salads and two medium pizzas, one with meatball, the other tomatoes, that could be reheated in the oven. He opened a bottle of Classico Chianti.

"They even provided freshly grated parmesan cheese for the salads and pizza. Cool, Russ."

He sat on the glider. The salad and wine was on the table in front of the glider. Maria was setting up the stereo. He wondered what she'd play. Then, he heard an old CD of Gershwin's Rhapsody in Blue by the New York Philharmonic, conducted by Leonard Bernstein and recorded at Lincoln Center. Maria had made a thoughtful compromise between classical and jazz.

The pizza was warming up in the oven when she joined him. He had wondered how he'd feel with her up here where he had spent so much time with Lucy. He touched his wine glass to hers.

"To you, Maria. You saved my life in more ways than one."

"To us," she said, and he again felt himself getting lost in those deep brown eyes.

Momentarily, he forgot about the Phantom, gangbangers and the danger.

CHAPTER FORTY

THEY FINISHED THE pizza, giving Itsy more than his share of the meatballs. He also nibbled at a portion of dog food, plainly miffed at them for not providing a complete meat dinner.

Rusty and Maria sat on the glider holding hands, listening to a magnificent Rachmaninoff piano concerto floating over them as the golden sun, promising a hot next day, inched below the horizon.

The temperature began to drop a few degrees at a time. "How about we take the beast for a short walk?" Rusty said.

"I told you, they hear. He's not a beast. He's part of the family, right, Itsy?"

The dog looked worshippingly at Maria, which was not hard to do. The air was as mellow as their mood, which didn't diminish even they strapped on Glocks in the growing darkness. They strolled slowly down the dirt road like ordinary people taking an after dinner walk.

Still, they didn't stray too far from the cottage. They settled comfortably on the porch glider, now listening to jazz coming from the dark cottage. Itsy decided to occupy Maria's lap, as the three of them watched the traffic on Highway 80 gradually decrease.

"You can't really lighten-up, even now, can you, Russ?"

"You're trying to read my mind again."

I'm not trying. I know exactly what you're thinking."

He challenged her. "Last time, about the music, you were wrong."

"I wasn't reading your mind. I was speculating about the past."

"So tell me what I'm thinking."

"You're thinking what's a great gal like this doing with me? She should be out looking for Mister Right, more her own age, about starting a family."

She was so accurate that Rusty couldn't keep some annoyance out of his voice. "Didn't your mother ever warn you not to constantly show men that you're smarter than they are?"

She laughed, "Yes. But my abuela told me that if I found a man unafraid of a smart woman, grab him."

"You're too, much, Maria. Now tell me what I'm thinking."

"You're full of lust. Thinking that you'd like to spank my smart little bottom, get the blood running and then ravish me to your heart's content."

"That wasn't mind reading. It was a self-fulfilling prophecy."

"Goody!"

The window above them shattered.

"Hit the deck!" Rusty yelled, picking up the scoped rifle as he flattened on the porch, looking for the next muzzle flash.

He saw two in close succession as a bullet whacked high on the roof. The third shot apparently missed the cottage entirely.

Rusty hadn't had time to get a good sight picture through the scope, but he squeezed off three shots, aiming right about where Pat Kelly had taken off the groundhog's head.

He jumped as Maria blasted away with the M 4, laying down a barrage roughly toward the same area. It was discouraging fire, rather than trying to take out the target.

Rusty felt her stretch out next to him, slipping a full magazine into the M 4, while he reloaded three rounds into the sniper rifle. She was smart to move, just in case the shooter had the bad sense to fire at where her muzzle flashes had come from. Rusty focused the scope on the spot where the first shots had originated. If there was another muzzle flash, he'd have a sight picture.

"What do you think, Russ?" Her voice was quiet.

"I think our friend didn't expect this kind of return fire. He's well on his way out of here."

"You don't think we got lucky, hit him?"

"I doubt it. We'd have to have been real lucky at this range. We really didn't have time to sight in."

"Yeah. I think you're right. But there might be more than one."

"I don't think so. We'd have drawn return fire. They would have spread out. Our return shots wouldn't have discouraged them."

"Of course, he could be lying there, waiting."

"I doubt it. This wasn't a Phantom, Maria. His first shot was high over our heads through the window. The second was higher. Hit up on the roof. And the third missed the cottage completely. He's no marksman, doesn't want to get into a shooting match with us."

They stayed still, patting Itsy, who wanted to hunt down the shooter.

"Obviously, we can't stay here tonight. But I need to call Sheriff Pat. Think we should go back, or find a hotel up here?"

"I want to go back," she said.

Inside the cottage, Maria sat cross-legged on the floor. Rusty sat next to her with his knees drawn up. He put the phone on speaker and dialed Pat Kelly's home number.

"Kelly," the sheriff answered on the first ring.

"Hope I didn't wake you up, Pat."

"Hell no. This Rusty?"

"Yeah, good voice recognition for an old geezer, thought you might have hit the sack."

"Well, for your information, I was watching this old movie, The Manchurian Candidate. You see it?"

"A long time ago."

"Well, all this stuff on the news about China expanding and all, I think we should be just as worried now, don't you?"

Rusty saw Maria's face in the dim glow of the phone's dial light. She was tense and drawn. Her eyes, flashing.

"Actually, Pat, I'm not worried about the Chinese right now. Someone just fired three rifle rounds at us in the cottage. We returned fire, probably chased him away."

"Us, we? Who's with you?"

"Lieutenant Hogan, you remember her?"

"Sure do. She helping you investigate out there in the cottage or body guarding you?"

"Little bit of both," Rusty smiled. Maria looked angry.

"Well, Rusty, I can get our copter up there in about thirty minutes."

"Not a good idea, Pat. With a scope rifle, a good shot could bring it down."

"I know. But these pilot guys get off turning on the flood-lights and swooping all over the place. I went up once with them, mandatory. Never get me up again. Now, I can get a couple of patrol units out there, but they'd be pretty vulnerable, and I don't know what the hell they'd be able to find in the dark if the bad guy is gone. 'Course if you thought he was going to lay in wait and bushwhack you on the way out, we'd give you an escort."

Waylay? Bushwhack? Pat, people haven't talked that way in a hundred years, except on a Hollywood set."

"Well, of course, you big city cops got all the jargon, but I remind you who got the DNA on that Phantom fella."

"That was great, Pat. Here's what I suggest. In the morning, maybe some of your people could look everything over. I think the shooter was around the spot where you hit the gopher. Also, one of his rounds went through the window. Probably lodged in the back wall. The other one went high, hit the roof. Third one seems to have missed entirely. I doubt if the spent rounds will be any good for ballistics with that velocity, but never can tell. Same with forensics, if it's possible to determine where he fired from."

"Don't sound like you was up against a sharpshooter. Anyway, we'll do our best."

"And Pat, can you have someone fix the window, and lock up? He can bill me."

"Anything else? Want me to have solar heating put in, stock up on vittles for your next visit? Repaint the barn or anything?"

"I don't have a barn, Pat."

"Well, we can have one put up. Send us the plans. And Rusty, you be damned careful, at least until you cross the county line. I'll give you a call."

Rusty turned off the phone.

"You two macho fools think this is funny?" Maria was furious.

Surprised, Rusty look intently at her.

"You think it's a fucking joke to see human flesh torn apart by lead, innocent people's lives taken by these animals?"

They packed quickly in silence. Rusty stole occasional glances at Maria, but her movements didn't soften. He drove the dirt road slowly without lights, turning them on only when they reached the highway.

Maria sat far away, leaning against the passenger door, her Glock resting in her lap. They were approaching the Bay Bridge when he tentatively reached over and took her hand. She didn't shrink away, but she didn't return his slight squeeze, either.

They reached her apartment without a word. When they left the car, she said, "I want to be alone. I'm going down to Laguna Beach in the morning to stay with my grandmother for a few days. You go back to Pablo's."

"Shut up, Maria. Do what you want tomorrow. Right now, pull yourself together. The first thing I want you to do is carefully check your alarm system. Make sure no break has been attempted. I'm staying downstairs with Itsy. You sleep upstairs. You'll be rested for the drive tomorrow."

Wordlessly, she turned and marched into her apartment. She was alert, holding her Glock along the side of her leg. None of the neighbors would see it, but it was ready. She looked over the front door carefully.

Rusty, equally ready if attacked, glanced at the windows. All he could tell was that they hadn't been broken. Maria opened the front door and quickly punched in her alarm code. Then she carefully inspected the system. She nodded to Rusty. It was intact.

Rusty fed Itsy some dog food and water. The dog tried to follow Maria upstairs, but Rusty tethered his leash so that he couldn't. Given the long drive, Rusty made for the bathroom. After relieving himself, he ran cold water on his face.

He was wide-awake. In a dark corner of the kitchen he deliberately chose a straight-backed, uncomfortable wooden chair, with a view of the sliding door. Itsy settled at his feet.

He heard the upstairs shower go on for a good fifteen minutes. Shortly thereafter, he heard the bed creak. Maria had retired, and he felt pleased. It was exactly midnight.

He sat wondering at her reaction. He had thought her strangely nervous here in her apartment the night the lights went out. On the other hand, in the hospital parking lot she was icy calm after gunning down a killer. But that was right after. Who knows what she had been like later? It's true that he and Pat had engaged in a little cop banter, but they were old friends. This lady's ups and downs were very strange.

And tonight had proven that this wasn't anywhere near over. How was he to handle Maria and the killers?

CHAPTER FORTY-ONE

AT SIX A.M., Maria was ready to go. She looked pale and wan. He dropped her at her car in the headquarters' parking lot.

"Take care of yourself. Give me a call, Russ." With that, she pecked him on the cheek, and pulled quickly away.

Rusty tailed her to the freeway. There was little street traffic. He was certain no one had followed. After she turned into the freeway entrance heading south, he drove wearily to Pablo's. He had breakfast with the busy family.

When they were finished, Teresa hurried out to drop the kids at their day camps. Pablo eyed him closely.

"You look like, crap, Rusty. You had a bad night?"

Rusty told him of the shooting up at the cabin. He left out any mention of Maria being with him, and let Pablo assume that he had just arrived home straight from Sheriff Kelly's investigation. Pablo listened intently.

He sighed. "It's one mystery after another. Somehow, someone found out you were up at the cabin. But they send a second string shooter. It sure wasn't the other Phantom, if there is another. You working on this at all, Rusty or just hoping to counter-attack every time they shoot at you?"

"I'm working a couple of angles, Pablo. I confess I haven't had time to get through those transcripts."

"Why don't you swim some laps. Loosen up, relax, have a shower and get some sleep. Meantime, I'll tell my guys to be extra alert. I'll give Henry a call to see if he's made any headway on the transcript."

Rusty followed Pablo's advice. He awoke in late afternoon, feeling logy and unable to concentrate. He swam for about half an hour. He showered, shaved and dressed in the new slacks and sports shirt that he had picked up at a department store before he and Maria had left for the cabin.

He was prowling the kitchen looking for something to eat when Teresa came in.

"Rusty, I heard you had yet another close call. Still," she scrutinized him closely, "you look much better. You know, last week, you were so down I was going to suggest a shrink I work with. She's excellent. But, now," she smiled, "there's something different in your face and body language."

"I guess getting shot at is therapeutic for me."

"No. I haven't seen you like this in years, it must be something's changed." She smiled again, but it was almost a smirk. "I'm taking the kids to a snack and movie. Pablo has a retirement dinner for his chief foreman. So you're on your own, tonight. Mrs. Monahan has made two huge baked tuna for the staff. She stored a dinner for you in the refrigerator and there's a selection of chilled wine. Help yourself to whatever. You know your way around. You do look a little sleep deprived, though."

"Thanks Doc. Put the bill for the diagnosis on my tab," he said dryly.

Teresa gave him a wink and left.

It was 8 p.m. Rusty decided to call Maria before he ate. She had had a long drive and he wasn't sure what would be a good time to call.

She said hello on the second ring.

"How are you, Maria?"

"Tired. A lot of miles, but I'm glad to be here and she's always so happy to see me. Anything more happen? You O.K.?"

"Yeah. I spent most of the day swimming laps and sleeping, about to have a snack."

"I'm taking my abuela to dinner, Rusty. I'm not into talking much now anyway, but I really do have to get going. She's not used to eating this late."

"Enjoy. I'll call tomorrow."

"Good."

He disconnected. She had sounded terrible, emotionally exhausted, flat. But at least she'd be safe down there, which was more than he could say for himself when he left Pablo's fortress

The next morning, Rusty's cell phone buzzed. He found his heart racing. Few people had this number. Had something happened to Maria?

"Rusty," he answered before the phone could buzz twice.

"Howdy, Pardna."

Hearing Pat's voice, Rusty relaxed. "What's up, Sheriff?"

"Couple of things, Rusty. I sent a crew out to your cabin. You were right about the shooter being lousy. And the two slugs that hit the cabin are probably too torn up for a ballistics match if we ever come up with the gun. Never could find his third round. But the one that whacked the

JOSEPH D. MCNAMARA

rooftop is a possible. Thought maybe you'd like to get Sally to send it to ATF in Washington to check against their data base of rounds recovered at crime scenes."

"Good idea, Pat."

"The other thing. I let Gloria do the crime scene, looking for where the shooter may have been. She loves that stuff. She recovered the three cartridges, but didn't get anything else. They should go to the ATF too."

"Right."

"Now Rusty, I don't want to get your hopes up too much. Gloria's pretty sure she found some good tire tracks from the shooter's vehicle. Apparently, he got out of there real quick when you guys shot back. I think maybe she's too optimistic this time. But we got two nice casts and pictures of them for you."

"How could that be, Pat? It's been bone dry up there for months."

"Yeah. But Gloria thinks we may have caught a break. We had a roadside grass fire along the pull-off lane on 80 the day before. That's apparently where he parked and walked to where he shot at you. Anyway, the firefighters really soaked the ground putting out the grass fire and making sure they doused all the hot spots so it didn't start up again. Ground was wet enough to get two terrific casts. Still, could have been another car."

"Yeah. But it's sure worth checking against the one with the license plate I gave you. I'll drive up this afternoon to pick everything up."

"Don't like to think you're right. That it was a law enforcement vehicle, but it's got to be checked. Look, Martha's pissed at me instead of you. You being up here and not coming by to say hello. She told me that if you want to leave with the evidence, you got to agree to let us take you out to dinner, have some nice wine, and stay the night at our place."

"If it was just listening to your hillbilly talk, I'd say hell, no, but it'll be good to see Martha again. I'll start up early enough to beat the rush hour traffic around the Bay Bridge."

Rusty called Maria just before he left Pablo's. "We just got home from playing tennis, Russ." She was animated.

"Tennis with your grandmother? How old is she?"

"You and the age thing. She's eighty. But she and her friends play doubles twice a week. In their day, they were all good players. You should see their spins, drop shots, tricky lobs and their anticipation."

"I hope you didn't annihilate them like you did me."

"No. We were giggling like a bunch of schoolgirls. I wish you had been here. She would have been flirting with you like crazy."

"I wish I had been too, Maria. I miss you. But you sound better. It's good for you to get away relax for a few days."

He told her about the possibility of getting some evidence from Pat Kelly, and having dinner and spending the night with them.

"Russ, you be real careful. I'm still brooding about how someone knew exactly when we'd be in the cabin. We're going to have to work that angle."

Pat and Martha took Rusty to a really good restaurant. He had anticipated Pat taking him to some roadside western steak house, but clearly, Martha had dictated a fine dining place.

Unlike Pat's rail thinness, Martha was pleasantly rounded, still pretty at her age. They had often gotten together at the California Sheriff's semi-annual meetings, and she had been quite friendly with Lucy.

Across the dinner table she studied Rusty. "What's up with you, big guy? You look really good. I thought you'd look frayed with all this shooting, but you're energized."

First Teresa, now Martha. What was it with these women?

"You didn't bring that Lieutenant gal with you, Rusty?" Pat was all innocence. "Maybe it's that, Martha. The gal's a whiz. Taking a lot of the investigative burden off Rusty's shoulders."

"Fist of all, you Boob, she's a competent woman, not a gal. Second, you're embarrassing our friend with your big mouth. And," she rolled her eyes at Rusty, "he talks about retiring. Can you imagine me having to listen to his dribble all day?"

The following morning, Rusty looked at the evidence. He hadn't expected much, but now realized that they had done a good job. The stuff had real possibilities. He'd again be listening to Sally chide him about maintaining the chain of possession. That is, if he turned it over to her. He'd have to think about that.

He called Arnie before starting back. They set up a meeting for late afternoon. On the drive south, his cell buzzed. He pulled to the side of the road. Once more, he felt anxiety about Maria. But it was Teresa.

"Hi Rusty," she said. "I was just wondering what time you'd be getting back this evening. Henry and Dolores are coming over for an informal dinner. It's been a long time since we all got together. We were all hoping you'd be here. Will you make it by 6:30 p.m.?"

"Sure. I think I'll beat most of the traffic unless there's an accident jam-up." He didn't mention his meeting with Arnie, and the possible importance it could have on all of their safety

JOSEPH D. MCNAMARA

"O.K. we'll look for you."

Rusty did stay ahead of traffic, but his meeting with Arnie would be tricky on time. He entered the Last Stop Saloon carrying the wrapped package of tire casts and the pictures with him.

Arnie watched him from the back booth, bourbons at ready.

"Arnie," Rusty, mindful of Teresa going to the trouble of telling him what time to show up, got right to the point, "someone took shots at me a couple of nights ago up at the cabin. I surprised them by blasting back, and they took off. Local sheriff's people got some good tire casts of what may have been their vehicle. Take a look."

Arnie carefully unwrapped the evidence package. He studied the photos. "These cast look good enough, if it's the same vehicle, Sheriff. What are you thinking of?"

"Well, I don't know how good your contacts are, and I don't want you surfacing and facing any risks. But you did I.D. which bureau that car came from when I gave you the license plate. Do you think it would be possible to check these casts to see if it's the same vehicle?"

"That might be tough. I need to think about it. But Sheriff, you get along with your successor. Why not simply let her investigate?"

"There are good reasons to keep this off the books, Arnie, but I don't want to put you in a position of knowing about them."

Arnie nodded.

"Also, once again, if it doesn't put you at risk, would it be possible to see if that car was signed out that night?"

"Everything's possible. Maybe cost some bucks. Nothing too extravagant, but you know, some people are more cooperative if they feel their efforts are appreciated."

"I know, all right. That's no problem. Do you need dough up front?"

"Not right now. I'll let you know."

Leaving the saloon, Rusty realized that he'd underestimated his travel time a bit. He was going to be fifteen or twenty minutes later than he'd indicated to Teresa.

When he got to Pablo's house, he heard laughing and talking from the dining room. Pablo stood near the entrance. Itsy demanded, and received, attention from Rusty. He straightened up from scratching the dog's ear.

He considered Pablo, standing aloof, frowning. Rusty realized that Pablo gotten a head start on the wine. Rusty glanced over at the people standing near the head of the dining room table, chatting away.

Teresa was telling a story that had Henry and Dolores chuckling. The other woman with her back toward him, turned slightly. Rusty was stunned. It was Maria.

He turned angrily on Pablo. "You pussy whipped bastard. You could have warned me."

Pablo, not meeting his eyes, walked toward the table and sat down. Teresa ruled the social calendar, among other things, with an iron hand,.

"Rusty," she had spotted him. "Come say hello." Her smile faded slightly when she saw Pablo sitting sullenly alone at the table.

When Rusty approached, she said, "Of course you know everyone including Maria, who was nice enough to join us."

Maria was having a hard time containing her laughter at Rusty's expression. Henry and Dolores looked pleasantly bemused.

"Let's all sit," Teresa commanded. "Rusty, help yourself to some wine. We're a glass ahead of you."

The dining table was adjustable and had been shortened to accommodate a smaller group. There were place tags.

Pablo had ignored his at the end of the table. He should have been facing Teresa at the other end. Instead, he sat across from Rusty, who had Maria directly on his left. She was quite jolly. Henry sat next to her, adjacent to Teresa and opposite Dolores.

Mrs. Monahan wordlessly moved the place setting from the head of the table where Pablo was supposed to be and set it in front of him. Teresa grimaced at Dolores, who didn't hide her amusement.

Rusty sipped his wine. He hadn't even greeted Maria, who must have been in on, and was obviously enjoying, Teresa's little surprise party.

"Rusty," Dolores said smilingly, "We heard from members that you and Maria played a match on the stadium court at the club last week?"

"You played singles with a girl?" Pablo blurted out, glaring at Rusty, from whom he had never been able to take a set.

His comment was amplified by one of those sudden brief lulls in conversations. Henry and Dolores guffawed. Rusty shifted uncomfortably, and Maria glanced down at her soup.

"Pablo, please." Teresa's tone was sharp.

It went right past Pablo.

"What was the score?" Pablo impolitely demanded of Maria.

"It wasn't really a match," she said. "More of a hitting practice."

"Pablo," Henry said, "it was 6-2, 6-1, 6-1."

Pablo nodded with smug satisfaction, taking a quick look at Teresa and Dolores.

"Maria won all three sets," Rusty continued.

"You got clobbered by a girl?" This time Pablo's loud voice drew laughter from everyone at the table except Rusty and Maria, who modestly sipped her tasty potato soup.

"Pablo," Teresa said with exaggerated sweetness, "not long ago Maria Lopez was one of the top ranked female pro players on the tour."

"Christ! You're that Maria Lopez." His soup was forgotten. "I saw you play at Desert Springs, when you won the tournament. How come you let this stiff win so many games?"

"He's such a hunk, Pablo. I kept watching his bod instead of the ball. Lucky, I didn't lose."

Everyone was laughing and Rusty felt like kicking Pablo for starting the conversation, but Pablo was now an awed fan. "And you, Dummy," he said to Rusty. "How'd you, with your crummy game, get sandbagged into playing one of the world's best players?"

"She used an alias," Rusty spilled a spoonful of soup on the tablecloth as he felt Maria firmly grope his balls under the tablecloth. Maria was innocently looking straight ahead at Pablo, with a small smile on her lips.

Red faced, Rusty placed his spoon back on the plate and extracted Maria's hand from where it didn't belong during dinner. "Also, she shamelessly groped me on changeovers, right in front of the stadium crowd," Rusty said.

"Er, Maria, will you pass the wine up here away from those two?" Teresa said. "By the way, everyone, Maria has generously agreed to hold a charity match against our pro, Roger. It will be in two weeks, for the benefit of the Children's Hospital."

Rusty looked at Maria, whose eyes were full of mischief. No wonder Teresa had been commenting on how well he looked the other day. He wondered just what else this bunch of females had discussed.

"Here's to Maria," Pablo held up his wine glass in a toast, "a great tennis player, and a great sport to help out with the kids. Teresa, how about Rusty being the ball boy for charity? That would bring in even more bucks."

Rusty reached across the table and passed Pablo's full wine glass up to Teresa, who couldn't stop laughing.

It turned out that Mrs. Monahan had outdone herself with servings of filets of sole almandine, and green beans. De-caffeinated coffee and a dish of fresh, ripe pineapple pieces finished off the meal, which had undoubtedly been selected by the health conscious physician at the head of the table.

"Leave your car. I didn't have any wine," Maria said to Rusty after they had done all the "good nights." "I'll bring you back in the morning."

"That certainly doesn't leave any doubt in anyone's mind about just what other games we're playing besides tennis."

She laughed. "But don't you see? It's written all over your face, and your closest friends find you as irresistible a straight man as I do."

He had waited until they were driving in the dark side streets before he adroitly reached under her skirt and probed between her legs.

"Oh," she said, spreading her legs wide open. "Go ahead, Cowboy. Help yourself. See how many times you can get me off before we get home."

He withdrew his hand. "O.K., I can see I can't win."

"You'll be fine as long as you remember that, Cowboy."

"A couple of slaps on your sassy bottom may remind you that I'm a lot bigger than you, Maria."

"Promise?"

CHAPTER FORTY-TWO

"YOU'RE STARING AT me, Russ," Maria said as she wheeled the car through the streets, taking care to check the rear view mirror.

"That's not hard to do, Maria."

"Talking like that will get you someplace, Big Russ."

"I'm counting on it. But I can't get over you linking up with Teresa, setting up a surprise dinner, and even a charity tennis match without me picking up a clue. How did they even know about us?"

"These are almost family to you, Russ. Don't you know how different you are since you loosened up after our candlelight dinner? Did you think they wouldn't notice?"

He turned serious. "I'm not so sure this charity match is a good thing. Security is still a problem, and they'll publicize it."

"Somehow, I don't think gangbangers would show up at the club. Besides, I saw you with those sick kids, and Teresa told me how depressed you were when she had to tell you that you couldn't visit them. This is a way for both of us to do something for those kids. I just hope you'll be aware of your duty to hit with me every day to get me in shape. Roger played on the tour."

"It's only a charity thing, Maria. No one would expect you to be as sharp as you were as a pro."

"You know better. I expect me to play well."

Rusty groaned. "You win all our arguments; isn't that enough? Besides, I might be the worse one for you to hit against. You need someone better."

She grinned. "Nice try. But you're just what I need, and you're not going to wiggle out of your duty to the kids. Then too, who could give me the kind of massages that you will after we work out?"

So, the next few days were magic. He did enjoy hitting with her. She told him exactly what drills she wanted and he saw her game get even better. He hadn't detected the slightest weakness in her stamina or speed when they had played. He didn't notice any change during the next few days, but since his fitness improved, he assumed hers must have, also.

It was like a honeymoon. They were conscious of security, and Pablo always had one of his men at the club when they played on the backcourts, where anyone approaching was immediately visible. The rest of their days were spent on relaxing swims, the very sexual massages Maria had hinted at, and light dinners at a number of good out-of-the-way restaurants. He spent every night at her place, and the intimacy of living together, and constant enjoyment of each other's company was a tonic.

In the second week before the match, Maria changed the routine, spending mornings at her desk in headquarters, and taking the afternoons off for tennis, using accumulated overtime. The gang shadow still lingered ominously, but gangs were keeping their heads down, and the lull was more than welcome.

One of Rusty's habitual breakfast haunts was the diner a few blocks from where his house had been on Rosebud Lane, the same diner where he had experienced the tense face-off with Maria the night of the fire. By 9 a.m. his favorite booth in the rear of the diner was almost always empty. Most of the breakfast eaters were already hours into their early morning jobs.

Since Maria had returned to working mornings, Rusty had been coming to the diner for breakfast. Sitting over coffee, he painstakingly worked his way through the recordings and transcript Pablo had brought from Mexico City.

This morning, his empty breakfast dish was quickly hustled away by the waitress. He sipped at coffee and was deep into carefully matching the recording to the English transcript that Pablo had provided. He was determined to get through it. The still unopened package from Arnie resting in his car trunk nagged his conscience, but the afternoons and evenings with Maria didn't leave time to dwell on the negative stuff he sensed he would find in Arnie's work.

The recorder was in his pocket and the thin wire to the amplifier in his right ear connected to the device was pretty much invisible, and totally inaudible to anyone else in the diner. As he listened to the taped interception, he followed the words on the typed page with his index finger, stopping and starting the player lodged in his pants pocket.

D.A. Herrera was deep into this, all right. But it was still opaque, and hard to follow. In the end, he knew they would have to rely upon Henry's legal expertise to determine the evidentiary value.

Rusty sensed someone slipping into the booth opposite him. He looked up from the document. Jacko's son, Ralph, sat across from him, both of his hands flat on the table.

Rusty kept his face blank. With his left hand, he reached beneath the table into his pocket and turned the recorder playback button off and activated the recording switch.

His right hand stealthily slipped the Glock from its holster.

"Ralph," he said, "under the table I have my Glock pointed right at your balls. If you start to move either hand, I'll get off at least four shots before you can do anything. It will be an agonizing and not particularly fast death."

"Cool it, Sheriff, I came here to talk, not to fight. I'm not trying to kid you. I hate cops, and maybe you even more. You and Jacko didn't like each other, either. Still, you did business together."

"We took years to find out how far to trust each other. And your father never tried to kill me like you've been doing."

"Yeah. And you had the Padre to negotiate, but there are no more padres. Anyway, hear me out. There are two carloads of my homies outside. If anything goes wrong, they'll spray this place with lead and kill us and everyone in here."

Ralph's eyes roamed the diner. "That would be, what?" he said, "Around twenty people? Even without them, you won't shoot. You're like most cops. Putas. Don't kill unless self defense, even then if there are bystanders like the ones sitting behind me. Me? I raise both my arms, and they'll start shooting. I don't give a shit how many of these nothings in here die."

Rusty briefly scanned the street. Ralph was telling the truth for a change. Two cars full of gangbangers were parked at the curb.

Rusty shifted his glance, looking into Ralph's eyes. He hid the chill that ran through him. This was a madman. One of the inner circle of sociopaths who ruled the gangs that Professor Bird had talked about. Individuals who, for whatever reason, had no sense of right or wrong.

"Don't kid yourself, Ralph. Only three pounds of pressure from my trigger finger stand between the slugs that will tear your manhood and life away."

"Today, Sheriff, you're safe. I have a proposition I want you to think about."

"Why should I listen to someone trying to kill me?"

"Because I'm calling a truce. For the next month, no one will go after you or your woman, unless you turn me down flat today. But before you do, I want you to look at some pictures in the left pocket of my jacket. You reach for them. I'm keeping my hands on the table where you want them."

Cautiously, Rusty reached into Ralph's pocket and pulled an envelope out. He spilled the photos onto the table. Looking at them, Rusty started to pull the trigger. Just in time, he took a deep breath, and moved his finger outside the trigger guard.

Briefly, he shifted his eyes from the various pictures, to lock back into Ralph's, watching for any sign of a trick. He examined pictures of Maria getting into her car at headquarters. A clear shot of the rear of Maria's car and license plate leaving the parking lot. Another of them driving out of the lot on their way to the cottage.

One of Maria, on the following day, giving Rusty a peck on the cheek just before she drove off to her grandmother's home. Separate images of Rusty and Maria driving away from the guard shack outside Pablo's gated community.

An additional picture of Rusty and Maria playing tennis on the stadium court. Rusty and Maria walking hand in hand, along the path to her townhouse. A crystal clear photograph of the cabin, obviously taken from Highway 80. Another photo showed Maria talking to Rusty in the Hospital parking lot a moment before the attack by the phony postman.

Rusty wanted to smash the smug smile from Ralph's face, and beat him to a pulp. Instead, he hid his rage. Steadily meeting Ralph's crazed gaze, Rusty waited.

"You're one lucky dude, Sheriff. Real lucky starting from the day that asshole, Jacko, let you drive away in your truck."

"The day you killed your mentor, the Indian?"

"The Indian, a fool all those years, so loyal to Jacko that we couldn't risk talking to him. He chose his own death."

"By trusting you to sit behind him in the mall parking lot?"

Ralph laughed. "I said he was a fool."

"But you screwed up," Rusty added. "You underrated Jacko. He got away."

Seeing the deadly fury in Ralph's face, Rusty knew he had pushed him too far. He slipped his finger back onto the trigger.

Then Ralph smiled. "But all of the money! I've got it, Sheriff, and more. It's the reason we're talking. The reason you're alive, as those pictures show." Ralph, ever so slowly, pointed his index finger at the picture of Maria in her pretty tennis dress.

JOSEPH D. MCNAMARA

"Most silly, Sheriff. As much a fool as Jacko was, he taught me early on, never let a ho get close to you. There are millions of them."

"What do you want from me, Ralph?"

"I mentioned there are no more Padres. No more messenger boys. I want you to talk to the FBI for me. I want the witness protection program."

Rusty took a plunge. "Why not use your buddy in the Sheriff's Department? He's under FBI protection. He can duke you in with the Bureau."

Ralph laughed. "You still hate him and his detectives for smearing your department. That's your trouble. You retired, but didn't know when to quit. You had to set the task force on us. It was my time to take it all over and you and the governor ruined it."

"You shouldn't believe everything you read in the newspaper, Ralph."

"I don't, but your friend, the captain, and his flunky Detective Peterson, who's on the task force, keep me informed."

Watching Ralph's egomania feeding his false sense of superiority because he thought he had inside knowledge, Rusty knew it would be futile to try to convince him otherwise.

"If you've got the money, and no rivals at the moment, why do you need witness protection, Ralph?"

"Because I deal with rats and whores who would sell their mothers. Word has reached me that I'm been ratted out on the Indian and a couple of other instances where scum had to be removed. If I disappear with the money, I'll always have to look over my shoulder on murders, because there's no statute of limitation, and they got DNA and shit that last forever. Why do it that way, when the government is stupid enough to let me off?"

"The witness protection program only works for people who can give up others. You may think you're a big man, Ralph, but I can tell you, you're nothing to the FBI. You haven't told me anything that I could get them interested in. I'm not going to make a promise to you today, when I know they'd just laugh at me. You'd think I double-crossed you and try twice as hard to get me. Besides, they already have a captain who's probably been ratting on you and Jacko for years."

Ralph's temper flared again. "On the way in the door, I almost stepped in dog shit. That's what your captain is. And if I lift my hand, he can be swept away just like the owner of this diner will sweep the shit away. When I tell the FBI what Captain Christian and his flunkie detective on their precious task force have been doing, they'll be shocked."

"They don't want to hear it. The FBI doesn't admit its mistakes. So far, you've got nothing, Ralph."

"No? You're so out of it. I can give up the Juarez Cartel, our blackmailing whore of a D.A., and the remaining Phantom, who also does work for terrorists. Of course, that's in addition to the peons outside, and their brothers. Children, playing gang games even into their old age."

"You know I can't speak for the FBI."

"I know. Neither can they speak for themselves. You tell them that I need the word of the U.S. Attorney in San Francisco. In writing."

Rusty pretended to be impressed and thinking. He drummed the fingers of his non-gun hand on the table.

"Look, Ralph, you've mentioned some heavy stuff. But I know these guys I can talk to. They're not risk-takers. They're not going to the U.S. Attorney without some more details than you've given me. Also, how do I know this isn't just a trick to get me and the lieutenant off guard?"

"First of all, off guard, on guard. It doesn't make any difference. The remaining Phantom took some of those pictures. He was along with Asshole Captain Christian and foolishly let him do the shooting at the cabin. If he had done it the way I told him, you'd both be gone."

"Christian panicked?"

"No brains. No balls, a maricoñ. He ran when you shot back. As to evidence, tell them, I've got tapes of D.A. Herrera and Captain Christian talking money with Jacko about fixing two of the jurors in that old Speed bust I took. Also, Herrera told him where he had hidden the gang-rat that had given me up. I know where Christian and Peterson buried him. "You know, when Jacko let me sit in jail for ninety days, stupid bastard, that gave Christian plenty of time to set himself up with me as the go-between.

"Later on, Christian warned me of two raids by the Task Force. A couple of times, Christian and three of his detectives rode shotgun, protecting the two biggest Meth deals the Cartel ever did here. I've got pictures of them helping unload the shit and standing outside the warehouse until I picked it up with my people. That enough?"

"I think it's enough to get their interest, but I'm not sure. Tell me about the Phantoms."

"They weren't brothers, of course, but I've got the Phantom who's alive stashed here and on my payroll. He demands as much as the whore Herrera. They expect ten grand cash every Thursday, so they can transfer it late on Friday. The federal budget worms don't work weekends. By Monday when they come to their cubbyholes, transfer records have been erased. Anyone else tell me exactly when I have to pay them, they'd be dead. And I can let the FBI know where we've stashed the Phantom, and where Herrera puts his money."

"And I can tell the FBI that the info is solid?"

"You bet. You see, you shouldn't have retired, Sheriff. It's too much heat to take out a D.A. or Sheriff, but a retired sheriff and his whore? Who cares? Gossip writers maybe. But because she's your girlfriend, there won't be heat. They won't want the publicity."

"All right, Ralph, I'll give it a try, talk to them. How do I contact you?"

Ralph wrote out a cell phone number. "It's good twenty-four hours a day for the next month. If I don't hear from you by then, look over your shoulder, not that it will do any good."

CHAPTER FORTY-THREE

RUSTY AND MARIA hit tennis balls that afternoon. After just an hour, Maria signaled that she'd had enough, and they went for a swim. They returned to her place, and did their usual massage routine.

Rusty hid his distress resulting from listening to Ralph in the morning, and the subsequent, less than satisfactory meetings with Henry and Pablo. Maria was slightly surprised that Rusty seemed uninterested in sex after the massages that usually turned him on.

"Later, then, Lover. It's part of my training program now," she smiled. "But to tell you the truth, we could both use an afternoon nap. Just an hour. Then, how about we order Chinese to be delivered?"

"Sounds good," Rusty agreed.

She was asleep almost immediately. Rusty stayed next to her for a few minutes, envying her face in repose. She was so beautiful, so relaxed, while sleep was unthinkable for him. Somehow, he had to ensure her safety.

Quietly, he slipped into shorts and sandals and went downstairs where he again listened to the tape of Ralph and made some notes on a yellow legal pad. An hour and five minutes later, he heard Maria in the bathroom upstairs.

Rusty got up and put the recording equipment in an empty, top kitchen cabinet, knowing that she'd have no reason to open it. He took the legal pad back to the comfortable Eames reading chair. He had jotted down various notes on the second and third pages, leaving the top page blank in case Maria happened upon it.

She appeared, smiling and refreshed. She gave him a slight hug and kiss. He held her tightly, his fury at Ralph and the others surging. She leaned back in his arms, meeting his eyes.

"What was that all about? Not that I'm complaining," she said.

He smiled. "It's just that sometimes I can't believe how lucky I am."

"That's sweet, Rusty." She affectionately touched his cheek. "When you order the food, will you get mine with pineapple?"

"Pineapple on Chinese food? Do they have that?"

"Of course."

"You had a bowl of pineapple for dessert last night in the restaurant. The night before, you had them prepare a bowl of pineapple for an appetizer. What gives? A special training diet?"

"In a way."

They both ate with gusto when the food arrived. Rusty had two glasses of Chianti with his. Maria drank a glass of milk. Rusty wrinkled his nose. "Milk with Chinese food? Do they go together?"

"Sure."

"You haven't had any wine since you returned from your grandmother's, but you've been on a milk kick."

"Good for a woman's bones, Russ."

"I guess. But I think I'll stick to the red wine."

"You should. Helps the heart, they say."

Maria settled on the couch with a magazine. She put a pillow behind her back and stretched her legs out on the couch. She was wearing a thin kimono and Rusty smiled at her bare feet and strong, shapely legs. Rusty was leaning back on the Eames chair with his own bare legs stretched out on the footrest.

"Something over here caught your interest, Russ?"

"As always, Maria."

"Wow, even on a full stomach. I'm impressed. I was beginning to wonder. You weren't hitting the ball with your customary accuracy and energy this afternoon. And you're usually more amenable to naps than I am. But you seem preoccupied today."

"I guess I am. We can't let this temporary pause in gang violence lure us into a false sense of security."

"We've stayed alert. The gang unit and patrol people have kept the pressure on. And there seems to be a leadership vacuum."

"Yeah, but do me a favor, Maria, don't relax. They're still out there, believe me."

She nodded and went back to her magazine.

Rusty went over his notes, kicking back and forth the ideas that were beginning to formulate. He was as uneasy as Pablo was about putting too much faith in a psychopath like Ralph's truce.

After all, how could you trust the logic of someone who was by definition illogical? He was convinced that they had to move immediately and was beginning to refine the plan he had mentioned to Pablo.

"What's all of the doodling on the yellow pad?"

Rusty looked up briefly, and shrugged, his mind deeply immersed in weighing various possibilities and consequences to different action.

"And here I was about to give you the good news that you're going to be a daddy, Russ."

"Yeah, right," he said, still thinking of ways to minimize the dangers to those who would help.

After a moment, he looked up at Maria. She was grinning at him.

"You into your weird sense of humor again?"

She smiled even wider. "Not at all. I just thought there'd be a little more reaction."

"You're not serious?" he frowned at her.

"You sound like John McEnroe."

"Maria, what the hell are you talking about?"

"I'm talking about how in about eight months we're about to be blessed with a baby."

"What? Damn it, Maria. You lied to me. Told me you were on the pill."

Her smile was gone. "No way, Russ. I never lied to you."

"I specifically told you that I hadn't come prepared. You told me not to worry about it."

"Right. I never said anything about being on the pill."

"Don't play lawyer's games with me, Maria. You know what you said."

"Yes. You said you hadn't come prepared. I said exactly: 'I'm a big girl. You don't have to worry about it.'"

"And now, you announce you're pregnant like it's nothing."

"It's everything. Not nothing."

"You deceived me, Maria."

"Your hard-on deceived you. You were thinking between your legs, not between your ears."

He tried to control his anger. He had suddenly been jolted from considering life and death questions to listening to Maria talk like she was nuts.

"You lied to me."

"I did not. I told you I was a big girl and you didn't have to worry. I'm telling you the same thing, now."

"You planned it."

She smiled her impish smile and happily nodded her head up and down.

"Did it ever occur to you that I had a choice in this?"

"Sure. You made it when you carried me upstairs. God Russ, I still get warm and fuzzy thinking that it may have happened then. Could anything have been more romantic?"

He stared at her, incredulously. He sat up and put his head between his hands. It was too much. Crazy Ralph, the Phantom killer, Herrera, Captain Christian, murderous gangbangers everywhere, and now this.

"You never told me," he said, once again glaring at her.

"Of course not. What would you expect me to say, 'Russ, let's go upstairs and make a baby? You would have run out the door. And I wouldn't have little Russ in here," she patted her stomach.

"Eight months, and I guess I'm expected to go smiling to the altar with you soon so we can pretend we didn't have to get married."

"I never said anything about marriage."

"What? You didn't think I might object to having a baby out of wedlock?"

"Out of wedlock?" she giggled. "Do people still talk like that? Russ, I have news for you, marriage is not a prerequisite to having a child."

"Yes, but I assume you'll be happy to marry me."

"No."

"No? What do you mean, no?" His face was red.

"I mean I have no intention of marrying you. I'm sure that you'll be as great a father as I'll be a mother, but it has nothing to do with getting married to you. I told you not to worry, and I mean it."

"Right. I'll be a great father. How old will I be when I take the little bastard to Little League games."

"I'll bet anything you'll still be the best athlete in the stands, except for me at tennis," she laughed.

"Maria, let me make myself clear. I admit I'm trying to control myself and not doing so well, but I'd like us to start planning to marry as soon as possible."

"No." She shook her head emphatically.

He leaned back in the chair totally frustrated. "You don't like the way we've been living together?"

"You know I love it. Except for now, we get along great, and have so much fun. And I often remember you reaching down and lifting me off the couch and get dizzy just thinking about it. It was a never before, and a never again."

"So why won't you marry me?"

"Because you never asked me until now. Until I told you I was pregnant. And you're so angry and hurt, and full of resentment. And you accused me of lying to you."

"Maria, I'm me. Yes, I should have told you before that I love you, but I know you knew it, didn't you?"

"Of course," she laughed. "Everyone knew it when they saw us together, all of your friends. People at work, asking me, 'Well, who is he?' Never guessing it was their former boss. But we need time. I have to consider what happened just now, about what I could have done different. I think you should go away for a while. We'll talk on the phone everyday, I promise."

"Forget it. You may be crazy, but I'm not. There're people trying to kill both of us, and I'm not leaving you alone for a moment more than I have to."

"You mean, I have to call the police to get you out of here."

"Maybe you can clear your head for a moment to think what might happen to Little Russ's father if you have him locked up?"

She was angry. "You're playing dirty, Russ."

"All's fair in love and war. Now come over and give me a smooch."

"No way. I don't want you to touch me."

"O.K., but think back to earlier tonight when you asked me why the special hug in the kitchen."

"Fuck you, Russ. You really have me pissed off." Maria stormed upstairs and slammed the bedroom door.

Rusty sat, emotionally drained. He had come dangerously close to showing her Ralph's pictures before she had dropped the bombshell. His hesitation then was due to the panic attacks and swings of mood she had shown after past dangers.

Now that he knew she was pregnant, he was even more concerned about her emotional state if she saw the pictures. She was too unpredictable before. Now, with her being pregnant, he certainly couldn't upset her more.

He would have to put the plan in motion first thing in the morning. He dialed Arnie Grime's number.

JOSEPH D. MCNAMARA

CHAPTER FORTY-FOUR

IT WAS 9 a.m. when Russ entered the Last Chance Saloon. Arnie was in the back booth with the usual two bourbons on the table. Three shabby looking men were already staring morosely into their whiskey at the bar.

Rusty tried to hide his disapproval of the drinks on the table, but he began to doubt if he should depend so heavily on Arnie.

"Don't worry, Sheriff, these are just for decoration. It doesn't hurt my rep in this neighborhood for people to think I'm just another drunk. Fact is, I rarely have more than three drinks a day."

His eyes were clear. Rusty thought he might be telling the truth. And if he had been a sharply dressed go-getter in this neighborhood, he would have quickly become a suspicious target.

"Arnie, yesterday I was having breakfast in the twenty-four hour diner near where my house used to be."

"I know the place. Just a few blocks from Rosebud Lane, right?"

"Yes."

"I was muddling through that transcript. You know my friend, Pablo Garcia?"

"The mega-rich guy who used to be a captain in Special Forces."

"Yeah. He gave me this gadget. You see this button—

—"I have one, Sheriff. I know how it works."

"Good. Ralph, Jacko's son unexpectedly slipped into the booth. I think the best way to go at this is to let you listen to it and then we can talk."

Arnie put in the earpiece and played the tape. When it finished, he rewound the cassette and took out the earpiece. He handed it all back to Rusty.

"He's as dangerous as he is crazy, Sheriff. It might be worth it to hand him over to the FBI. If they deal, you get him and the remaining Phantom off your back."

"Here are the pictures he gave me."

"Arrogant bastards, aren't they? These in the police parking lot were shot from the jail. I'd wager from Captain Christian's office. Makes you long for the good old days when cops could handle these gangsters without ever going to court. I never heard about the lieutenant and you, so not too many in the Department know. Her rep is a real good boss, tough and smart. She doesn't catch a lot of the crap that some of the woman get, including Sheriff Sally who, in my opinion, paid her dues. Have you read the info I put together yet?"

"No, Arnie. I wasted a lot of time on the transcript which we now know can't be used. And the other attacks and stuff have kept me busy."

"Well, you might do yourself, the lieutenant and me a favor, if, when you start looking at the package, you toss the sheet on her without reading it."

Rusty frowned, knowing that the first thing he'd do would be to read Arnie's report on Maria.

"I take it you showed the lieutenant the pictures and told her about Ralph so she knows the danger?" Arnie asked.

"No. I haven't."

"I'm surprised. Under the law, cops have to warn potential victims."

"We're not cops, anymore, and dealing with these animals, we're doing a lot of things that aren't exactly under the law."

"I know, Sheriff, and I'm certainly not arguing with you but . . ."

"Arnie, this stays between us, O.K.?"

"Right. Everything."

"Well, Maria is as cool as they come during an emergency. But after a couple of close calls were past, she reacted kind of weird, real emotional, and hard to deal with, let alone to anticipate how she'd react. Still, I was about to show her the pictures even though I was real concerned about what she'd do. Maybe make things even more dangerous."

"They do think different than we do, Sheriff."

"To say the least. But last night, she dropped this bombshell on me. She's pregnant."

"Isn't she kind of old enough not to let that happen?"

"She wanted it to happen. Told me that I didn't have to worry. So I thought she was on the pill. But that wasn't what she said at all. Just not to worry."

"She never seemed like the type to trap a guy. Seemed very independent."

"She is, absolutely too independent. I said we should get married. She said, no way, tried to throw me out. Won't even talk to me."

Arnie smiled, shaking his head. "What's the old saying, 'You can't live with them, and you can't live without them?'"

"Well, I'm kind of glad to hear that I'm not the only one in the dark about women. But her safety is one reason I'm not willing to go along with Ralph."

"A guy like him would get into trouble even in the witness protection program."

"No doubt about it. My concern is that sooner or later, if he needed leverage, he'd let the other Phantom or the cartel know that Maria was the one who took out the Phantom in the hospital parking lot. Some of those animals would never stop hunting her."

"Especially, because she's a woman. They're so damned macho and disrespectful of women that it's fanatical. So what's the game plan?"

"When I listened to the tape on Ralph, he used the word that he "stashed" the other Phantom. It struck me as a kind of strange word. You stash stuff and people in special places, right?"

"Yeah. The rep of the Phantom brothers, who ain't really brothers, is that they did dirty work all over the world. Those guys found their own way around. No one "stashed" them. Of course, this is an unusual job for the one Phantom still here, in that it's so extended. He would be looking for a safe, long-term pad. That way, he wouldn't have to keep moving around and maybe call attention to himself."

"Exactly, my thought. Then, on the tape from Mexico City, I heard Herrera tell one of the cartel guys who was coming for a visit that they had a secure place where no one would look for him or anyone else."

"I see what you mean. It's a little too much of a coincidence, but I can't think of where they're talking about."

"Here's one thought. Remember the Sureños little store on Fourth Street that got blown up?"

"Sure do. Whoever took them out did all of us a favor."

"When I was in uniform on patrol, the narcs had a tip on a shipment of cocaine being stored there. They got a warrant. I helped, but it turned out that a court clerk handling the warrant had warned them. We came up empty. What stuck in my mind, though, is that the entire block was owned in the name of a sleazy law firm that represented gangbangers and dope dealers. And guess what? Herrera worked some cases with them and was real tight."

"So you think maybe this firm is a front for some other gang property where a Phantom could stay indefinitely, and not be conspicuous?"

"You got it, Arnie. It's a long shot, but Ralph promised a month cease-fire, so we have some slack time. I'll have to see him again, to stall a little. Make sure the screwball doesn't get impatient. But I think he really believes his plan is clever."

"I can run down the real estate holdings of the firm easily enough. I'm sure that there won't be a lot of locations where the Phantom could hide. But what do you do if I find him?"

"Just talk to him, Arnie."

Arnie shook his head. "That's like saying you're going into a cage with a thousand pound gorilla for a chat. Why would he even talk to you? And the guy's supposed to be so good that, no disrespect, Sheriff, none of us should take him on alone."

"I agree. You heard the tape. What do you think the Phantom's reaction would be to hearing Ralph's voice on tape talking about giving them all up?"

"That's beautiful, Sheriff. Still, this guy wouldn't even give you a chance to play the tape."

"He would if I caught him right and had a Glock in his face, telling him I just want him to listen."

"You need a backup. I'll take your back, Sheriff."

"Thanks. You and I have always been straight with each other, Arnie. I want to ask a question."

"Go ahead."

"If it was you, and you had a choice of taking on the Phantom with Arnie Grime, or with Pablo Garcia at your back, who would you pick?"

"Pablo," Arnie answered without hesitation. "But you'll need a driver. I'll be there. That is, if we can find this guy, but I've got a good feeling about it. I'll start this morning. If all goes well, I'll nail down his location by tomorrow."

JOSEPH D. MCNAMARA

CHAPTER FORTY-FIVE

RUSTY DID HIS best to stay out of Maria's way. He was gone before her in the morning, cruising the residential area on foot. He believed that he had pinned down the location of the photographer who had caught him and Maria walking the path.

A bench on the periphery of the small artificial pond provided perfect cover for a scout pretending to watch the swans, while snapping a surreptitious photo of Maria. It was the first place Rusty checked in the morning.

Unknown to Maria, he had made several quick nocturnal rounds of the housing complex, making sure that no one was near her car. She rarely altered her route to headquarters.

Rusty waited on a side street and followed her at a distance. If she spotted him, she never showed it. He'd check to confirm Pablo's assurance that Maria would be covered at the club.

After he was sure that she entered the headquarters parking lot in the morning, Rusty wound his way to the diner for breakfast. He had discarded the transcript and finally opened Arnie's report.

Arnie had reacted to Rusty's rambling request by giving a rough rundown of detective units using the copying machine from which the flyers had come. He had included common hearsay about the various units' practices, efficiency and staff.

Rusty's first selection to read was on Maria Lopez-Hogan. Arnie had written that the twelve-year veteran of the Department was well regarded.

Rusty read with interest that she had changed her name when she quit tennis a year before she joined the Department. So, there had never been any divorce from a Mister Hogan, as Rusty had naturally assumed.

The next line jolted him. Maria had changed her name soon after the tragedy in which she had lost her mother and her ten-year old brother. The case came back to Rusty in a flash. How could he have not connected her to it?

When Ramundo and Ricardo had bolted the Norteños to lead the Sureños following their clash with Jacko, according to investigators, they had gone on a drive-by shooting binge, fatally gunning down two Norteños standing on the corner. The barrage of wild shots had penetrated the Lopez's modest home, unfortunately taking the lives of Maria's mother and ten year-old brother.

Rusty had pulled out all stops, assigned extra detectives, and launched a major crackdown on the Sureños. He had attended the chapel rosary for the deceased and expressed his regret to the family. He also attended the funerals which had been held in St. Sebastian's.

He dimly recalled it all, now. Right before he had approached the family at the rosary, Sally had told him that the other child, Maria, had been away playing tennis. He remembered the anguished grandmother and the girl who looked to be about fifteen.

In fact, he now realized she had been several years older. He had never become aware that she was an up and coming tennis pro. Since her name was Hogan when she quit tennis and later joined the Department, no one realized who she was.

He did recollect sincerely assuring the family after the rosary that the Department would make every effort to bring to justice those responsible. And Rusty had been good to his word, keeping the investigation going for years. He recalled that detectives had been sure that Ramundo and Ricardo were responsible, but couldn't make the case for indictments.

Arnie's source offered the opinion, without any proof, that the flyer proclaiming a reward for a hit on Rusty probably came from the homicide unit.

Rusty sat stunned in the diner. It was nothing more than a rumor in the report. He really couldn't understand why, or believe that Maria had known about the origin of the flyer.

But if he had opened Arnie's package first, instead of the transcript, he would have had a much more wary attitude toward her. Rusty would have steered well clear of Homicide Lieutenant Maria Lopez-Hogan. A totally different life than he had now!

Reflecting on her sudden temper flaring, when he and Sheriff Pat had seemingly taken the cabin shooting casually, it was now more understandable. Her mention of innocent flesh being ripped apart by bullets had puzzled him at the time, as if coming from a victim, not a tough homicide cop. She had more than once expressed deep animosity toward gangbangers, but he had taken it as simply a typical police attitude toward gangs.

He read further. Her excellent performance in the academy, and very youthful appearance, caused the Narcotics Enforcement Unit to grab her. Immediately, Maria excelled, making many undercover buys, and setting up a number of major drug cases.

When she was promoted to sergeant, she was assigned to the Gang Enforcement Unit. Given her heartbreaking family history, Rusty probably would have assigned her elsewhere, but Lucy's illness had sapped a lot of his attention. He had left most of the routine decisions to Sally by then.

In the anti-gang unit, Maria had served under then Lieutenant Christian. Six months later, she requested a transfer without specifying a reason. Arnie's source believed that she had verbally reported suspicions of Christian's crimes to Undersheriff Sally.

She was picked up by the homicide unit. Once again, her performance was outstanding, eventually leading Sally to put her in charge of the unit when she was promoted to lieutenant after Rusty's retirement.

Rusty couldn't remember exactly what had triggered the sting operation that nailed Christian. But he had been furious when the FBI, without consulting Rusty, made a deal with prosecutor Herrera.

Christian and his gang walked. Rusty didn't believe for a moment that the FBI had gotten their money's worth out of the agreement. His previously good relationship with the Bureau had cooled considerably during his last year in office.

In Maria's apartment, he pored over the remainder of Arnie's preliminary investigation involving the flyer.

All in all, there wasn't much there, aside from the stuff about Maria, and he wasn't sure what to make of it.

Around noon, his cell phone buzzed. He wondered if it was Maria and was undecided about taking the call. He needed time to digest Arnie's report. In the end, he answered and was surprised to hear that it was Teresa calling.

"Rusty," she said, "could you possibly stop by for coffee?"

"Now?"

"Yes, if it's convenient."

"No problem. I'll be there in about twenty minutes." He disconnected. What could this be about?

Teresa opened the door herself and led Rusty to the kitchen. They took two mugs of coffee out to the pool area and sat under the shade umbrella. Pablo and the kids were absent, but staff members moved through the house and grounds.

"Rusty, I saw Maria hitting on the ball machine this morning at the club. She was really banging away furiously. I didn't want to distract her, but when she stopped to refill the machine, I went over to say hello."

Rusty was surprised. He thought Maria would work at headquarters in the morning and practice in the afternoon.

"Well," Teresa continued, "when I went up say hello, I teased her, asking where her hitting partner was. She looked pretty miserable."

Rusty didn't say anything.

"I asked her if anything was wrong. She burst into tears. I had to put my arms around her to calm her down. We went over and sat in the shade. I couldn't get anything out of her."

"Don't look at me. She won't even talk to me."

"Rusty, you're one of the most gentle men I've met. Please don't misinterpret this, but many pregnant women go through an emotional rollercoaster. There are tremendous physiological changes taking place in their bodies. Have you noticed her sudden hunger for pineapples?"

"Yes. She told you she was pregnant?"

Teresa looked puzzled. "I told her, Rusty. She came to me for the examination. You didn't know that?"

"No. It was only last night that she told me she was a month pregnant."

"Oh. Was there a problem?"

"That would be understating it."

"Look, Rusty, I don't want to pry. I simply want to tell you what I'd tell any expectant father. You have to be very understanding, very careful not to upset a woman at this time."

"I'm afraid it's a little late for that."

"I'm really surprised to hear that from you, Rusty. I thought you'd be very sensitive."

"And your patient didn't tell you the circumstances, just cried on your shoulder and made me the bad guy."

"Rusty! Please. What in the world has gotten into you?"

"Maria, for one thing. In addition to any number of people trying to kill me and her."

"Still, you must be considerate."

"I tried, Teresa. But I guess I failed. When I asked her to marry me, she told me to go fuck myself and to leave or she'd call the police."

"As I told you, you have to be extra careful not to upset her."

JOSEPH D. MCNAMARA

"Well, it's difficult to do when you're trying your best to save her life, and she's not only not cooperating, but taking really stupid risks like going to the club unescorted."

"My God! It's that serious? I don't understand about these threats. Pablo tells me nothing except to be careful. He thinks he's being protective by not having me worry. We're women, but not children, Rusty. And I can see you're more miserable than she is. How did this happen? I would have thought you'd be happy. I know how you love children, how hard you and Lucy tried."

"Before you condemn me to be hanged, Teresa, you might ask Maria how she deceived me about being on the pill, deliberately deciding to have my child without discussing it with me."

She shook her head. "I can't get into the middle of this. Obviously, you two need marriage counseling."

"Are you kidding? If I mention marriage again, she's liable to shoot me."

"Damn Pablo, I never would have set up the charity match if he had told me how serious the danger is. I'll cancel it."

"Teresa, let me gently suggest that you think about it before you do it. I'm really concerned about what impact that might have on Maria. Maybe playing this match will cool her off. Pablo and I have discussed security, and I'm going to ask Henry to call Sally and make sure there's a uniform presence. In addition, I've done some things behind the scene that I can't tell you about that makes me believe we'll be safe for a couple of weeks."

"Henry's going to call Sally, not you?"

"I seem to have totally lost my ability to communicate with women."

"Well, at least you're aware of how you're coming across."

"Thanks for the coffee, Teresa." He got up and left, ignoring her frown.

CHAPTER FORTY-SIX

THE SUNDAY OF the match, Pablo and Rusty nervously checked security at the club. Sally had not only come through with a couple of marked units in the parking lot, but two uniformed deputies inside the club. And Sally herself was sitting front and center with Teresa.

"I've got three people inside as well, Rusty. And I'm going down to sit next to Teresa. For some reason, she's ticked off at me," Pablo said.

"There's not only a gang war going on, Pablo, there's a war between the sexes."

"Oh, yeah. That reminds me. Teresa said I should pass on a message from Maria that if you're in the stands, she'll walk away from the match."

"Well, that's the least obscene message from her lately."

"You shouldn't have upset her, Rusty. If she loses, it's your fault."

"Loses? She's so mad, she going to kick poor Roger's ass."

"I doubt it. The guy was a male pro; he'll overpower her."

"I'll bet you ten bucks that she takes him in straight sets."

"Make it a hundred. She might win in three, but it will only be because he's a gentleman."

"Two hundred?"

"You're on, Rusty, although you're making me feel guilty taking advantage of you betting silly just because you're pissed at her. You've got to learn to be more diplomatic with women."

Rusty stayed in the parking lot. He stood in the deep shade where he was inconspicuous. He wanted to make sure the deputies weren't regarding this as just ceremonial crowd control. Satisfied that they were alert, he entered the club and stood in a walkway where he couldn't see the court, but could see the scoreboard.

He rocked back on his heels. Maria had won the first set six to love. It seemed like they had just started the match a short time ago. She wasn't taking long to demolish Roger.

Carefully, he edged forward. Maria's back was to him. Roger had hit a nice approach shot into her backhand and quickly gotten into a good position at the net. Maria zinged a backhand rocket of a passing shot. Roger lunged, but never got a racket on it. He slipped to his knees and was slow getting up. Rusty went back into the parking lot.

One of the deputies came up to him. "How's our side doing, Sheriff?" he said.

"She won the first set, six zip. Ahead, in the second."

"Good. It's nice to see our side winning, no?"

Rusty nodded. You should only know which side is winning, man.

Twenty minutes later, he heard the crowd applauding. The loudspeaker came on. The blah, blah would take a few minutes, before the crowd moved in for the champagne reception. Pablo came out shaking his head. He handed Rusty two hundred dollars. "The poor guy didn't win a single game."

"It was a pretty shitty thing for her to do. He's a nice guy, playing for charity. She embarrassed him in front of all the members. It will really help him to get requests for lessons."

"Here, she comes, Rusty. She didn't even shower or stay for the reception."

Maria walked down the corridor, carrying her tennis bag. She didn't look at them.

"Congratulations, Maria," Rusty said. "Want to get married? I'll buy you a pineapple ice cream Sundae."

She gave him the finger. "Get lost!" she stormed toward her car.

"You sure got a touch with ladies, Rusty," Pablo said, watching two police cars speeding to keep up with Maria burning rubber on the way out of the lot.

Downstairs at Maria's townhouse, Rusty stayed especially alert that night, knowing she would sleep soundly after burning off energy in the tennis match.

He had no idea what she would do the next morning, but he followed her as far as the Department parking lot. He was pleased to see an unmarked detective car with two deputies also following her. Sally was paying attention. Rusty exchanged waves with the detectives and pulled away to have breakfast again in the diner.

It had been a full week since Ralph had accosted him there. He didn't want to call him too soon, wanted to let Ralph sweat a little. But he didn't want him getting nervous, either. Rusty, hoped that his following the routine of eating in the same place would calm Ralph.

Reading the paper with his coffee, Rusty wasn't surprised to see Ralph arrive with two cars full of gangbangers. He just couldn't wait to be called. Rusty pressed the record button. His Glock was pointed right where it had been last week. Ralph sat down, and waved the waitress away.

"Just checking in, Sheriff. Got some new pictures for you. He tossed three photos at Rusty. One showed Rusty standing in the parking lot during yesterday's tennis match, another pictured Maria during the warm-up, and the last one was of Maria this morning, leaving her car in the Department parking lot to go inside to work.

"Last one's hot off the press. Had any luck getting in touch with the FBI guys?"

Rusty kept his face expressionless. "Yeah. I talked to one guy. He's interested. Going to take it to his boss. If that boss goes for it, they take to the SAC."

"Special Agent in Charge, right?" Ralph, showing how smart he was, sneered.

"Yeah. If the SAC approves, he'll take it personally to the U.S. Attorney." Rusty was playing it delicately, letting Ralph think he was controlling the conversation.

"So what'd he say that makes you think he's interested?"

"For one thing, he said he was. But he asked me a couple of questions."

"Like what?"

"Well, remember I'm just repeating what he said. He wanted to know about the Thursday payoffs to Herrera and the Phantom."

"What about them?"

"He told me to ask you if you'd wear a wire when you gave them the dough?"

"Jesus. Are they really that stupid?"

"I told you this would take a while, wouldn't be easy."

"I can't believe they think I'd personally carry money."

"What can I tell you? That's what he wanted an answer to."

"Look, tell the shithead that the Phantom likes young girls. I send him this same ho three times a week. She's fifteen, stays all night, Monday, Thursday, and Saturday. She's so dumb she thinks he loves her. Gonna take her to Mexico when he leaves."

"Well, I know what they'll ask next. Will she wear a wire?"

"For Christ's sake, I just told you she thinks it's love. She'd tell him. He'd kill her and disappear in a minute."

"Cool it, Ralph. I said these are their questions, not mine. You'll have to deal with these same jerks yourself, if they buy in. What about Herrera?"

"Same thing. We use a ho. Cops don't search them like they do chicos."

"Same one every week?"

"Absolutely, they're so dumb, you don't want to take a chance of breaking in a new one. Get the address wrong or something. You think I should send the Phantom a new cunt? One I can count on?"

"How the hell do I know? But you're trying to set up a deal. If the bullshit about the Phantom is true, he might be sharp enough to get suspicious. If he kills anyone or flies, it would queer the whole thing. The FBI is drowning in red tape. Any little thing like the Phantom taking a powder would turn them off on the whole deal."

"The Phantom ain't bullshit. And that's what I just said, about being careful. We don't want to get his ears up. But you can tell them, Herrera doesn't take the money himself. His brother does. Supposed to be office manager. Can't even manage to zip his fly. Anything else?"

"No."

"How come the feds are laying off us?"

"I told them it might be a good idea if they want to show good faith in this deal."

"Good. Another thing you can tell them. By leaving us alone, they give me time to set things up. If they start busting people, breaking balls, how am I supposed to do all these things they want?"

"I'll pass it on. One thing, Ralph. Knock off the shit with the pictures. You already made your point. If some cop spots one of your people and shooting starts, the FBI will kiss you off so quick you won't believe it."

"Nobody's spotted us so far."

"Wrong, Ralph. I'm trying to keep things quiet, but I'm not God. Can't tell what some individual cop might do any more than you can be sure one of your assholes outside doesn't blow someone away who drives in front of them."

"O.K. How long is this gonna take?"

"As long as the fucking FBI takes to get its head out of its ass. If they think I'm trying to give them orders, they'll fuck both of us up."

"Yeah. Yeah, Sheriff. But just remember we'll be around and I don't trust your ass one bit."

"Anytime you want to deal with those assholes yourself, Ralph, you just go ahead. I can't tell you how much fun it is trying to work with them."

A moment after Ralph and his gangbangers pulled away, Rusty dialed Arnie's number.

"Arnie, can I meet you in about fifteen minutes, usual place?" he said, when the P.I. answered.

"I'll be there."

JOSEPH D. MCNAMARA

CHAPTER FORTY-SEVEN

RUSTY FOUND THE Last Stop Saloon had the same stale, dank smell of cheap booze and customers who, soon enough, would be making their last stop. The waitress deposited bourbons to Arnie's rear booth. This time she put down generously full glasses without ice.

"Why don't you have a taste, Sheriff? You look like you could use a boost."

Rusty wrinkled his nose, and shook his head.

"It's Jack Daniels, Boss."

"That's not what it said on the bottle."

"I know," Arnie smiled and winked. "You didn't think I drank the rotgut they serve these poor guys, did you?"

Rusty took a sip. It was Jack Daniels. He took a swallow, enjoying the warm glow as it made its way down to his stomach.

"I wanted to let Ralph sweat a little, not call him too soon, but I didn't want him to get antsy, so I've been having breakfast in the diner. That way he knew he could talk anytime he wanted to."

"Yeah, I know about the diner. Me and my op shadowed you there twice. You were clean. No tails."

Rusty was skeptical, but he continued, "Anyway, he showed up this morning; listen." He handed Arnie the recorder and earpiece.

After hearing it, Arnie said, "Yeah, he sounds nervous. Do you have the new pictures with you?"

Rusty gave him the pictures. "Two were at the tennis match yesterday."

"Right. My op and I were there. The lieutenant is one hell of a tennis player."

"You were there? How'd you get in?"

Arnie smiled. "We do this stuff for a living, Sheriff."

"Spot the photographer?"

"You bet. Got his license plate. Guy's legit. Runs a photo shop and business. Ralph must have hired him. I didn't think any of those gangbangers could take pictures that good. I bet he even supplied the digital equipment for Captain Christian. Christian got those pictures of you two in the parking lot right from his office window. E-mailed the one of her going to work this morning to Ralph. Ralph wanted to shock you."

"It's one thing to sneak a picture, another for a sniper to set up for a long range shot without being noticed. Still, they made their point, and I'm getting uneasy. I can't seem to convince Maria that she's got to be super careful. We have to start moving now."

"I liked the way you conned him about the Feebies. Have they really pulled back?"

"Yeah, pulled everyone out for a big Las Vegas operation."

"Still, if the Department or DEA turns up the heat, Ralph will panic."

"That's why I came. I'm wondering if you think it's possible for us to shadow the fifteen year-old chica this afternoon. Ralph said Monday, Thursday and Saturday. Today's Monday. My guess is that she leaves from the Sureños main clubhouse on East First Street. I can back you up."

"You're probably right. My op and I have cased it a few times. It's like a beehive. They're in and out all the time. No offense, Sheriff, but we don't want you or Pablo or any of his people within miles; you'd be like a flashing sign."

"Isn't that a little risky, Arnie, for you guys to be that close to them? It's one thing to tail me, another these gangbangers. They spot you, you're dead."

"Sheriff, I haven't been made once in all these years. My top op is even better. She's invisible."

"A woman?"

"Right. She's spent hours on you. Passed right by, even talked to you. You never made her."

"Are you sure, Arnie?"

"Absolutely; this is the third time she served you bourbon. Can you remember her face?"

"The waitress in here?"

"Actually, the owner. In fact, she owns the whole block. My partner. We've been living together for ten years."

Rusty tried to bring the woman's face to mind and couldn't. All he could remember was that the first time she had served them her apron had been stained.

JOSEPH D. MCNAMARA

Arnie grinned. "I bet you're remembering her stained apron."

Rusty laughed.

"That's part of the reason she's so good. Sometimes uses a little something that people focus on instead of her face. Then next time, it isn't there."

"You're willing to risk having her tail someone as good as the Phantom?"

"I think she already has, Sheriff, but we can't be sure. That's why this new info from Ralph is gold. If we pick up the fifteen year-old chica this afternoon and follow her to the guy we think is the Phantom, then we've got him."

"Right."

"Doris and I will work as a team this afternoon. We have closed circuit wireless devices in our ear, transmitters in our lapels. I traced the property to the law firm, and Doris has followed the guy to dinner three times. Once, she even ate in the place."

"Arnie, that's really pushing it."

"Naw. She was in there well before him. Almost finished her meal when he walked past her and sat down. As good as he is, he follows a rigid schedule. Five minutes after he sits, she finished her meal, paid, and left. He didn't know she was alive."

"You sure?"

"More important, Doris is. If we see him with the chica today, that means you and Pablo can hit the pad on Thursday when she takes him the money."

"Great."

"One other thing, my source matched the thread to a jail car. Vehicle sign out sheet for that day is missing. Brazen using a Department car, no?"

"More than brazen. Reckless, almost panicky, which makes them all the more scary. You're a whiz, Arnie." Let's just keep our fingers crossed that it's the right guy."

Rusty left, scrutinizing the bar. A non-descript woman in her sixties was behind the bar, pouring whiskies for the silent drinkers. Rusty had no idea if she was Doris. He hoped Arnie was right that the Phantom was as oblivious of her.

Otherwise, he and Pablo might get a big surprise instead of delivering one.

CHAPTER FORTY-EIGHT

DESPITE HIS RELATIVE confidence that his afternoon meeting with Ralph meant that the truce was still holding, Rusty made his usual cautious approach to Maria's apartment. He found her sitting on the couch, watching television. Rusty went to the refrigerator to get a beer. Annoyed, he turned to her.

"Maria, did you toss the six pack I had in the fridge?"

She came and stood with her hands on her hips. "Yeah. And I also chucked the pineapple ice cream, and the fresh pineapple you brought for me. I though maybe you'd get it through your thick skull that this is my place and you're not welcome."

Rusty walked past her and sat in a chair. She had turned off the television set.

"And who the hell do you think you are, going to Teresa and telling her personal stuff about us?" She stood over him, hands still on her hips.

"She summoned me, Maria," he kept his voice calm. "Gave me the lecture to imbecile fathers that pregnant women are highly emotional. Dumb Alpha males, like me, need to be sensitive."

"She wasted her breath on you. You don't even know what planet you're on. And where do you come off asking Sally to put all these backup cops on me? You forget that it was me who saved your dumb ass, not the other way around?"

"I haven't forgotten, and I haven't talked to Sally since I gave her the statement on the hospital shooting."

"You're playing at something, Russ, and I don't like it. I'm the cop here, not you. I don't have any confidence you know what the hell you're doing. But I have confidence that I have the authority to investigate, and am fully capable to investigate homicides."

Rusty didn't respond.

"So you're just going to sit there like a dummy?"

She glared at him for another minute and then stomped up stairs. He heard her switch on a television set. There hadn't been one in the bedroom before.

Maria was preparing for a siege. At least, she hadn't had the locks changed. He wished Teresa had been present to advise him which was more insensitive, his calm replies, or verbal silences.

His cell phone buzzed. It was Arnie.

"Bingo, Sheriff. Can you and Pablo meet me at the usual place tomorrow at 1700 hours? You need to see the setup."

"You're on, Arnie."

CHAPTER FORTY NINE

P ABLO LISTENED TO the latest recording of Ralph while Rusty drove a zigzag route to The Last Stop Saloon, cautiously checking for a tail.

"Arnie thinks he and his op have located the Phantom. They were going to follow Ralph's fifteen year-old whore from gang headquarters to see if she linked up with the guy they think is the Phantom," Rusty said, when Pablo turned off the recording.

Five minutes later, Rusty parked. He and Pablo joined Arnie in the saloon. The waitress put three glasses of bourbon on the rocks in front of them.

Arnie raised his glass, "To crime, Gentlemen. It's kept the sheriff and me employed for quite a few years."

Pablo was surprised, but not to be outdone by Rusty taking a sip of cheap bourbon. Pablo took a ceremonial sip. He tasted again. "This is Jack Daniels; that's not what it said on the bottle she poured from."

"Can't always tell from appearances, Captain." Arnie might well have been cautioning Pablo, who hadn't been at all impressed by the joint or Arnie's appearance. Rusty had studied the waitress' face this time and still couldn't make up his mind about whether or not he had ever seen her before.

"Anyway, after this little taste, I'd like to take you to look at the Phantom. The young hooker practically ran up the stairs to him. It's got to be the guy."

The three men left by the back door and made their way through a series of alleys to a padlocked chain link fence that appeared to house a group of cars ready to be squashed. Arnie unlocked the entrance. Inside, they got into a washed out Cadillac parked in the middle of the sorry collection of cars.

Arnie started the motor. Pablo and Rusty immediately recognized that whatever the rest of this vehicle looked like, under the hood was a well-maintained, powerful engine. The P.I. took a circuitous route to a neighborhood that had long ago lost the fight against the broken windows syndrome.

They parked in a lot manned by a skinny kid of an attendant, surrounded by a pack of teeth-baring mutts who looked anxious to attack. The boy came forward to take fifteen dollars from Arnie, who kept a respectful distance from the snarling dogs.

Rusty and Pablo followed Arnie through a series of alleys leading past the rear windows of six-story run-down tenements. He entered the rear cellar of one of the buildings and led them up steps to a hallway from which they looked out at a similar building across the way.

"This place we're in is abandoned. We can pretty much count on no one bothering us while we look over the building across the street. That one looks like shit, too, but unlike this dump, there are two luxury apartments inside that are top drawer, best of TV, entertainment centers, bar, fancy bathrooms. You name it. If you have to hole up, this is the place to do it."

"Which floor is he on?" Pablo, who knew something about surveillance, asked.

"Second. We can take a look at his door in ten minutes. He walks half way down the street and has dinner in the same restaurant three nights a week at this time. Two other nights, he eats in the restaurant on the next block. Other than that, he never goes out. Has food delivered the other nights. Twice a week, a chico delivers groceries for him to the apartment."

"Lookouts?"

"We been on him four days now, Captain. No lookouts. My guess is that he and Ralph don't trust any gangbangers to know who, or where, he is."

"Who's our lookout if we go to take a peek at what kind of door and locks he has?"

"My op. She's crossed in front of us three times in the fifteen minutes we've been here."

"I haven't seen her," Pablo said.

"She's right in front of you, now, Captain."

"That old woman with the shopping bag and the droopy stockings?"

"That's her. The same one who served our bourbon in the saloon. She could take out the Phantom in a second if you gave her the word. He'd never know who did him."

"Cool." Pablo smiled. "Why not tell her to do it, Rusty?"

"Wouldn't help us with Ralph and other problems."

"There he goes," Arnie nodded toward a slim, nondescript man in his forties, but looking thirties. The guy glanced around, casually.

Doris was heading in the opposite direction; his eyes slid right over her. The Phantom's worn clothing wouldn't raise eyebrows in this hood. Without lingering, he made his way a short distance and entered a Mexican restaurant.

"He'll be there for about an hour. The restaurant people call him Señor Valdez. We should cross the street one at a time. I'll be first. If you don't hear anything from me, follow separately. Not many people live around here. There's almost no traffic."

"Suppose he changes his mind about dinner and comes back?" Pablo said.

"Doris is watching. She'll let me know by wireless signal," he touched the earpiece in his left ear. "I'll be lookout in the ground floor hallway. I'll come to you. We go up and over the roof to the next building. Down the stairs, exit the rear of the building into the alley. Doris will have voice contact all the time."

Arnie touched his ear. "He just ordered soup. I'm on my way. Give me a minute, and then come separately. No hurrying, we don't need attention."

And that's the way it went. Rusty followed after Arnie had disappeared into the building. A minute later, Pablo joined them. Arnie guided the group to the door of apartment 2C.

He handed Pablo a powerful flashlight, and went down the stairs to guard the entrance. Pablo thoroughly inspected the doorframe from top to bottom.

Using his knuckles, he tested the texture of the wooden door. On his knees, he carefully studied the metal lock. He and Rusty started down the stairs. Arnie, hustling up the steps, halted and held up his hand, obviously listening to a message from Doris.

"Cops," he said, "a cruiser circled the block twice. Doris thinks they're trailing a young punk, maybe a mugger. We don't want them to eyeball us coming out the front. We better go up and over the roof, if you're finished."

Arnie cautiously opened the roof door. All of the other rooftops seemed empty. They moved to the adjacent roof. Arnie tried the door.

"Shit," he whispered, "It's locked. Should we try one of the other roofs?"

"You know this building is unoccupied, but you're not sure about the others?" Pablo said.

Arnie nodded.

"We don't want to get reported prowling around here. Let's open this one," Pablo grabbed the door handle. With his powerful arms he pulled on the door, bracing his left foot against the building for leverage.

The lock held, but the door opened a crack. Very quickly Arnie stuck a long thin steel rod through the crack and pushed up against the hook lock inside. It gave suddenly. A group of junkies shooting up, looked at them. Startled, they stampeded down the stairs leaving their burning candle, needles, and cookers scattered on the landing.

The three men waited until they were gone. Arnie fastidiously stomped on the candle the hypes had left behind, extinguishing it. Minutes later, they made their way to the parking lot. Arnie talked through his lapel speaker, telling Doris to break off surveillance.

"Whatcha think, Pablo?" Rusty asked on the drive back to The Last Stop Saloon."

"Door looks almost too flimsy to be true. Do you know if there's a deadbolt lock inside?"

"Yeah, there is. I stole a look through the firescape window, deadbolt, but there's no alarm system," Arnie said.

"O.K. Could you tell if the deadbolt was fastened to the same thin wood? I can batter the door, maybe the wood holding the deadbolt is just as thin and it will give. If not, I have something that will take care of the deadbolt in a jiff." Pablo frowned. "Thing is, if this guy is as fast as he supposed to be, he'd be ready for us, if we get held up by the deadbolt."

"I think the deadbolt is fastened to the same weak wood, but I can't be sure. On the other hand, twice Doris was outside the door listening when the young hooker went in. Doris says they were going at it within five minutes."

"She got that close?"

"I told you Captain, she's invisible. She even nodded to the girl, who was in heat, didn't even notice her."

Pablo shook his head in admiration. "O.K. On Thursday, if the birds and bees and hormones are racing as usual, we should be all right."

CHAPTER FIFTY

THE DAYS CRAWLED by. Rusty and Pablo had talked over in detail their plans for Thursday evening. The stalemate at Maria's continued. Wednesday night, she confronted Rusty.

"What gives with you? The last couple of days you've been as skittish as a cat sensing a coming earthquake," she said.

Rusty sat, silent.

"Taking the Fifth?"

"Maybe you should consult Teresa. Find out about the behavioral changes expectant fathers go through."

"And maybe you should get out of my face, let me get some peace."

"Soon enough, my Sweetie."

She looked at him curiously. "What's that supposed to mean?"

"Nothing, just rambling on. You know how old people are."

Maria shook her head and retreated upstairs to her bedroom.

The next day, Thursday, Rusty decided to hell with it. He couldn't just sit around fidgeting all day. He strapped his Glock under a running outfit and took a long jog. Returning to the empty townhouse, he did some calisthenics, and enjoyed a long shower. He ate a light salad, and left at 1700 hours to pick up Pablo.

The fifteen year-old girl carrying the money was supposed to arrive between 1800 and 1815 hours. He and Pablo were in place in the hallway across the street fifteen minutes early. Arnie was behind the wheel, waiting around the corner. He had provided Rusty and Pablo with wireless connections. They had four-way communication. Doris was shambling up and down the sidewalks in the vicinity.

Rusty hated waiting, thinking of all the things that could go wrong. Pablo stood next to him, his keen eyes roaming the street, but other than that, totally relaxed.

"Bring back memories, Pablo?"

"Yeah. Some good, some bad. Thing is, that this isn't the time to brood. We went over our plans. Now we concentrate on executing the plans. I wish we were executing the bad guys, but it was your call."

"If all goes well, they'll take care of each other."

"And our hands will be clean? You got a strange way of thinking about it, Amigo."

Rusty could see Pablo's point. He hadn't experienced any regrets over the two gangbangers he had taken out at Rosebud Lane and the other at the tennis court. Clear self-defense. He had made up his mind on the Fourth Street take-out only after much agonizing.

He had tried without success to get the FBI and DEA interested, and also considered the sheriff's Department as a means of getting protection. But the Department clearly had failed to keep him out of danger, and was somehow, itself, compromised in all of this.

Rusty knew well that his actions at Fourth Street plainly didn't fit the law of self-defense. It had made sense to him at the time as a last resort, yet afterward, the danger had increased.

The recording of Ralph made it certain enough to him that he and Maria were marked for death. But the recording had been obtained in violation of California's penal code. It was almost certainly inadmissible. Even if they got it in and Ralph was held for trial, he would keep the contract on them active from behind bars. Nevertheless, Rusty shrank from further preemptive killing in favor of a very iffy plan.

"She's on foot, wears a money belt probably. You should sight her any second." Doris was as calm as a master spy.

Pablo nudged Rusty, "There she is. Get ready. We give her five minutes to get her drawers off, before we hit the door."

Although she had been described as fifteen, Rusty was still shocked at how young and frail the girl was. She wore the excessive make-up and attire of a whore, but you saw some of that on TV nowadays as fashion. Under her tasteless clothes, she had the boyish body of a young teenager who should have been sitting behind a desk in junior high. Rusty's misgivings increased, he was putting her in danger. He sighed. In reality, she had put herself in danger, joining a gang, where, on any given day, she could become just another casualty.

Rusty and Pablo quickly crossed the street and made their way without delay to the door outside the apartment. They heard the young girl excitingly exclaiming her pleasure over the sex. "Yes. Yes. Deeper. Harder. You're getting so big!"

Both men stepped back and hit the door as hard as they could with their shoulders. As they had hoped, the whole flimsy door jam splintered. The deadbolt lock popped out. Rusty and Pablo were at the head of the bed instantly. The girl went from ecstasy to fear, opening her mind to scream. She remained soundless when she saw Pablo's razor sharp bayonet at her lover's throat.

The man who had been on top of her flopped onto his back. His right hand started to reach up under the pillow but stilled when the edge of Pablo's blade hovered over his wrist. He moved his hand down to his side.

"Senor, Valdez," Rusty said calmly, "we will not harm you or the girl. We simply want you to listen to us for a few minutes and then we will leave. Please tell the girl, that everything is all right. She should go into the bedroom and not listen. You will call her out in ten minutes."

The man blinked when Rusty used the name he was going under. He spoke reassuringly in Spanish to the teenager. She went without protest with Pablo, who, on his way, propped up, and closed, the front door. The girl displayed no shyness over her naked body. Pablo checked to make sure there was no phone in the back bedroom or access through the window to a fire escape. He was back in an instant. He reached under the pillow and took out a semi-automatic Beretta. He ejected the magazine and tossed it into a corner, and the gun into the opposite corner of the room.

The man on the bed had, of course, recognized Rusty as his target, but he ignored him and his Glock. His eyes were fixed on Pablo. The two brothers, no strangers to taking of lives, had made instant recognition.

Pablo's voice was soft, polite. "Senor Valdez, please sit on the end of the bed. All that we ask is that you listen to this recording for a few minutes, and we will be gone."

The man said nothing but slid to the end of the bed. He sat naked and unembarrassed, his eyes never leaving Pablo. Pablo dragged a wooden chair over and placed the recording device on it. Gently, he put the earpiece in the man's right ear, his bayonet never far from the Phantom's throat. Pablo pressed the play button.

The man on the bed listened. His eyes flickered once he recognized Ralph's voice, but he was otherwise, expressionless. He nodded to Pablo when the recording ended. Pablo removed the earpiece, ejected the cassettes from the device and placed them on the chair. He pocketed the recording apparatus.

"We wished only for you to hear what you heard. We leave the cassettes with you. Also, today is Thursday, we wish you to be gone by noon on Saturday and to never return," he said.

JOSEPH D. MCNAMARA

The Phantom frowned. "You want me to go, but not until Saturday?"

"No senor," Pablo told him. "You may leave now or whenever you wish as long as it is before Saturday."

"I don't understand."

"We don't want you to regard this as personal, as you might if we said that you must leave now. We recognize that you may need tomorrow to make travel arrangements. Adiós, Senor."

Rusty and Pablo carefully backed out the apartment door, never losing sight of the Phantom. They quickly descended the stairs and walked around the corner to where Arnie waited. He pulled away once they were in the car.

"We're clear, Doris."

"Good. I'll keep an eye on the place. He usually takes the girl to dinner at 1830, about twenty minutes from now. I'll watch."

"Take no chances, Doris. If any neighborhood creeps bother you, get out of there quick," Arnie said into his transmitter.

"If they bother me, it will to their everlasting regret."

He smiled and shook his head in admiration. "She's not just making noise. You can't imagine what the punks would look like if they took her on. Rusty and Pablo put the listening gear Arnie had provided in the glove compartment.

Arnie drove his car into the padlocked lot and walked with Dusty and Pablo to where Rusty's dented vehicle was parked. Just as they were about to get into Rusty's vehicle, Arnie held up his hand, listening to his earphone.

"The Phantom and the girl entered the restaurant, right on time, like they always do. Doris is shutting down surveillance."

"That's good, my friend," Pablo said. "When you have time, I wonder if you would do a job for me. I've had consistent theft from one of my local building projects. I'm pretty sure it's from the inside."

"Sounds like something we could handle. I'll take a look, Captain. Sheriff, nothing to do but wait, now. My source will let me know as soon as anything happens. I'll buzz you right away."

"Thanks, Arnie,"

Rusty dropped Pablo at home. "Well, the die is cast," Pablo punched Rusty lightly in the shoulder. "I'll stay loose, just in case, but it went down the way you planned. Let's hope that the results are what we want."

CHAPTER FIFTY-ONE

RUSTY COULDN'T SLEEP all night. In the morning, he dutifully shadowed Maria until she arrived safely at headquarters. He gave the usual friendly wave to the detectives tailing her. They would have told her about him, if she hadn't seen him herself. She hadn't commented on it, but he knew she must have been aware of him.

He arrived at the diner shortly after 9 a.m. Consciously, he acknowledged that it was too soon to be hearing from Arnie about whether or not the Phantom had taken the bait. All the same, his apprehension was growing. Had the Phantom informed Ralph of Rusty's betrayal? Had the Phantom simply vanished into Mexico?

Rusty couldn't concentrate on the newspaper he had purchased from the rack outside. His phone buzzed. He quickly answered. It was Arnie.

"Sheriff, I just heard. The Sureños headquarters clubhouse went up in flames, an explosion. It's a very preliminary report. I'll be getting more soon, let you know. But word is that Ralph left just before the blast, and the Phantom, who was parked in the vicinity also took off."

Rusty leaned back in the booth. Murphy's Law. Whatever can go wrong, will. Murderous, paranoid Ralph was still out there. The Phantom who he had hoped would turn into the avenger was in the wind.

Rusty was staring absently at the entrance when, a few minutes later, Ralph barged in followed by two gangbangers. Rusty drew his Glock, keeping it out of sight under the table. Ralph's face was a combination of confusion, suspicion, and anger. He was halfway to Rusty's table when the Phantom, who had followed them through the door, called, "Ralph!"

Ralph spun around, as did the gangbangers with him. There were three quick pops as the Phantom's pistol, equipped with a silencer, expertly took them down. By the time the Phantom's eyes searched for Rusty as his next target, the retired sheriff was flat on the floor, his Glock braced for firing. Anticipating that the Phantom was probably wearing a Kevlar vest, Rusty fired five shots at his head. Two hit their mark. The assassin fell to the ground, his body twitching as life drained out of it.

Rusty slowly rose to his feet. The four bodies on the floor were motionless. The diner was in pandemonium. People screaming, fleeing, taking cover. Rusty holstered his weapon, picked up his coffee cup and went behind the counter to refill it. Couldn't really expect waitress service right now. He returned to the booth and sat sipping coffee. Before he finished the cup, sheriff's patrol cars, lights flashing, and sirens blaring, screeched to a halt.

Deputies quickly determined that the danger of additional shooting was gone. They began herding the witnesses outside for questioning and cordoned off the area. They left Rusty where he was. Within a short time, Maria arrived and took charge of the crime scene. A sergeant, who had been one of the first to arrive, told her what he had learned. He inclined his head toward Rusty. She spotted Rusty sitting in the rear booth.

Maria approached, and Rusty stood.

"Russ, are you O.K.?" Her eyes showed concern.

"Yeah."

"Listen," she said. "I want you out of here, before the media descends. Go out the back door. These two deputies," she pointed to the team that the sergeant had sent to the booth, "will take you to the hospital. This has been real trauma. I want your heart checked.

"Stick to him like glue. We need tight security until we see what the hell is going on," she told the deputies. She turned to Rusty, "Russ, I'll need your gun for processing the crime scene."

Rusty handed her the weapon, and followed the deputies to their patrol car. He grunted. More doctors probing and poking. But it was beginning to sink in. Ralph and the Phantom were gone.

CHAPTER FIFTY-TWO

THE FOLLOWING AFTERNOON, Arnie, Pablo, and Rusty gathered in Pablo's den to discuss the previous morning's events. "A Margarita today, instead of bourbon, Amigo?" Pablo asked Arnie, who readily agreed.

Tapping the glasses in a silent toast, the three men settled in comfortable chairs.

"Well, most of this info comes from Doris. You two guys understand women," the private eye began.

"Arnie, that has to be the most incorrect statement of the year," Pablo said.

Arnie didn't respond. "Despite my strict instructions to stay away, Doris was too curious. She haunted the area around the Phantom's pad. Around 0400, he drove to the Sureños clubhouse."

"You weren't curious as to where she was?"

"She usually closes the bar, Captain. She's kind of a night person. I'm kind of a day person. But you're right. I was getting a little worried, called her on her cell. I met her a block from the clubhouse. She took the back. I took the front. Only lookouts, a couple of kids who were high. Ralph doesn't run things as tight as Jacko did."

"I'll agree with that," Rusty said.

"An hour later, Doris buzzes me. Lo, and behold, Captain Christian and his buddy, Detective Peterson, just went in the back entrance. Another hour or so goes by. It's getting light and I'm getting nervous about us being spotted. Then, the Phantom leaves the front door and gets into his car. Tough decision, but I decide to leave the clubhouse, follow him. The son-of-gun drives around the block, parks where he can keep an eye on the front of the clubhouse."

"That means you can't do the same without him seeing you," Rusty said.

"Right. So I watch the Phantom. Another half hour or so, he drives off. I follow and realize that he's tailing Ralph and his two goons in the car ahead of us."

"And Doris?" Rusty asked.

"I buzz her and tell her what's happening. We, or I should say, she, decides that since she has the two cops' car in sight she should stay put. I'm keeping well back from the Phantom, but from the route, I guess that Ralph is probably heading for the diner where he'll find you having breakfast."

"Why didn't you buzz me and let me know?"

"Well, Sheriff, they suddenly reversed directions, and I don't know that you're in the diner. Turns out, it was a trick to make sure they weren't being followed. Anyway, just then, Doris calls, tells me that there was an explosion and a big fire at the clubhouse. I call you, let you know, but since we're still winding around, and I'm concentrating like hell on not being spotted by the Phantom, I didn't have time to chat."

"So how the hell do they all end up back at the diner?"

"They did so much twisting and turning, and I had to stay so far back, that I lost them. I immediately drove directly to the diner just in time to see Ralph and his gangbangers walk in. I called 911. I was still telling the dispatcher to get units there, Code Three, when the Phantom went in. Bang, bang, bang. It was over in seconds. I called 911 again and told them, 'Shots fired'."

The three men sat there in silence, contemplating the events.

"You know, Arnie, you and Doris did an amazing job. And Rusty, you're turning into a modern day Wyatt Earp."

Rusty rubbed his chin. "But what was going on?"

"I don't think we'll ever know for sure, since the players are all dead," Sheriff.

"My money is on the Phantom planting a bomb in the clubhouse. He's the only one of them who had the expertise," Pablo said.

Rusty frowned, "With Ralph and two cops present?"

"Why not? C4, a timer, and a detonator in his pocket, he says he has to take a leak, sets it up. Then he leaves and sits to watch. Bad luck, the cops stay, but Ralph bugs out unexpectedly."

Rusty grunted. "Could have happened. But what were Christian and Peterson doing there?"

"These guys have been doing dope deals with the gang for years. Maybe, the Phantom called them. Didn't want to leave any loose ends after the explosion and fire," Pablo said.

"You know, I can see that. And no doubt after he heard Ralph on the recorder, he was going to whack him. But why didn't he just turn and slip out of the diner? Why stay to come after me?"

"Protect the brand name," Pablo said. "Remember, Rusty, word was around that the Phantoms had accepted the contract on you. Then Maria blows one of them away. Sure, the Phantom takes out the rat, Ralph, but how does it look for the Phantom's rep if the old Sheriff is still standing?"

"It's certainly plausible, Captain," Arnie said.

Rusty's phone buzzed. It was Maria. "Russ, I'm in headquarters with Sally. Can you and Pablo come to her office? We'll send an unmarked car."

"Hold on. I'll ask him."

He told Pablo. "Ask her if we need to bring Henry."

"Hell, no," Maria said when Rusty passed on the question to her."

"She says, 'Hell, no,' Pablo."

"Good. Then we'll go."

Arnie left. A few minutes later, two detectives in an unmarked car picked up Pablo and Rusty and drove them to headquarters.

Sally greeted them in her office. She had a wide smile for Rusty. "Thank heavens, you're O.K., Rusty. Permit me to introduce Mexico's Deputy Attorney General Guillermo Avaro Acevedo, who just flew up from Mexico City."

Acevedo, in his early thirties, was tall and trim in a dark pinstriped suit and blue. He politely shook hands with Rusty and Pablo.

His demeanor was quite serious. "Gentlemen," he said, "I am representing the Attorney General. He desired that I personally convey certain facts to you. Señor Garcia, I believe that the Attorney General has previously disclosed information to you on wire intercepts our government has made of the Juarez Cartel. Sheriff Henson has been quite gracious to host our meeting today. If I may, I would like to show you the following:

Acevedo pushed a button on a projector set up on Sally's conference table. For a disappointed moment, Rusty thought he was going to present a power-point presentation. But the projector flashed a picture of Mexico City's airport.

Acevedo froze the frame showing D.A. Herrera walking down an exit ramp to the airport's waiting area. "We were observing the arrival of this flight as the result of an intercept of a call from the Juarez Cartel to your District Attorney Herrera, early yesterday. Our experts concluded that the coded message issued an urgent demand for Señor Herrera to meet members of the cartel in Mexico City."

Pablo and Rusty watched the screen showing Herrera's unpleasant surprise when met by three thuggish looking characters. Herrera shook his head vigorously from side to side when one of the men spoke into his ear. The man slipped his arm under Herrera's, and with the other two men, nudged Herrera toward an exit.

Herrera resisted, turning his head from side to side, apparently looking for someone to intervene, but his large escorts pressured the much smaller Herrera toward the exit. Acevedo halted the tape.

"As you know, we have been quite interested in Señor Herrera's past dealings with the cartel. Because of other intelligence, we anticipated that something like this might occur at the airport. We made a decision not to intervene based on the fact that Herrera would not be cooperative if we tried to arrest the suspects, and because we had two cars of plain-clothes agents positioned to follow the cartel car."

He activated the projector. The final pictures showed Herrera being forced into a large black limo by the three big men who also entered the vehicle.

"It was our plan that we would intercept them on the outskirts of the city after what was apparently a kidnapping at the airport. We believed that, by then, Herrera would be frightened enough to provide evidence that could be used to prosecute the cartel. We had no way of knowing that the cartel had somehow learned of our work. They very cleverly staged a traffic accident between two large trucks which blocked our intercept vehicles. Our energetic efforts to determine where Senor Herrera is, and what happened to him have thus far been for naught."

Pablo sighed. "Señor Acevedo, can you tell us the details of what Herrera might have been up to here on behalf of the cartel?"

"Based upon our interpretations of past intercepts, we believe that Señor Herrera has moved from providing useful information and sabotaging your prosecutions of drug dealing cartel members to the role of planning and overseeing quite large shipments and disposal of amphetamine. It appears that the cartel is most unhappy with the local gang's mishaps, the death of the Phantoms, and most of all the loss of the latest large shipment in a fire at the Sureños headquarters. They blame Herrera, and unless he is a most persuasive advocate for himself, the cartel, in all probability, has already administered the usual punishment. My superior also wanted you to know that two of your police employees appeared to be facilitating the last shipment, a Captain Christian and a Detective Peterson."

The men made their goodbyes to Sally. Acevedo lingered for a moment in the corridor before getting on the elevator. "I apologize for being the bearer of bad news on the corrupt policemen, Gentlemen. Also, I must explain why the meeting had to be in Sheriff Henson's office. Your government, the FBI, the DEA, are, at times, very difficult to deal with. We depend heavily on United States aid in working against drugs, as you know. The two agencies I mention can be quite vindictive if they find that we communicate here in your country outside law enforcement. So," he turned to Pablo, "the Attorney General was quite happy to speak directly with you in Mexico City, but here the meeting had to be held in the Sheriff's office. The FBI and DEA will still be quite unhappy with us for not going through them, but will hesitate to offend the sheriff."

Maria had been standing a distance away, waiting for the Mexican deputy attorney general to leave. She approached after he got on the elevator.

"Pablo," she said, "the deputies will take you home. I'll transport Russ."

Pablo, out of sight of Maria, who had turned to give the deputies their instructions, gave Rusty a big lewd wink that was totally unappreciated.

CHAPTER FIFTY-THREE

BEHIND THE WHEEL of her car, Maria said to Rusty, "I'm starving. How about you?"

"I'm in your custody, Maria."

"Don't forget it. Here," she handed him a new Glock in his old holster, in which he had turned his weapon over to her in the diner. "This is a loan until we can return yours."

Holding the gun, Rusty asked, "Is this really necessary?"

"Are you kidding? You attract flying lead like a magnet. I expect you to be in the delivery room when little Russ arrives."

"As your husband, or as a witness?"

"You haven't asked me to marry you for awhile."

When they were seated in a small, but nice seafood restaurant noted for its good food, Rusty said, "Maria, will you marry me?"

"That wasn't very romantic, Russ."

"I guess not. But after your last obscenity laced responses . . ."

"Oh, come on," she smiled, "they weren't really obscene, not like some deliciously obscene lovemaking we've had. Your proposal raises the same old question. Do you want to simply make me an honest woman, or to love and cherish me for the rest of my life?"

"Let me count the ways I want to love and cherish you forever, Maria."

"Now, that's more like it. Of course, I want to marry you."

He blinked. "No kidding?"

"Of course, no kidding, Silly. Did you ever doubt it?"

Rusty decided not to answer.

"There are conditions, though," she said.

"Why does that not surprise me?"

Maria smiled, still chewing on a shrimp from the shrimp cocktail she had chosen for an appetizer.

"Well, don't keep me in suspense, Maria. What are your outrageous demands?"

"First, I want you to give me a baby brother and sister for little Russ."

"Sure. See how easy it is when you ask me first?"

"Ha! Big fibber. Also, I want the beautiful white gown. And the marriage, it has to be by a priest, of course."

"Fine with me, if you can find the priest for a non-religious guy."

"No problem. I know the one. He doesn't speak English. He'll think everything is fine. And, I want a nice reception with family and friends."

"O.K."

"You don't have to sound like it's going to the dentist. And finally, I want to live in a nice safe house. Can we afford one in Pablo's gated community?"

"I think so. Henry has been working on the insurance and sale of the Rosebud Lane property. When will the wedding be?"

"I set it all up for two weeks from tomorrow."

CHAPTER FIFTY-FOUR

F OR THE FIRST time in people's memory, gangs were absent from Silicon Valley County. So was the district attorney, but no one seemed to care about him.

Maria was a whirl of activity preparing for the wedding. Rusty was spared from decision-making, except for asking Pablo to be his best man. Rusty braced himself for what he envisioned as a demanding ritual to be endured.

But on the day of the wedding, he was almost as excited as Maria, and it turned out to be a touching and thoroughly delightful day.

During the reception, after his waltz with Maria, he danced with her abuela, who was having the day of her life.

"You are both so fortunate to have a wonderful mate," she said to Rusty before returning to her table amid applause that came close to what had followed the bride and groom's dance.

The following day, the honeymooners took a non-stop flight from San Francisco Airport to Kona on the Big Island of Hawaii. Rusty had booked them into the Orchid resort, which had a highly rated tennis program, beautiful beaches, and good restaurants. They stayed in a luxurious ocean front room with a lanai looking out on a long green lawn leading down to the Pacific Ocean.

The days rolled by. He and Maria fell into the island's languid rhythm. Early every morning, they hit tennis balls for an hour. The first day, he found she was playing just as hard as she had in Silicon Valley. After a few minutes on the court, he had come to the net, and beckoned her.

"Maria, is it safe for you to play like this?"

She laughed. "Yes." Gently, she touched his cheek. "My protector, my husband." She kissed him softly, retreated to the baseline, and smashed the next three shots for winners.

Following tennis, they swam for twenty minutes on the resort's beach. Waves broke on an offshore reef, leaving the water ideally calm for swimming. Wire mesh strung between rock jetties kept out the random shark wandering inside the reef.

After long sensual showers together, they fought the impulse to make love, saving it for the mellow nights. Some days successfully abstaining, some days not, but even on those nights, they couldn't get enough of each other.

One day, a light brunch followed tennis. Then, a ride in the glass-bottomed boat to peer down through the crystal clear water at the amazing variety of exotically colored and oddly shaped fish. Maria looked away when the occasional ominous shark glided under the boat.

"Miss your Glock?" Rusty teased.

She wrapped her arms around him. "I've got you. Those sharks wouldn't know what hit them."

Another day, they skipped lunch and scuba-dived in the area protected from sharks, actually swimming through schools of small tropical fish. In the late afternoon, the heat diminished, they went back on the tennis courts. Maria actually drew small crowds. The resort's pro had recognized her, but respected their privacy, and didn't disclose her tennis identity to the guests who realized they were watching a pro.

Rusty suggested that she might want to play a couple of mornings against the club pro. "I only have time for you, Russ," she demurred.

Most nights they sat on their private lanai and watched sunsets made unique by the windswept absolutely clear air over the dark blue Pacific. Maria claimed to see lucky green streaks when the sun finally sank, lighting the ocean into a golden ball of fire, but Rusty never saw any green streaks.

Rusty let Maria select which one of the three restaurants they would then dine in. With Maria abstaining from alcohol, Rusty found that a couple of glasses of wine with dinner satisfied him.

Being Hawaii, there was always fresh pineapple available for Maria at every meal. After they had sampled each restaurant, Maria suggested on the fourth evening that they order room service for dinner. They dined on the lanai, enjoying the sunset.

The next night, they returned from a dinner of fresh fish to sit in complete darkness of the lanai and gaze upward at the constellation of stars. "I've never seen them as brilliant," Maria said, "but, of course, we're looking up through clean air from a little spot in the middle of the ocean." She had turned the room's music system onto soft Hawaiian music which drifted through their open screen door.

His lounge chair was just a few feet away. From time to time, he stole a glance at her glowing beauty, lit only by the bright moon. But it was still there, buzzing through his mind.

Even after four full days of heavenly, total relaxation, memories of the ugly underbelly of violence that had coursed through their brief, intense courtship hadn't vanished like the fog did from the Pacific air.

"You haven't spoken a word in three hours, Big Russ. What's bothering you?"

He could barely make out her beautiful eyes in the mellow darkness.

"You planned the whole thing, didn't you?" His voice was quiet, but even to him, the words exploded through the night.

Maria looked out toward the ocean. Her voice was soft. "I always knew that you were too good a detective to not have eventually realized what I did. But the whole thing, no. You had more to do with what happened than I did."

"I really don't understand, Maria. You printed and delivered the flyers. You had to know that those dumb animals would try to kill me."

"Russ, believe me, we had Rosebud Lane covered like glue. A marked unit was at each end of the street, and one parked in front of your house that morning. But because you hadn't used your truck to return from tennis, no one, including the bad guys, thought you were home."

"Murphy's law."

"Or as we say on the job, shit happens. The two deputies in front of your house disobeyed orders. When a call came over of an armed robbery in progress in the nearby shopping mall, they left their post. The gangbangers would never have dared to break in if they had been there."

"You wanted to stir the gangs up because of your mother and brother."

"Of course, you had promised to get them. I believed you."

"What?"

"When you came to the rosary. You told us, they would be brought to justice. You were so tall and straight in your uniform. I quit tennis to join the Department to come and help you get them."

"Maria, you know we never gave up. The entire Department did everything they could."

"I know, Russ. I never blamed you. Even when you retired without nailing them. I knew what Lucy's illness did to you."

"I was in such deep mourning, distracted from the job."

"It made me respect you more that you grieved so hard. But you have to understand, I grieved even more, Russ. Lucy had many good years with you. My mother and brother's lives were stolen by young animals without a conscience who had continued to kill. My little brother was only ten, Russ. And, it's hard to explain, but I believed that even if something went wrong, you were invincible. And you were."

"So the flyers were just a device to start a gang war?"

"I found out through my years in the Department, that Ricardo and Ramundo were the actual shooters who took my mother and brother away. It was Ralph, the Judas Norteños, who told the R. & R., the upcoming Sureños, where Jacko's two top guys were hanging out."

"And by horrible coincidence it was near your house, and your family was cut down by stray shots."

"Yes. Ralph encouraged the Sureños shooters, so that he could oust Jacko and merge the gangs. I held all three responsible."

"All those bodies, Maria, I've lost count."

"There were thirty-one all together. Some you never knew about."

"Does that include Doc Hoffman?"

"Yes. I am dreadfully sorry about him, Russ. He was such a good man. His death will always be on my soul." She was crying softly. "We knew about the tennis in the playground. Just like your house. We had it completely protected, even better than Rosebud Lane that first morning. Both ends of the street next to the tennis courts were covered."

Her tears brought Teresa's warnings to be sensitive back to him, but he couldn't stop.

"But they came from the gym?"

"We were going to put people in the gym, but it was locked every day. Only afterwards did we find out that the animals threatened to kill the custodian's family if he didn't let them in the night before. I was overconfident. Even if a stray gangbanger slipped into the tennis area, I knew you and Pablo would be armed, and were expert shots."

She sighed, "No one expected three of them to come from the gym. Even so, as I anticipated, you and Pablo took care of them. But the shots led one of the cruisers guarding the street entrance to race to the tennis courts.

"That allowed a gang car to crash through. The other cruiser chased them. Deputies blew the gangbangers to hell, Russ. Just one of the gang's wild shots got through. It came nowhere near you guys on the court. The awful thing is that Doctor Hoffman was so dedicated that he got close to the street. Put himself in range because he went to help the man who was already dead from your shots. The doctor died because he was too good a doctor, and I wasn't a good enough cop."

"Something must have made you optimistic enough to decide to start our family."

"I guess I deserve that. But again, you're right. The cross dressing kid who I broke down in the interview room, later told me that there was bad blood between Christian and Ralph. One of our narcs was also convinced that the Phantoms were really working for the cartel, which was convinced that Ralph and crooked deputies had cheated them. The Phantoms were probably hired to clean house after they had taken you out. All we had to do was to protect you, and let them do the dirty work, against the gangs and Christian."

"So what set you off against me?"

"You can't accept what Teresa said about pregnancy?"

"No. Not completely."

She remained silent for a few minutes. Rusty guessed that she was carefully choosing her words.

"I'm not going to talk to you about whatever you may have been involved with on Fourth Street. I'm not even certain about all of them. But I was frantic. I knew you were hyper about protecting me, and that you were up to new things. Some by yourself. Some with Pablo and Arnie. I was terrified that you were going to get hurt, or go over the edge and openly execute the vermin."

"I admit to being tempted."

"There is some truth to the emotional upheaval in being pregnant, Russ. I was so happy when Teresa confirmed I was pregnant. It was foolish of me to expect you to be as thrilled as I was, but I flipped at your reaction. Also, I came to hope that putting on the chill would freeze you. Maybe you'd take a cruise or something to think things out while the gangsters blew each other away."

"You came up with this elaborate plan to get others to bring about the justice you wanted."

"But I never violated the law. Russ, don't you remember what you preached to us all those years: those who enforce the law must obey it. You never said anything about what those who retired should do."

Startled, he gaped at her.

"Why are you looking at me like that?"

He didn't say anything.

"Come on, Russ tell me what you're thinking."

"I'm wondering if you're insane." He had spoken impulsively, but now, as she smiled and began giggling, he grew unsure about how true it might be.

Maria jumped up and leaped into his lap, almost knocking over the lounge chair.

"That's good, Russ." She continued laughing. "In a few months when I'm fat and ugly you'll still be fascinated by me."

She nestled into his arms, her head resting on his shoulder.

He stroked her hair and whispered into her ear, "You'll never be ugly, Maria. And, to me, you'll always be the most fascinating person in the world."

Other Books by Joseph McNamara

Fatal Command
The Blue Mirage
The First Directive
Code 211 Blue

CPSIA information can be obtained at www.ICGtesting.com
Printed in the USA
BVOW070001271212

309173BV00002B/5/P